STARS, STRIPES & SUMMER NIGHTS

Stars, Stripes & Summer Nights

CELESTE DADOR

Delacorte
Romance

Delacorte Romance
An imprint of Random House Children's Books
A division of Penguin Random House LLC
1745 Broadway, New York, NY 10019
penguinrandomhouse.com
getunderlined.com

Editor: Wendy Loggia
Cover Designer: Casey Moses
Interior Designer: Cathy Bobak
Production Editor: Jamie Johnson
Managing Editor: Tamar Schwartz
Production Manager: Liz Sutton

Library of Congress Cataloging-in-Publication Data

Names: Dador, Celeste author
Title: Stars, stripes and summer nights / Celeste Dador.
Description: New York : Delacorte Romance, 2026. | Audience: Ages 12 and up | Audience: Grades 7–9 | Summary: "First Daughter Abby Cary-Alzona wants one normal summer before college—until she meets a carefree small-town photographer, a boy who is everything she never saw coming"— Provided by publisher.
Identifiers: LCCN 2025048852 (print) | LCCN 2025048853 (ebook) | ISBN 979-8-217-02973-0 (trade paperback) | ISBN 979-8-217-02974-7 (ebook)
Subjects: CYAC: Children of presidents—Fiction | Romance stories | LCGFT: Romance fiction | Novels
Classification: LCC PZ7.1.D224 St 2026 (print) | LCC PZ7.1.D224 (ebook)

The text of this book is set in 11-point Maxime Pro.

Manufactured in the United States of America
3rd Printing

The authorized representative in the EU for product safety and compliance is Penguin Random House Ireland, Morrison Chambers, 32 Nassau Street, Dublin D02 YH68, Ireland, https://eu-contact.penguin.ie.

For Mom, who gave me a public library card
and a love for exploring new worlds through books.

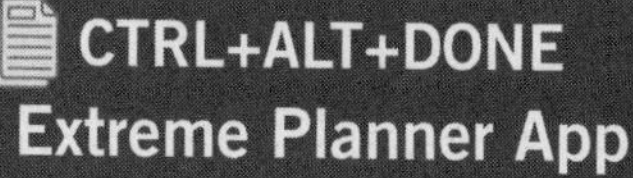

Abby's Personal Summer Endeavors List

- ❑ 1. Add senior year schedule to academic planner
- ❑ 2. Complete senior year AP English summer reading
- ❑ 3. Demonstrate "character and commitment"
  - ❑ 3a. Volunteer with Pod Patrol: dolphin rescue group
  - ❑ 3b. Lead Hawaiian community service project with Senator Sina
- ❑ 4. "Gain new perspectives"
  - ❑ 4a. Travel (Hawai'i! Italy!)
  - ❑ 4b. Broaden culinary palate
  - ❑ 4c. Shop local
- ❑ 5. Enriching activities outside of academics to be "well-rounded"
  - ❑ 5a. Community events
  - ❑ 5b. Cooking class
  - ❑ 5c. Art lessons
  - ❑ 5d. Team sports
  - ❑ 5e. Do something nature-y

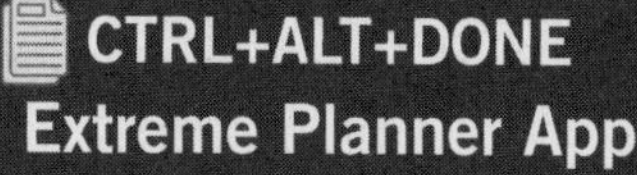

Abby's <u>Unofficial</u> Summer Bucket List

↓ (Pg. 2 For My Eyes Only)

- ❑ 1. Enjoy a laid-back picnic
- ❑ 2. Veg out at the beach
- ❑ 3. Get brain-freeze induced by fancy whipped-cream-smothered coffee latte (the perfect summer drink)
- ❑ 4. Chill and savor ice cream in a huge waffle cone (the perfect summer indulgence)
- ❑ 5. Dine at top foodie restaurant (no parents)
- ❑ 6. Stay up all night (not studying)
- ❑ 7. Watch the sun set (not rushed)
- ❑ 8. Go stargazing (no agenda)
- ❑ 9. Dance under the stars (alone or with someone special . . .)
- ❑ 10. First date?
- ❑ 11. First kiss???
- ❑ 12. Be spontaneous. For once. 

CHAPTER 1

"Smokeshow" and "hot guy" are phrases you don't typically hear during Mom's work parties, but of course my sister missed that memo years ago. Fortunately, we're in the privacy of my upstairs bedroom, away from spying eyes and gossip-hungry ears.

I lower my phone, where my feed shows most of my classmates at end-of-the-school-year parties. Not me. I'm mentally preparing myself to keep an eye on the "rambunctious" member of the family. My head tilts sharply as I beckon my little sister away from my bedroom's second-floor window. The royal-blue curtain, which Mom's designer selected, provides a stark contrast to Elle's sparkly citrine-yellow ball gown, the gown she and Mom eventually compromised on.

Since I'm the "dependable" one, no one had to weigh in on my dress. My white-gloved hands flatten my lavender sheath dress against my thighs—very Jane Austen meets Jackie O. It's classic and maybe a little predictable, but I prefer playing it safe.

A stubborn strand of my sister's brown hair has fallen from her updo. "Tsk tsk," I say as I tuck it back into place for the millionth time. Oblivious, Elle continues to talk about the "hottie" outside like a reporter live on the scene. I sigh. Freshman year has turned my sister boy crazy. To her, the "American dream" refers to a cute guy. For the rest of my family, it's what everyone in this country deserves.

I force all five feet, two inches of myself to stand tall. "Young lady"—my voice is overly crisp and clipped as I impersonate our mom—"you mean *attractive* and *smart.*"

Elle smirks as she fans herself with her neon-green nails, a color she picked despite my repeated suggestions for Essie's Ballet Slippers—my go-to pale pink.

"Nope. I definitely mean smokeshow," she says.

"Smokeshow? Hay naku. Is something burning?" I throw up my hands, this time imitating Mom's sister Tita Karra's sonorous accent when she slips into Tagalog to scold us.

Elle's giggle is my reward. Only Elle knows that imitating voices is my thing. I've got several governors and many of our teachers down pat. Impersonations are one of the few things that have gotten her—and if I'm being honest, also me—through the years and years of monotonous VIP functions.

I wrestle Elle's sequined dress straps back into place; she was too busy with her amateur red-carpet fashion analysis of our guests to notice. "Hold on," I protest as she turns away.

"He might be gone," Elle groans as she rushes back to my window to press her nose against it. My pearl earrings jostle as I shake my head at my sister.

"Like I said, total hottie," Elle continues. "Loving the dark wavy hero hair. And sweet! Are those Chuck Taylors with his tux?" Exhaling loudly, I stand behind her and follow her gaze, where guests in predictable black tie and grand ball gowns parade about our manicured lawn below. It's a perfect June evening, meant for showing off the historic grounds of our home under the star-spangled night sky—but most guests aren't stopping to smell the fragrant flowers in our rose garden, they're rushing to get inside to the party instead.

"None of these guests strikes me as hot unless balding and boring is your thing," I say.

She huffs. "He must be inside already. I'll find him when we get downstairs."

My cheeks flush. That's the last thing I want her to do. An awkward encounter with one of Mom's VIP guests orchestrated by my sister. *Hey, Abby, meet this hottie*, Elle would shout across the room, causing people to stare. My number one rule in life: Don't create any headaches for Mom. She's got enough on her plate. "Please don't. I'm not interested."

A wicked grin curves her lips. "I'm just wondering if you're 'not interested' because of your date tonight?" I fiddle with my amethyst necklace.

Heat spreads across my cheeks. "Sorry. I'm not sure what you mean." But of course I do. Whether Oliver Darby is officially my date tonight is something I've been worrying about too, and something my sister has been teasing me over for years.

Oliver, my entire family, and his entire family know my parents' rule. None of the Cary-Alzona girls are allowed to date until senior year of high school. A rule that is apparently inconvenient to Elle but hasn't bothered me because Oliver has always been my partner. It's our unspoken default.

I bite my lip, recalling that he hinted about asking me something important this past week. After school today, he even made me promise to save him a dance. Is this the night he asks me to be his girlfriend?

Elle's eyes gleam. I adjust some nonexistent wrinkles on my gloves, not wanting to give her the satisfaction of calling me out. "You know the rules about dating," I remind her.

"I do indeed." She moves her arms like she's making a grand reveal. "Ta-da! You're officially a senior now."

"In the fall. I'll be a senior in the *fall.*" Even I wince at my sharp tone, which sounds as grouchy as one of Mom's overworked lawyers.

My sister raises a finger like a reporter with a *gotcha* question. "If you believe that, then what about your unofficial summer bucket list?" I stiffen like the upper lip of a pretentious guest. Why did I let Elle read my summer bucket list?

And worst, the pesky thing swiped right and saw page two with my private goals—aka my "for my eyes only" list, which bullets all the normal teenage things I want to experience before senior year. This is the last summer before I'm an official adult—along with all the expectations of being my mother's daughter.

Elle waggles her brows. "Goal eleven? That was"—she pauses dramatically—"first kiss, I believe?"

My cheeks burn. What a mistake it was writing that down.

"That was a draft!" I practically shout. "Page one is the official summer list." The enriching activities that colleges will like when I apply this fall. I glance at the antique clock on my dresser. "Speaking of official, we don't want to be late." I reach for the brass doorknob, anxious to stop this discussion about my bucket list.

"But Abby—" Elle protests.

I cut her off. "Promise me you won't tell anybody about my list."

She frowns but agrees with a tiny huff. "You know, you shouldn't feel guilty for wanting to do stuff for yourself."

Her words make me pause for a second. Everything I do is for my family. How is that not more important? I fling the door open, pretending not to hear her, and step out quickly, nearly bumping into the burly man guarding the door.

Without missing a beat, Agent Shaw steps aside. By now Shaw's all too used to my near collisions with him and by default moves away whenever he hears me approaching. "Nice tie tonight, Shaw," I say sheepishly. He's always in a black suit, his tie the only thing that changes. Tonight it's gray with green dots.

He nods at me before speaking into his earpiece. "Rapunzel and Rhapsody are on the move."

Nessa, the other agent assigned to my and Elle's security detail, joins him. She's wearing a navy pantsuit, flats, and a simple silver watch. I can't see it but I know she has a secured firearm under her jacket. "Ready to party?" Elle asks with a giggle. We're rewarded with a tight smile from Nessa. And a grunt from Shaw.

I glance one last time at the privacy of my bedroom before turning toward the sounds of laughter and conversation as our guests mingle about the White House's Residence.

My back straightens and chin lifts high as I switch into "First Daughter" mode. Elle stands next to me. I check her hair again, and everything is where it should be.

Taking a deep breath, I nod at my sister, then give her my usual pep talk before one of Mom's VIP functions: "We are Abigail and Eleanor Cary-Alzona, the sweet and charming daughters of Constance Alzona, president of these United States of America—and it's performance time."

CHAPTER 2

The second floor of the White House, formally known as the Residence, has been my family's home for the past five years. Elle and I are part of the ultra-exclusive sorority of First Daughters who've lived within these storied walls—likely all having been mildly exasperated by the occasional tourist craning their neck in hopes of glimpsing our bedrooms.

I smile pointedly at a couple whose gazes linger a moment too long before they veer off toward an incoming senator.

As we enter the Residence's Center Hall, which functions like a long living room, it's bustling and full of laughter and loud guffaws with guests waiting for tonight's state dinner to commence. Dad wanted us to meet inside the Yellow Oval Room at 19:00, and as he's a former navy pilot and astronaut, this means no later than 18:45. Because if you're not early, you're late.

My ears pick up hearty Italian accents, which makes sense because tonight's dinner honors the prime minister of Italy. My stomach rumbles, excited for Chef's menu—I love pizza, and I heard a fancy version will be served this evening.

Mom's guests mill about with wineglasses in hand, admiring the artwork on our walls—by celebrated artists modern and historic, from Claude Monet's *Morning on the Seine* to Georgia O'Keeffe's *Mountain at Bear Lake—Taos*.

Some guests wander toward the Lincoln Bedroom, where an actual copy of the Gettysburg Address resides. For Elle and me, it's kind of creepy in there, with stories of Lincoln's ghost. Not that ghosts exist.

As we make our way through the crowd, Elle and I grin politely. The guests up here have an extra *V* designation, as in *VVIP*. These are the select people invited to our private living space before tonight's main event on the State Floor of the White House.

While presumably everyone here is important in some way, the White House Residence is still an extra-exclusive space for visitors, which explains the curiosity. After all, they're mere steps from where the most powerful person in the world sleeps. Of course, Elle and I just call her Mom.

"Shoot," Elle mutters as she kicks a candy wrapper under a side table. Elle has the poor habit of dropping things, including a Snickers wrapper from her dress pocket just now. Telling her to pick up after herself never seems to sink in.

"Elle, that table belonged to Teddy Roosevelt," I snap.

She rolls her eyes. "Whatever. I'm sure his kids ate Doritos on it too." She laughs at her own joke. I hold back my "the White House is also a museum" speech. Not that the White House's staff would let our home be out of order.

Fortunately, I don't see any other signs of Elle's snacks, schoolwork, or personal items. If not for our bookshelves, which display a collection of our family photos going back several generations to Mom's family in the Philippines and Dad's Irish roots, you wouldn't know a real family lives here.

As the rest of the guests circle one another in a game of "who's most important," I'm able to spot the route that will take us to the Yellow Oval Room fastest. "Come on, Dad's waiting," I say to Elle.

"Hold on to your gloves a sec. I need to find Enzo," Elle says, her eyes circling the room. Enzo isn't a friend—he's one-fifth of an Italian teen boy band who's on tonight's guest list. And he's not the only celeb: Hollywood director Tyler Storm and his date (pop star Lil' Shady) and former NBA legend turned famous podcaster Jax Romeo have also been invited. Most of the time we don't know who's attending the dinners until the last minute since the guest list is constantly being updated, but Elle got the inside scoop about Enzo a couple hours ago.

I look at my gold watch, a Christmas gift from Oliver. He should already be here. Elle's grinning as she looks up from my watch. "See, I have five whole minutes," she says.

"Wait," I say uselessly to her back as she flits away. Nessa and Shaw remain a polite distance across the room. They're usually not up here when we're in the Residence, but with tonight's guests they must have been asked to stay close.

Elle weaves in between a Supreme Court justice and the Speaker of the House. I'll give her three minutes. She deserves to enjoy herself. It's not easy being a First Daughter, especially on nights like these with all of Mom's high-profile guests, and the media waiting downstairs. Up here, we need to behave, but at least there are no cameras.

My back prickles in that "someone is watching me" way. I know this anxious feeling too well. Sure enough, a couple across the hall are looking in my direction, trying to make eye contact. Judging by his impeccably well-tailored tux and her conservative designer dress, I'd say they're rich corporate-donor types looking to get in a good word with my mom by making nice with me.

Ugh. Those are the encounters I desperately try to avoid whenever possible. I back away slowly, annoyed that my dress is not compatible with making haste. My constricting silk skirt pulls against my legs. Note to self: Go with a stretchy material next time.

From the corner of my eye, I see the shark couple headed toward me. Alarm bells going off in my head, I turn abruptly.

But my escape is blocked. I gasp as I smack into a wall. Or rather, a guy.

I rock back in shock, losing my balance, but instead of falling, I feel firm hands grip my arms. "I got you." The voice is low, comforting, and warm.

I go on autopilot as I utter multiple "I'm sorrys" while I regain my footing. I'm relieved to see my skirt hasn't ripped, but my relief turns to curiosity as I spy white Chuck Taylors near my heels.

My eyes rove upward, taking in black pants and a trim waistline, then a fitted black button-up shirt underneath a tux jacket that emphasizes a broad chest and abs (which aren't hard to imagine are like one of those muscled marble statues in the National Gallery of Art). As my gaze reaches his face, I'm greeted by full, inviting lips and intense copper eyes framed by unfairly thick lashes. His skin is a sandy beige and his features look mixed like me and Elle. His dramatic dark brows arch with concern.

My body burns ten degrees hotter than the summer night outside as I realize this is the "smokeshow" Elle was referring to. She's right. It takes every ounce of effort to keep my jaw from dropping faster than a judge's gavel. He's so hot, it's almost criminal.

"Are you okay?" he asks.

"I—yes," I stammer. Very uncharacteristic of me. But who can focus when a guy like this has his full attention on you? My gaze flicks to his hands still holding my arms. "I'm—I'm . . . good."

He seems to notice at the same time. "Sorry, I didn't mean to." He removes his hands fast. I momentarily miss the pressure and warmth of his touch. His face grows red as he looks away. "I should. Um . . ." He doesn't finish his sentence as he turns to leave.

It takes me five whole seconds before I finally respond, which, again, is very un-Abigail of me. "Wait," I call after him.

He pauses and I can't say I'm not admiring the view of his back. He runs a hand through his thick wavy hair as he turns to face me like he's suddenly self-conscious or something.

I smooth some imaginary wrinkles from my dress. First Daughters are always polite and gracious. "Thank you for the save."

He winces. His face is the very definition of awk. "I'm sorry, I didn't mean to grab you—it was a reflex. I know you would've regained your balance on your own."

I do my best to act chill. Me regaining my balance would've been unlikely, but I'm good with him not knowing that. "I meant you saved me from the shark couple who were about to make me their first course," I say, trying to sound light and funny but obviously failing given the confused look on his face.

"Shark couple?" he echoes.

I laugh nervously. "The power couple behind me."

He looks over my shoulder. "The guy who looks like the Monopoly dude without a top hat?" His eyes sparkle. "And his partner, who looks like that mean mom from *Titanic*?"

My hand flies to my mouth to suppress my giggle. I looove *Titanic*. My eyes narrow. "Rose, you are not to see that boy again. Do you understand me?" I say in a haughty tone.

The boy's surprised look reminds me he's a stranger. I never do impersonations with anyone except Elle. My face flushes hotter than debate stage lights. I don't even know his name.

I hold out my gloved hand. "I'm Abby, by the way."

He looks uncertainly at my outstretched hand, making me feel a bit self-conscious. Seconds ago, we were so close I could smell his minty toothpaste, and now he doesn't want to shake my hand?

I frown as a panicked look crosses his face. My hands instinctively go to my own face. "Do I have something in my teeth?" I ask.

"No, I . . . there's a smudge on your arm." He points where seconds ago his hand gripped my right elbow. He's right. I see what looks like black ink on my skin.

We both stare at his hands and find the evidence on his fingertips. He grimaces. "My pen must've leaked. I'm sorry," he says.

"It's okay, I'm sure it'll wash off." I look at my watch. Four minutes to get to Dad. Finding a sink will have to wait until after I check in with him, but fortunately I have a quick solution. I tug my white gloves upward to cover the stain. "There. All better. 'Be prepared' is my motto." I stop myself after I realize I'm babbling. Me? Babbling?

The boy nods politely as he goes for the inner pocket of his jacket and pulls out a black pen and a small notepad with scribbles all over it. "The culprit," he explains. He tosses the leaky pen in a small, ornate trash can.

I tilt my head, curious. Most folks at this party aren't taking actual notes. "What were you writing?"

He looks embarrassed. "I was checking out this collection of photos on the bookshelf and taking notes on their age and provenance."

"Provenance," I repeat. "You mean the origin of the photos?"

He nods. "Yeah, there are some awesome images in this collection."

I beam as I walk over to the bookcase of family photos I personally curated. "Thanks, I worked hard on locating and placing . . ." My words trail off as I look at the frames. To my annoyance, I realize four of them have been rearranged to different spots. "Hey, did you move my frames?"

My back tingles, sensing him behind me, but my frustration at seeing my photo collection out of order is more galling. "Each of these photos was placed with intention," I say with irritation.

I pick up a wooden eight-by-ten frame with a photo that's particularly important to me. It's a sepia-toned portrait of my mom's grandma, Lola Liwayway, when she was about my age in the Philippines.

The photo's angle captures her profile as she sits on a rock off to the side of a mountain road. There's a great valley below and mountains in the distance.

A year after that photo was taken, World War II would reach the Philippines and my great-grandmother would become a nurse and a resistance fighter, starting a tradition in our family that would eventually lead to Mom's military service, then public service as a champion for veterans and small businesses, and now the White House. Lola Liwayway was a hero, and I'm not happy seeing the photos surrounding hers moved around.

I can sense him frowning. "I'm so sorry, I thought I placed them back in order."

"These four aren't where they belong," I say, putting Lola's photo carefully back in place and rearranging the others.

"Four?" He sounds amused. "There's like fifty frames here and you're upset about four?"

"Everything has a proper place," I say primly. That should be reason enough to explain his error, but instead he doubles down.

"I know a little something about photography. I can usually tell the era based on a photo's characteristics. Those four photos were out of place."

I scoff. "I had an archivist from the National Archives help me."

He lifts his hands in surrender, but now it looks like he's trying not to laugh. "Well, you might want to get a second opinion. I put them in correct chronological order."

We stare at one another. I can't tell if I'm more irritated by him suggesting I'm wrong or the fact that he doesn't care when things are out of order. Or maybe it's the tiny, annoyingly cute smirk emerging on his face.

As we stare at one another, it's like the air is as thick as on a hot and humid DC summer day. I suddenly wish I wore more deodorant.

"Everything all right here?" I jerk back at the sound of a familiar calm and confident voice.

My best friend steps forward, looking magnificent in his tuxedo. He barely acknowledges my brief hello as he angles himself in front of me. "Hi, I'm Oliver Darby," he says, extending his hand to the boy in Chuck Taylors.

The boy's eyes widen. "Darby? As in Darby Hotels?"

Oliver's face pinches in dismay. That is his family, but it's not how he likes to be identified. "As in, son of Vice President Darby."

CHAPTER 3

"Should I bow?" the boy asks as he looks between Oliver and me. His lips twitch and I'm pretty sure he's trying not to laugh. At our expense.

"That won't be necessary," Oliver says, his eyebrows drawn together with confusion.

I sigh. Oliver has never been good with sarcasm. I'm guessing the boy recognizes Oliver now, because everyone in America is obsessed with the possibility that Oliver and I are dating.

Ever since our parents began campaigning together as president and vice president, there's been plenty of stories about me and Oliver. From the clothes we wear becoming instant bestsellers to more recent stories about us dating. The press went wild when we attended junior prom together. And I get it. The eldest daughter of the First Family and the eldest son of the Second Family makes for a good story.

Plus, Oliver would pretty much be an ideal boyfriend. He's smart, kind, and organized. We have the same class schedule. And perhaps most important, he understands how to operate in our shared world of fancy functions, Secret Service, and family duty.

Still, standing between Oliver and this boy feels like I'm in a passive-aggressive game show.

"Gabriel of the Mystic Hollow Calabreses," he says with a pompous bow and a wave of his hand. A quick glance at Oliver and I know from the twitch in his smile that my friend is puzzled and low-key annoyed. It's actually amusing to see. Oliver rarely gets thrown off.

Meanwhile, Gabriel rises from his bow, returning to his full height. Though he's not as tall as Oliver, you wouldn't know it. His athletic build and attitude make him feel much taller.

Gabriel? Calabrese? My head tilts as I try to figure out how he made the guest list. My mind races to high school prize winner or artist—he certainly has that vibe about him—but likely he's someone's plus-one.

Mystic Hollow sounds familiar but I can't place it. I try not to stare as I study him for some kind of clue. A rectangular object inside his tuxedo jacket catches my attention. His phone? Whatever it is, it's not dangerous since the Secret Service would've checked him.

"See something you like?" Gabriel asks. My gaze jumps from his chest to his face to find his lips upturned into a satisfied smile.

My nostrils flare, but my response is cut off as Oliver's hand grabs mine. "We need to go," he says to me, his grip tightening.

He isn't wrong. "It's 18:55," I gasp. Dad won't be happy. With one last look at Gabriel, whose gorgeous face is as unreadable as the unsmiling portraits hanging on the White House's walls, I let Oliver tug me away through the crowd.

Gabriel is Trouble with a capital *T*. I should stay away from him. With any luck, I can avoid him the rest of the night despite my lingering questions, like why does he know about old photos? Why is he even here tonight? And what's with the Chuck Taylors? Didn't he get the dress code instructions? Does he even follow instructions?

My mind hardens with resolve. *No, Abby. You are not to see that boy again.* Of course, that ultimatum didn't work out too well for Rose and Jack.

I do my best to match my stride with Oliver's—again cursing my restrictive dress. I'm going to Hawai'i soon, and for a moment I picture myself walking along the beach in a sundress and flip-flops. I can't wait.

I frantically scan the room for my sister. "I already directed Elle to the Yellow Oval," Oliver confides. Oliver and I have been friends for so long he can practically read my mind. He grins at me, and thanks to our unspoken best-friends mind-melding abilities, he knows I'm grateful.

I follow behind him quickly, holding up my skirt to allow myself to keep up. It's not like me to be late. "And what's your story? You're cutting it close," I tease.

Oliver winces. "Sorry, my dad was going over some Hawai'i plans and I tried to make it clear to him that you and I are going to have some downtime while we're there."

"Did it work?" I ask.

He grins. "I managed to negotiate about half of our to-do items away. We've got dolphins to swim with, right?"

I smile. Ever since we watched a bunch of National Geographic marine life documentaries on the campaign trail, whales and dolphins have been our thing.

The Yellow Oval Room is where mom likes to entertain VVIP guests before they make their formal entrance into the State Dining Room. True to its name, the room is painted a soft yellow in homage to First Lady Dolley Madison's color scheme when this was the Ladies' Drawing Room. Today it serves as a formal sitting room. Elle is not allowed to eat Doritos here. I've always loved the room's long windows, which overlook majestic views of the South Lawn and the tall, marbled Washington Monument piercing the sky.

I spot my parents instantly—surrounded by people orbiting them like planets around the sun. Mom shines in a sleek navy ball gown, rose-gold-tinged pearls glowing softly against her brown skin. President Connie Alzona has led with distinction, integrity, and respect, but it's in these personal moments—when she's laughing, connecting one-on-one—that she truly lights up the room. Her deep, joyful belly laugh, now a viral meme, rings out above the crowd.

Beside her is my father, the First Gentleman, charming a small circle of guests. I catch the tail end of one of his signature stories—something about life in space, no doubt. It's classic: He keeps everyone entertained while Mom gets a breather from the endless spotlight.

They're a team in every sense of the word. They just get each other.

Mom sees Oliver and me and motions us forward. I am

comforted by her jasmine-and-freesia scent as she wraps an arm around me and gestures at the couple next to her.

A friendly-faced man who reminds me of an owl and a stately blond woman in a glamorous designer dress nod in my direction. Mom beams. “Mr. Prime Minister and Mrs. Mariano, may I introduce my eldest daughter, Abigail? And Vice President Darby’s son, Oliver.”

“Ah, the beautiful Abigail Cary-Alzona,” the prime minister exclaims. “A national treasure, no doubt. Lovely to meet you, my dear.” I blush, admiring his musical accent.

“Buona sera, Signor Prime Minister e Signora Mariano,” I say graciously. “Non vedo l’ora di visitare la sua casa.”

The prime minister grins, obviously pleased that I greeted him in his language. “And I look forward to your visit to my country, signorina,” he replies.

I nod in agreement. After the White House’s Independence Day Gala, our family is off to Italy for a state visit, which means my Hawai‘i trip is my best chance to check off my summer bucket list items. I’ll be under a microscope in Italy.

I flush as I look at Oliver. He’s chattering away with Mrs. Mariano. Oliver’s Italian is much better than mine, but he’s been a world traveler since birth. Helps when your family owns hotels all over the globe.

“You two are such a lovely pair,” Mrs. Mariano declares in the direction of Oliver and me. Oliver smiles, while my immediate response is a very mature nervous giggle as I remember Oliver had a question to ask me later tonight.

Fortunately, Dad jumps in. "Time flies, doesn't it? Abby's still in pigtails as far as I'm concerned." Okay, not sure I'd go that far, but I'm thankful for his intervention. Mental note, need to develop a new talking point regarding the status of me and Oliver. It used to be a simple *best friends*, but from the way Oliver is looking, I'm not so sure anymore. And I'm certain *it's complicated* isn't a relationship status Mom's press secretary would approve.

"Where's Elle?" I whisper into Dad's ear.

His bushy eyebrows pinch together. "Giving a history lesson to some kid on the balcony," he says. "Bozo?"

I stifle my laugh. "You mean Enzo," I chastise him. The Truman Balcony is just outside the Yellow Oval, and sure enough, I see Elle pointing excitedly to something in the distance. A floppy-haired boy in a gold-trimmed tuxedo who must be Enzo leans against the balcony with her.

A woman next to Elle in a gorgeous red gown makes my smile stretch even wider. I squeeze my mom's arm. "Tita Karra is here! I thought she wasn't going to make it." Mom leans out of her conversation and her lips quirk in that way they always do when she refers to her younger, pluckier sister. "She apparently had an important guest she wanted to bring." We exchange meaningful looks.

We never know who Tita will bring as her plus-one to Mom's functions, but no doubt it's someone connected to a cause she supports, like puppeteers for world peace, or even a service animal, which happened to be a potbellied pig one year. So long as the guest passes a security check and doesn't cause any controversy,

Tita is allowed some grace. It's the least Mom can do for her sister, who is a fundraising goddess and practically raised Elle and me during Mom's campaigns for Senate and twice for president.

One of our military social aides whispers in Mom's ear. She smiles at the news and claps her hands, drawing everyone's attention. "Who's ready for dinner?" she asks like we're about to have an intimate meal in our home, not a fancy political-people dinner where even the salads have last names. I cast a look at Elle, Enzo, and Tita, who are slowly exiting the balcony.

I'll lecture Elle about paying too much attention to Enzo when we're seated at our table together. As for Tita, I hope to get a few words with her alone before her plus-one steals the spotlight.

The energy amps up higher with anticipation as the White House staff helps usher everyone from the Residence to the floor below us, where the State Dining Room is located.

Mom, Dad, and the prime minister and his wife make their way toward the Grand Staircase, where they'll make their entrance, but not before Dad hugs me and shakes Oliver's hand. I'm wary of the knowing look Dad shares with him. Like everyone is in on a secret except me. Oliver offers me his arm. I look into my best friend's eyes and feel nervous.

Didn't I write page two of my unofficial bucket list anticipating us dating? Even our first kiss? Haven't I already decided that it's time for Oliver's best friend label to switch to boyfriend? I feel an elbow bump me and am glad to see Elle. I lock my other arm with hers and the three of us make our way to dinner.

As we enter our grand State Dining Room, where Mom prefers to host official functions, I'm stunned. The White House staff have outdone themselves with turning this historic ballroom into an elegant party space, with soft pink uplights, golden platters, and lush floral centerpieces. Toward the back, a few members of the press stand to capture tonight's event.

It's hard to imagine First Lady Abigail Adams used to hang her laundry here. The room has hosted official state dinners for over a century, the first one in 1874 when President Grant honored the king of Hawai'i. Where I'll be soon. I push the thought of balmy breezes out of my mind for now.

As we make our way to our seats, my sister and I do our best to smile, but not *too* wide. Stand tall, but not too rigid. Don't flinch or look like you're annoyed by the thousand lights flashing in your face. You're happy, your parents are great, and you're gracious and humbled to serve the American people.

As the flashes begin to slow down, I notice one photographer who doesn't fit in. My chest thumps. Gabriel is standing with the press taking photos with a pocket-sized but pro-looking camera.

Wait. Is he with the press? Why was he in the Residence?

And if that wasn't strange, his camera seems to be aimed at the walls behind me. Everyone else is taking photos of me. What's so interesting about the walls?

Oliver nudges my shoulder. "You're frowning," he whispers between his toothy grin. Oh no. I do my best to recover, but the damage is done. Sometime tonight or tomorrow a photo will be posted of me side-eyeing a guest. And then the internet will decide I've personally offended democracy, and criticize my parents for whatever is the issue of the day.

Mom and Dad will say it's not a big deal, but I know these kinds of things are not helpful either. Rule number one: Don't make Mom's job harder.

Our procession continues until we're escorted to our table by one of the White House's military social aides. Our round table is clothed in rose gold with twinkling crystal glasses and Mom's White House china—the ivory-and-gold design was one she and Dad picked out together.

As I approach the table, I see my name is handwritten in flowery script on a tiny name tent where I expect to find it. Next to me is Oliver, where I expect to find him seated. I glance at the name placard on the other side of me.

Gabriel Calabrese, the script on the name tent reads. My stomach does a backflip. Not what I expected.

I turn to my sister for an explanation. She rewards me with a sheepish smile as she grabs a chair at the table behind me. I try not to scowl as she sits beside Enzo.

Of course, she must have begged to be seated next to him. I always knew Tom, Mom's social secretary, liked her more than me. I know the seating charts are always changed up to the last minute, but Elle could have at least warned me we were at different tables. Feeling petty, I decide to make sure she doesn't get her favorite ice cream flavor when we're on vacation. I'll eat all the pineapple sorbet out of spite (even though I hate pineapple).

I summon my inner yoga girl. It's not that I mind talking to strangers—it's practically part of my job description as a First Daughter—but Gabriel Calabrese? He's the rare type of person who makes me tongue-tied, and now I have to sit through an entire five-course dinner with him?

If Oliver noticed Gabriel's name, he doesn't say anything. Instead, he's already turned on the megawatt Darby charm as he greets the other guests at our table, all of whom I've already done my homework on. There's Secretary Luis, our commerce secretary, and his wife, Penny. Sitting next to her is a military veteran; then a green-energy entrepreneur; and finally, an Italian arts philanthropist and his guest, a fashion influencer.

And now, seated on my right, is Gabriel Calabrese, who's into photography, doesn't care about keeping things in order, and is a possible member of the press. Oh, and is ridiculously hot.

Being on time doesn't seem to be his thing either, since he's nowhere to be seen.

Oliver's cool hand touches my arm, snapping me out of my thoughts. "You remember the name of that town we visited last summer?" he asks from his seat—my best friend's way of looping me back into the moment.

Flustered, I slide into my chair, offering polite nods and smiles around the table. My gaze lands on Secretary Luis as I answer. "Oh, in Virginia? We did that whirlwind trip through the countryside. So many cute towns—I remember it being beautiful, but they blur together."

"Including Mystic Hollow," a low, warm voice says. I look up and see a smug Gabriel Calabrese standing behind his chair. "That is, you passed through. You didn't stop."

I fiddle with my gloves, avoiding eye contact. I don't control my family's itinerary, but I still feel bad for not stopping at his town even though it's impossible for us to stop everywhere.

Oliver snaps his fingers, not missing a beat. "Mystic Hollow. That's why I remember that name. It's unique."

"And I think you'll be hearing a lot more about that town," says a loud and very familiar voice. Tita Karra places her hands on Gabriel's shoulders and beams. "I'm working on a new project in Mystic Hollow with my godson's mother."

Godson? I look at Tita and then Gabriel and back at Tita as I bite my tongue. Now is not the time to grill Tita about some mysterious godson I've never heard of. But wow, my blood is boiling at this breaking news. How long has this been a thing with Gabriel and my aunt?

As Gabriel takes his seat, Tita greets Secretary Luis and the others at our table. Apparently, she was supposed to join our group, but Mom has Tita seated next to an Italian businessman.

Gabriel doesn't say a word as he sips from a glass of water. I force my gaze away from him and focus on the dinner menu atop my plate. I barely register the upscale Italian-sounding names: prawn carpaccio, tricolore salad, lamb agnolotti, and pizzetta contemporanea, which must be the pizza dish I'm looking forward to.

As the group discusses farm-to-table menus and where tonight's food was sourced, I scan the room. My parents are seated at the head table with Italian prime minister Mariano and his wife. The two couples look like old friends. Is that me when I'm older?

I glance at Oliver, who's now confidently engaged in a

conversation with the table. It's practically predestined for Oliver and me. Everyone knows it.

The topic must've moved on to our upcoming trip to Hawai'i, as Oliver's discussing our plans, from snorkeling to sunset boat tours.

"Sounds like a blast," Gabriel says.

I turn to him, annoyed that even his profile is gorgeous. I try to keep myself from frowning. "What's a blast?"

"Your summer. A luxury trip to Hawai'i." His expression is flat, but those copper eyes shine with intensity. The judgment in his voice will not do.

"It's not just for recreation. I'll be leading a community service project for Senator Sina while I'm there." In fact, it's one of my top three activities on my official personal summer endeavors list, but I don't tell him that.

Gabriel nods. "Hmmm. While sipping virgin daiquiris at your boy's infinity pool?"

My face burns as he chuckles. *My boy?* What does that even mean? I stiffen and lean forward, so only he can hear my response. "My entire summer itinerary is jam-packed up to the minute. If I can get away to the beach it would be a real treat."

He stares at me for what feels like an eternity. I can't tell what's going on in his gorgeous head except that he's probably forming opinions of me. Finally, he exhales. "I'm sure you'll do that alongside a picnic of fancy Michelin-starred food."

So that's it. He thinks I'm super fancy. I chuckle. "No. I'll pack a charcuterie board—no, I mean peanut butter and Oreos, thank you." I wince. In my effort to pick everyday food, I went with Elle's favorite.

Gabriel's expression goes from shock to the IRL version of a laugh-cry emoji. "Peanut butter and Oreos? You ever go on a picnic before?"

"Of course I have," I retort. Community gatherings on the campaign trail count, don't they? I just haven't gone on one with people my age, hence item one on my unofficial bucket list.

"You all just seem into really fancy food." He gestures at the menu card.

I frown. What does he expect to eat at a black-tie event? "Well, there is pizza on the menu. Our chef knows it's my and Elle's favorite."

"Your favorite food is pizza?" he asks.

I lift my chin. "Absolutely. Comfort in a box."

The expression on his face is still annoyingly amused and attractive. I straighten my shoulders, employing a strategy I learned from Erin, one of Mom's campaign staff: If you don't like the topic, change it. "What's with you standing with the press pool? Are you media?"

He looks around the room, then back at me. "No."

I narrow my eyes. "You sure you're not reporting for your high school or posting pictures somewhere? Because if so, you'll need the right credentials." My gaze lands at the bulge in his tuxedo jacket where his camera must be.

"Definitely not with my school paper," he says with a force I wasn't expecting. "Or with the media. I'm a fine arts photographer," he says. "Or I want to be."

The wistfulness in his voice surprises me, but before I can respond, Oliver taps my hand. Maybe I'm imagining it, but he looks annoyed. I inhale, remembering we need to help each other during these social occasions—just like Dad helps Mom out.

"Actually, Abby's the bookworm in our group," Oliver says with a grin.

I force a smile. That's my cue. And I almost missed it—too distracted by Gabriel. First Daughter 101: Always make others feel seen. I mentally scold myself.

The rest of dinner I stay sharp—engaged listening, laughing at the right moments with everyone *except* Gabriel. Maybe he's picked up on it. Maybe that's the point.

The first course doesn't help my "I eat everyday food" argument. The prawn carpaccio is beautiful but is designed so the delicate meat is still inside the prawn's fully intact body, beady eyes and all. The second course is a salad arranged to look like a butterfly. And the third dish is basically four ravioli, but dressed up with flower petals.

Gabriel, as it turns out, isn't bad at adding to the conversation. While I ignored him, he held a pleasant discussion with Luca, the Italian arts philanthropist.

I didn't know Florence was home to many fine arts schools, and there's a prestigious photography program that Gabriel seems to know a lot about. The philanthropist practically invites Gabriel to a private tour.

"Maybe Signorina Abby can take you," Luca says. "You'll be stopping in Florence this summer, no?"

My cheeks warm. Gabriel is quick to respond. "Nah, she'll be basking in the sun in Hawai'i. Besides, I'm needed at home this summer," he says. "Family business" is all he offers. I frown, detecting a hint of reluctance in his voice.

Our servers arrive with the fourth course. I perk up. This is the pizza course.

But when the plates land in front of us, I do my best to contain my shock at the small square crust on my plate. There's no sprinkled cheese. No tomato sauce. No toppings.

Instead, there's a green sauce, a sliced eggplant that has a white sauce spread atop, then piled with tomatoes, radishes, and alfalfa sprouts like a salad.

"Pizzetta contemporanea," Secretary Luis says. "Contemporary pizza." He takes a bite of the tiny slice and nods with approval.

"Ah, yes. This is not what my mama would call *pizza*, but it's very fashionable," Luca says, and he and his date tell us about the latest food trends in Italy.

I can practically hear Gabriel's thoughts: fancy food for a fancy girl. I sigh. People form their opinions about me all the time. I shouldn't care about his, but for some reason I do. The tension between us doesn't get any better when Mom stands up to give a toast. I blush as she shares how excited she is to take me to Italy to help bridge our cultures and how fast I've grown from the shy girl in pigtails to a vital voice for young people across the country.

All of it is super flattering and even funny at times, but on the inside, I wish I could sink into my chair. On the outside, I flash my megawatt smile. Rule number two: When your parent is president, everyone's expectations of you are high—fair or not.

Gabriel grumbles. I cut him a sharp glance meant to shush him, but the concerned look in his eyes is not what I expect. "No wonder you're so high-strung," he murmurs. "That's a ton of pressure on you."

My jaw drops with shock from his sympathy. As Mom proposes a toast to our two countries' friendship and bright future, all eyes are on her, except Gabriel's.

Instead, he angles his glass like he's toasting me. His copper eyes hold mine as we raise our glasses, and I'm struck by the recognition in his expression. How can he look at me like that when we've just met? When two hours ago, all I wanted was to avoid him?

My chest tightens with realization: Even if we never meet again, I don't think I'll ever forget this moment, or his face.

CHAPTER 4

"Well, that was superb," Luca says, placing his napkin on his plate. "Abby, you'll have to save a dance for this old man after you two do a few rounds." His eyes go from mine and then, to my surprise, to Gabriel.

My body warms as I realize what Luca is saying. He thinks Gabriel and I will dance together.

Why would he assume that? Didn't he get the briefing? Oliver and I are supposed to be a couple. Not me and Gabriel.

Gabriel laughs. "She's all yours. I don't think I can handle this one."

I gasp and glare at him, which earns a chuckle from Luca. Meanwhile, Gabriel couldn't look more pleased with himself.

Thankfully, Oliver is still engrossed in his conversation with Secretary Luis and didn't hear our exchange. Good. Let Oliver focus on trade policy and not the barbs being traded between me and Gabriel.

Music begins to play, beckoning guests to the East Room. I recognize a jazzy version of a Frank Sinatra song. Ready to end this conversation fast, I rise. I offer friendly but curt smiles to everyone at the table except Gabriel and make my way to the ballroom, trying to lose myself in the swanky tunes of the US Marine Band.

I hear Elle's giggle before her arm links through mine. "Enzo is the absolute—"

I cut my sister off. "I can't believe you did that to me," I hiss so only she can hear.

She gasps. "Did what?"

"Switched seats."

She snorts. "You looked completely fine with the person who I switched with."

I follow her gaze and see Tita Karra locking arms with Gabriel.

I groan. "Have you heard of him before? I had no idea Tita had a godson."

"And one that hot." Elle giggles. I give her a little nudge. Elle huffs. "What? Tita's allowed to have a life outside of us."

I roll my eyes. After we got into the White House during Mom's first term, Tita very happily went back to her roots as an angel investor—a person who provides seed funding for businesses. She works with a group of angel investors whenever she finds a good business case. Tita has helped start up many female veterans and local small businesses in underserved areas, urban and rural. All causes Mom believes in too.

Tita has a lot of new ventures, but who knew landing a godson was one of them. Hopefully while everyone's dancing I can pin her down and get the story on Gabriel.

Despite my mood, even I can appreciate the White House's largest room, the East Room. The space already embodies glamour and historic charm, but the room is practically glittering this evening with its three grand chandeliers and guests in colorful ball gowns. All underneath the watchful eyes of President George Washington, whose portrait First Lady Dolley Madison famously saved when the British burned the White House in 1814. Yes, another woman who saved the day.

The US Marine Band is set up beside a small stage, playing their merry tunes. Apparently later tonight Enzo and a couple other singers will also be performing. Elle is breathless trying to figure out which songs he'll sing.

I shoot her a warning look. "Please don't fixate on just one person."

She bursts out laughing. "Says the girl who can't stop staring." She gestures—not subtly—over my shoulder.

I turn. Tita Karra is heading straight for us, practically towing a reluctant-looking Gabriel behind her. Do I really have to spend more time with him?

Tita grins. "I'm so glad you two connected over dinner." She reaches up to pinch Gabriel's cheek, clearly delighted. He endures it with a mortified smile.

"Your mother has a few people she wants me to meet. Will you girls make sure Gabe behaves himself?" Tita teases. "I'm counting on Abby's discipline and good manners to rub off on him."

Elle snickers as she whispers in my ear, "I think you'd rather rub something else on him." My face pales. I hope no one heard that.

I glance at Tita, trying to hide my annoyance. "Happy to help, Tita, but first, do you have a moment?" *As in a moment for me to politely but firmly inform you that "Gabe" has been voted off the island and he has to pack his bags?*

Tita wraps an arm around my shoulders and pulls me aside. "Yes, anak?" Her gaze meets mine and I feel at a loss for words.

This is Tita Karra, who was there when I broke my arm falling off the bleachers during a campaign rally. This is Tita Karra, who helped me overcome my shyness at my first debate club meeting in the fifth grade. How can I be upset with her? Keeping her godson company should be the least I can do.

I stammer as her eyes search mine. "Nothing. You look great tonight."

She tsks. "You're almost an adult, Abby. You're allowed to share your opinions with me. Even if I disagree."

If she notices me frown, she doesn't stop her commentary. "Thank you for being nice to Gabe. It's been difficult—" She stops mid-sentence and grins. "Oh, look who's here."

With a startle I turn to find Oliver urgently beckoning me. I give a pointed look at Tita as she pushes me toward him. She's another Oliver and Abby shipper. "Go, we can catch up later," she says with a wink.

Oliver reaches me first. "Your folks want us to join them for the first dance," he says, doing his best to hide his giddiness.

My body stiffens as I look from him to Tita. Participate in the first dance? We both know that's a first. Usually Mom, Dad, and the visiting head of state will dance the first dance.

Protocol must've slackened now that Mom's in her second term.

Oliver holds out his hand, which I stare at for a fraction longer than I should.

I don't look at Gabriel directly, but from the side of my eye I can feel his gaze laser pointed at me.

Meanwhile, the crowd around us parts as Oliver leads me to the dance floor. I hear curious murmurs and excited gasps along the way.

Oliver leans in. "Don't be nervous," he whispers. "We'll just do our prom moves."

My grip tightens. Oliver thinks I'm nervous about dancing, especially given my gift for being a human tumbleweed. But it's not the dancing, which we've rehearsed many times, that's got me worried.

It's pretty much the optics of pairing Oliver and me together on the world stage with my parents and the prime minister and his wife. Practically declaring to the world our impending coupledom.

When we reach the floor, Mom, Dad, and the prime minister and his wife greet us with the friendliest of smiles.

My parents lean in for a hug, but Dad pulls me close. "Sweetie, do you want to sit this out?"

"Won't that embarrass Mom?" I murmur so only he can hear.

"No. I've asked Oliver to move you to the front of the room to watch us." He holds his breath. "But he asked if you two can join the first dance. Your mother is fine with that, if you are."

I stare into Dad's concerned eyes. "I thought this was something Mom's team wanted for positive press," I say.

Dad scoffs. "They always want nice human-interest stories, but you're not a prop." He smiles encouragingly and I know I have the best father in the world.

I glance at Oliver, who's having a heart-to-heart with my mother, and I know dancing with my best friend is the right thing to do for our family.

I give Dad an encouraging smile. "No problem. I'm up for it."

He tugs my hair playfully. "I still see pigtails."

My father reaches for Mom's hand and that's my cue. My parents head to the dance floor, and so do the prime minister and his wife. And I'm not imagining it: The uproar in the crowd is loud as Oliver leads me to the floor.

Though the rapid-fire clicking of cameras may be louder than the people, I tune that out and focus my attention on Oliver's smooth and steady hand over my right and his other hand at my back. His touch so familiar it's reassuring, like my favorite childhood blanket.

The music begins and the familiar dance commands fill my brain as I count the steps. One-two-three, one-two-three . . . I fall into a well-practiced rhythm.

My face freezes into a pleased and pretty smile. An expression also well-rehearsed.

My body on autopilot might've stayed perfectly composed, except for the tiniest glances I steal at Gabriel, who stands near the corner of the room like a dark cloud.

I force myself to not react. Not let him rain all over my sunshine, which unfortunately makes my brain cue up cheesy montages of the two of us caught in a summer storm together.

Gabriel's hands move and I see a bright flash. Did he take a photo of me?

It's not until the prime minister's wife, Mrs. Mariano, cuts in that I realize the song is over. I look up to see Oliver beaming at me—completely over the moon.

"You were amazing, Abby," he whispers as he hugs me. "My parents will be thrilled!"

I hug him back, because Oliver is my best friend and I want him to be happy. And pleasing our parents is one of our top priorities.

Mrs. Mariano coos in Italian as she squeezes both our arms. Oliver, ever the diplomat, asks her for the next dance.

I look over to Mom, who's now partnered with the prime minister.

Naturally I head for Dad—only to find Elle already claimed him.

Ugh. I guess Enzo must be somewhere rehearsing his song.

Now that the dancing has officially started, couples are heading toward the dance floor. I lower my gaze, dodging eye contact with anyone who might ask me to dance. Dancing with Oliver works because we're a well-oiled machine. Dancing with complete strangers who want to talk my ear off? Also something I like to avoid.

But because it's me—clumsy Abby—trying to escape, I promptly bump into Gabriel Calabrese. I take a deep breath as I lift my eyes to meet his.

"We seem to keep bumping into each other," he says, those lips of his upturned into a devastating smile.

"Seriously. You need to wear reflectors or something," I scold him. My eyes widen as I see the Monopoly guy beelining toward me. His partner appears to be chasing Secretary Luis down.

I exhale. Why can't I catch a break? I look Gabriel over and make a snap decision as I reach for his hand.

He hesitates for a millisecond before wrapping his hand around mine. I tingle at his rough and warm touch.

He looks at me, puzzled. "You need help walking or something?"

I look over his shoulder, where Mr. Monopoly is still making his way toward me. I turn to Gabriel with a tiny smile. "Care to dance?"

His brows lift. "Do I really have a choice?"

"Of course you do. It's a democracy." But I already know his decision as he follows me to the dance floor.

He moves into the starting position for the dance with ease. I cock my head. "Do you know what you're doing?"

He rolls his eyes. "You're not the only one with Filipino heritage. My mom was all about beauty pageants and debutante balls."

My eyes crinkle with appreciation. "Tita almost entered me into a beauty competition, but my dad put a stop to it."

He snickers. "I don't blame him. Besides, there'd be no competition. You'd get first place automatically."

My face goes hot, and when I glance at him, he's just as red. As the music begins, we're an awkward pause away from issuing a formal apology to the nation. Meanwhile, I'm sure my Secret Service detail is taking notes on my spectacular lack of chill around this boy. I nod and focus on his outstretched hand and place mine in his. The firmness of his grip, the way his left hand holds my back, firm yet gentle, makes my body tingle like electric sparks dancing across my skin.

Just inches away, I appreciate his scent like a blend of mint gum, fresh-cut grass, and smoky wood. He smiles down at me and I can't help the one spreading across my face.

As he squeezes my hand, he steps forward and I follow his lead. We do a few steps and I'm amazed at how he's able to guide me.

With Oliver, it was a matter of me remembering my steps and syncing with him. With Gabriel, I just fall naturally into step.

"You okay?" he asks.

I meet his smiling eyes. "Yes. I usually am not able to think or talk when I'm dancing. My brain . . . I usually count my steps."

His chuckle is wry. "Yeah, that explains the Thor look on your face," he says.

I do a double take. "Thor look?"

"You look very intense while you're dancing."

I scoff. "Seriously? Like 'You're big. I've fought bigger' Marvel Avenger Thor?" I do my best Hemsworth impersonation.

He eyeballs me. "Okay, that's unexpected."

"What?"

"You know your popcorn movies."

I shrug. "We have a movie theater in the White House. My dad's a movie buff."

"Mine too," he says. I wait for him to elaborate, but he doesn't. The silence stretching between us reminds me of the questions I have about him.

"So, my Tita Karra is your godmother? Lucky you," I tease.

He chuckles. "She can be a bit much, huh."

I roll my eyes. "Tell me about it. Between my mother and my tita, I'm under more surveillance than someone on the FBI watchlist."

"Must be nice being famous—without the fan club or merch," he jokes. He twirls us so we're facing opposite directions, my back now to my parents, who're in the middle of the room.

"Your mom's toast was kinda epic. I felt like you were the chosen one or something."

My cheeks warm. "She was just saying how proud she is of me."

"You're practically the voice for young people," he says, and I'm pretty sure he's making fun of me. "Hanging out with world leaders, vacationing at luxury hotels, and eating pizza with alfalfa sprouts. So relatable."

I bristle. "All of it comes with being the First Daughter," I say, taking a deep breath. "And I don't vacation all that much."

He spins me with ease, then pulls me back into his orbit. "Especially when your vacation sounds like one big community service project?"

"Right, I'll mostly be working this summer."

My head lowers and I'm suddenly aware of how easy and nice it would be to lean my head on his chest. I inhale his soothing musky scent and am so tempted.

Gabriel clears his throat, snapping me out of my trance. My eyes widen as I meet his. "Seems some folks are starting to watch us," he says. I follow his gaze and notice a reporter with a camera looking in our direction instead of at Mom, who everyone else is watching.

Gabriel stops dancing. "I have an idea," he says.

Still holding my hand, he pulls me off the dance floor, and we weave in between guests. I try not to read too much into the smile he shares with me as we make our way out.

I feel flustered as I follow him from the East Room and eventually find a quiet corner in the White House's Red Room.

"Am I seeing red?" Gabriel jokes.

"Yes, welcome to the Red Room." I flourish a hand. "Aptly named after the rich red decor and red silk wallpaper that adorns all four walls. Abraham Lincoln was known to relax in here. Also"—I lean in to whisper—"your godmother accidentally spilled red wine in here."

Gabriel shakes his head, amused. He takes his camera out—turns off the flash after I warn him—and shoots more photos of the room. I tilt my head. Most folks take a couple shots of the room and ask for a selfie. Gabriel seems completely absorbed in the details. "Sounds like something my mom would do too. Your aunt is one of my mom's oldest friends. They were in the same sorority or something together," he explains.

"Is that how you became her godson?" I ask.

"Yeah, something like that," he says quickly. Again he goes quiet. My forehead creases; I'm worried something happened to his parents, but he doesn't say anything further.

I smile, trying to lighten the mood. "You said something about an idea?"

He reaches inside his jacket and retrieves his cell phone. "Let's order a pizza," he says with a grin.

I can practically feel my face transform from puzzled to disbelieving. "We just had dinner."

He stares at me. "And do you feel full?"

I think about the bite-sized pizzetta. It was delicious, but not comfort in a box. "Honestly, not at all."

"I bet there's some good pizza places around here," Gabriel says. He taps his phone. "What kind of toppings do you like?"

"Toppings," I repeat like it's an obscure SAT word. He hands me his phone. My hands shake as I review the choices. "I like mushrooms and ham," I manage to say.

"Ham?" He smiles. "I got this." I return his phone and he punches his screen.

"Wait, are you having the pizza delivered here to the White House?"

"It's 1600 Pennsylvania Avenue, correct?"

"Yes."

He grins. "It'll be here in fifteen minutes."

My jaw drops. "Fifteen minutes? But—"

"But you've never ordered pizza before." His tone is smug.

My face burns. I imagine how pathetic I would sound if I responded, *No, because my mom has staff who've done the ordering for us since I was six.* Gosh, it sounds terrible in my head. Maybe he's right to question whether I'm a suitable "voice for young people." I've never ordered my own pizza before.

My hands cover my face as I try to reconcile all the feels going through me.

I should be upset. Totally against this idea . . . but honestly, I'm also having fun.

"Abby?" I jerk up, hearing the concern in Oliver's voice. He walks toward me, his lips pressed into a thin line as his gaze goes from me to Gabriel.

"The performances are about to begin," Oliver says. Meaning my folks would like the entire First Family to sit together to demonstrate our appreciation.

Gabriel looks at his phone and sighs. "Thirteen minutes," he says, his voice clearly annoyed.

Oliver glares at him. "Is everything okay?" he asks me.

Gabriel snorts. "Excuse me?"

"I wasn't talking to you," Oliver retorts as he places a hand on my arm. "You look upset."

"No, I was just . . ." I throw my hands up. For once at a complete loss for words. "Gabriel and I ordered a pizza."

Now Oliver looks stunned. I continue practically babbling. "We were discussing how we're still hungry."

"But we just had dinner," Oliver says, confused.

I laugh nervously. "I know that. I know. It's just a fun idea."

"But you have kitchen staff who could whip you up anything you want," Oliver says.

"Hey, dude. She just wanted to order out," Gabriel says. "No big deal."

Oliver has daggers in his eyes. "Sorry, *dude*, but we can't just order out. Our parents are very important people—"

Gabriel rolls his eyes. "Right, you're very important people."

Oliver groans. "My dad would have a fit if I did anything to jeopardize security or public relations. Abby's in the same boat."

I glance at an increasingly defiant-looking Gabriel as Oliver keeps going. "If your father was vice president, you'd have an appreciation for all the precautions people like me and Abby have to take."

"My father?" Gabriel says incredulously. I cringe as he glares at Oliver and looks in disbelief at me. Despite the anger in his face, I also sense pain.

Gabriel turns to leave. "I'm out of here. You two have a nice important life together."

"Wait," I say after him. "Let me explain."

Gabriel bows, imitating the one he did when he first met Oliver, and walks out the door.

My chest fills with anger. "Oliver, why did you say those things?"

He looks at me. "What, Abby? It's true. We can't just order pizza!"

But I don't let Oliver finish his thought as I head toward the front entrance. "Where are you going? The performance is about to start. Your parents?" he calls after me.

But I don't care. Right now, all I can think of is one thing.

"I'm going to pick up my pizza."

CHAPTER 5

"Abby, wait," Oliver calls. His footsteps echo over the marble floor of the White House as he catches up to me.

Agent Shaw and Oliver's Secret Service agent exchange glances when they see Oliver and me head to the front entrance instead of the East Room to join my family for the performance.

I glance in that direction, wondering if Gabriel went back, but see no sign of him.

I inhale deeply. He's probably long gone by now and I don't blame him. Oliver treated him badly, and I said nothing. I feel terrible.

Maybe I can get Tita Karra to send him a note for me because I doubt he'd want to see me again. And I doubt I'll have a chance. Oliver and I leave for Hawaiʻi this weekend.

My shoulders sag. Realistically, never seeing Gabriel is likely for the best. My chest tightens and I'm overcome with a strong urge to run.

"I just need to get some air," I say to Shaw as I attempt a smile.

"*We* need to get some air," Oliver adds.

Our agents don't say it aloud, but I can read their thoughts:

Lucky us having to babysit two teenagers and their drama. We don't get paid enough.

Shaw opens the door for us.

The warm summer air is a relief as I step outside, inhaling a blend of blooming flowers, sunbaked earth, and fresh-cut grass. The evening hums with Friday-night energy as Washington, DC, bustles with laughter and life. The rhythmic chirp of crickets fills the air.

Even Oliver seems appreciative as he takes in the scene. "It's a nice night for a walk," he concedes.

"Oliver, I'm going to get my pizza," I say with a resolve that surprises even me. But, I rationalize, this is in bucket list territory—trying new foods and new perspectives. This counts.

My statement is clearly not what Oliver wants to hear.

"Abby, I really think that's a suboptimal choice. What if we get in trouble?"

I nudge him with my shoulder. "Let's walk and I'll just happen to stroll over to security and pick up the pizza. I'll say you have nothing to do with it."

He inhales deeply as he mutters, but to his credit goes with it.

I survey the lawn and our surroundings. The North Lawn features a large water fountain in front of the White House and a semicircular driveway that is framed by trees and boxwood hedges.

Our timing is perfect. Everybody, including the press, is inside watching the performances. The only people outside are us, our agents, and the security guards at the gates at the bottom of the driveway.

And it's a given there are always people passing by the tall black fences that guard the perimeter of the White House. Fortunately, no one appears to be looking our way; people are just walking past, minding their own business. If Oliver and I keep to the driveway and behind the trees, we should be okay making our way to the security gate.

"How do you know which security gate the delivery guy is coming to?" Oliver asks.

It's a good question because we have several. "Not sure, guess I'll wait and see?"

He nods. "Actually, I'm glad we're alone. There's something I've been meaning to ask you."

My step falters and my heart skips a beat. Is he going to ask me to be his girlfriend? I laugh nervously. Shouldn't I be excited? Shouldn't this be one of those moments I'll cherish?

"Abby," Oliver says. "I don't think I have your full attention."

A red scooter approaches one of the gates. "Hold on," I say, holding up a finger. I silently cheer seeing the square "boxes of comfort" strapped to the back.

I look back at our agents, who are several feet behind, then at Oliver, who looks uncertain. I make a split-second decision.

Lifting my constricting skirt, I kick off my heels and hurry to the gate.

"Abby," Oliver hisses, but nothing's stopping me now.

As I approach the gate, the poor guard who's stationed there looks my way, bewildered. I ignore him and turn my attention to the scrawny college-aged guy carrying a red pizza delivery bag.

"I've got a delivery for a Jack and Rose Dawson," he says, scratching his chin.

Gabriel sure has a sense of humor. "Yup, that's me, I'll take it," I say, and the guy slides a cardboard box out of the bag.

By this point, the security guard has stepped in front of me and a furious Agent Shaw has caught up with us.

"There's a mistake," he says, looking from me to the guard to the pizza delivery guy.

"No mistake," I say, and reach through the gate to grab the box from the stunned delivery guy, maneuvering it sideways through the gate. It's a tight squeeze but thankfully it fits.

"Abby!" Oliver warns, but I ignore him as I open the lid to smell my pizza.

My nose wrinkles. "Um. Maybe a slight mistake," I tell the delivery guy. "Why is there yucky pineapple on this pizza? Gross!"

Still bewildered, he shakes his shaggy head. "It's a Hawaiian pizza."

Hawaiian? My laugh is thunderous. Oh, Gabriel is too much. "Is there another pizza in that bag? One with mushrooms and ham?"

"If there is, keep it," Shaw barks at the guy, and shoots me a look. "Back inside," he orders me and Oliver, grabbing the box from me. "We'll have to get this analyzed first."

I frown, knowing he means they need to check if the food is safe before I can eat it.

"Don't bother," I say, rolling my eyes. I wave at the delivery guy and suddenly feel guilty for all the trouble. "I'm sorry. Did we pay for the pizzas?"

"Yes, on the app," he says, voice squeaky. Still, I feel bad for him. I pat my nonexistent pockets. "I don't have a tip." I look at Oliver, who shrugs.

"Wallet's in the house," he says.

I twist my mouth and swiftly remove my watch and give it to the delivery guy. Oliver stares at the exchange, wide-eyed, while the delivery guy is equally speechless as he takes the watch.

"Abby, we've got to go," Oliver says tersely.

I follow his gaze and notice a few excited onlookers with their phones up. They're outside the gate and several feet away, but they're definitely close enough to see something going down.

Oh no. I gulp, hoping no one posts those.

Shaw looks like he's about to have a meltdown. He motions for me to hurry up and I follow his lead back to the Residence, questioning everything I've done this evening and wondering what has gotten into me.

Maybe the better question is: Who got to me?

CHAPTER 6

"Enzo rocked!" Elle says, dancing into the kitchen in her Hello Kitty slippers. She reaches for the cereal box on the counter. It's 08:30 and I was enjoying a quiet breakfast in our family's private upstairs kitchen up until now.

Last night, after the incident with the pizza, I went straight to the Residence after learning that Tita Karra and Gabriel had already left the party.

Tita apparently had to get back to Mystic Hollow for business and to drop her godson back home. For a good hour I wrestled with the idea of calling Tita so I could get Gabe's number.

I wanted him to know how much I appreciated the *Titanic* reference. And I wanted him to know how wrong he was to order pineapple on pizza. Seriously? Who does that? Gabriel Calabrese.

After knowing him a whole two hours I pretty much ignored my security detail and could've created an embarrassing story for Mom. Gabe's not a good influence.

Fortunately, I've checked all the papers, and the ones that mention me focus on me and Oliver.

Our About Town profile has a predictable photo of me and

Oliver dancing at the state dinner. The caption: *Here's something the ENTIRE country has been predicting for years! FDOTUS and her date, Second Son Oliver Darby, looking cozy. Is it time to officially crown them "Abliver"?* Abliver? Really? Sounds like a body part.

It's hard to know what's more annoying, the media already dubbing us a couple or the fact that this is something the entire country has predicted for years . . . That's me, boring, predictable Abby.

No pics of me dancing with Gabriel, or the pizza incident.

"Earth to Abby," Elle says. She waggles her brows. "I'm sorry you and Oliver weren't feeling well and had to bail from the party for the rest of the night." Her voice is anything but sorry. My eyes narrow, not appreciating her innuendo.

"For goodness' sake, don't people have better things to worry about?" Mom's voice cuts through the air before she even appears in the kitchen in her plaid pajamas and silk robe. "Abby. A pizza delivery? Really?"

She holds up her phone—a photo of my face frozen mid-scowl at a pizza box. Must have been when I discovered it had pineapple. "But I searched online. I didn't see anything about the pizza," I mumble.

Her hands fly to her hips. "Honey, maybe I have an entire press team monitoring news for me twenty-four seven."

I sigh. She's got me there.

Mom continues, "They're calling it Pineapplegate."

"Pineapplegate," I squeak.

My mother groans. "Abby, it's bad enough you ordered a pizza without running it through the proper channels. You know food deliveries are handled by designated staff. It's not as simple as a delivery driver pulling up and handing over a pizza!" she continues. "But why of all the nights did you have to order it the same night we served pizza at the White House to the Italian prime minister?"

My stomach roils with guilt. "Mom, I'd hardly call the garden salad on bread pizza. I was hungry, and wanted gooey cheesy *pizza* pizza."

She tilts her head the way an eagle studies its prey. I've always felt bad for anyone who gets that look of hers. Pity it's me this morning. Her eyes narrow. "Did you. Because you very visibly are making a yuck face in this photo," she says.

I inhale deeply. "You know how I feel about pineapple." My hands cover my face. "I'm sorry, Mom, I wasn't thinking about the optics."

"No, you weren't thinking," she says. I cringe when she goes quiet. I can practically see her brain calculating my punishment. Woe to the person about to get punished by President Alzona.

Dad pops into the kitchen grinning ear to ear in his REAL MEN BAKE COOKIES T-shirt. He makes a show of an exaggerated double take when he sees everyone. "I wasn't expecting a full house this morning. Abby, it's nice to see you awake. Heard you and Oliver weren't feeling well last night," he teases as he heads to the coffeepot.

When no one responds, he sighs. "What did I miss?"

Mom sniffs. "You got here just in time."

Dad wrinkles his nose and pats the chair next to him. I scoot my cereal bowl over and join him.

"Last night's state dinner made quite the impression," Mom says. She unfolds the front page of the newspaper tucked under her arm. The top image is her and the prime minister's formal greeting. The headline is favorable, even complimentary of my mom's diplomacy skills.

"This looks fine. Great coverage, even," Dad says. "They're focusing on your trade deal. Good job."

She shows him her phone next. Dad's eyes widen. He reads, " 'While the president excelled with honoring our guest's country, First Daughter Abigail Cary-Alzona was caught carrying out her own brand of diplomacy by ordering a pizza pie despite being served one during the state dinner.

" 'In a blow to the guest country, Cary-Alzona ordered an American-style pizza alongside her boyfriend, Oliver Darby.' "

I protest aloud, "He's not my boyfriend."

Dad continues reading the article.

" 'She then tipped the delivery boy with a ridiculously expensive Cartier watch.' "

Mom pinches the bridge of her nose. "Why would you do that?"

I stammer as I realize my error. "I felt bad for the delivery boy and wanted to give him a tip. Oliver has given me so many watches and bracelets, I guess I didn't think much of it."

"Honey, most people your age don't own a watch that costs more than their entire wardrobe, let alone leave it as a tip." I flush. Oliver gave me that watch. He gives me lots of presents—usually stuff I suspect his parents don't want.

Mom closes her eyes. "Abby, you can ask the chef to make you whatever you want."

I inhale slowly. That's exactly what Oliver said. "I know. I just wanted to do something normal. Something a regular teenager would do," I say, my voice sounding small and defeated.

Silence. My parents exchange worried glances. Elle catches my eye and mouths something. I squint and realize she's saying, "Bucket list."

No. She wants me to tell them about my list? So they know I want to do "normal" teenage things? Yeah, that's not going to happen when they're already upset about me ordering pizza. I'm sure the other items on my list will light their fuses, and I've experienced enough fireworks this morning.

My dad sighs. "How did you even know how to order a pizza?"

I bite my lip. "I used an app." I'm pretty certain if I mention Gabe that'll create more questions and headaches. Better to omit that part.

Elle groans. "An app? Then a tip was probably automatically included in your order, dummy."

"Elle," Dad warns, then squeezes my hand. "It's okay, honey, you're a teenager. You're allowed to make mistakes now and then."

Mom takes a deep breath. "I'm not angry, sweetie, just surprised. This isn't like you."

I stare into my cereal bowl, where my milk is turning pink and orange from my Froot Loops—one of my few vices. I feel so lousy about disappointing Mom. She sacrifices so much, and here I am embarrassing her because I wanted a pizza.

No, if I'm being honest, I wanted to prove to Gabe that I could be normal—but why? Caring what he thinks of me over my responsibilities isn't like me at all. I sigh. My cereal's gone soggy, which feels like my life right now.

★ ★ ★

By lunch, it's clear that my pineapple story is gaining steam. The pizza delivery boy has now spilled the beans about what happened, alongside memes that flood social media comparing me to Marie Antoinette saying let them wear gold as I toss a Cartier watch. Leave it to Elle to very sagely point out that it's the opposite of Marie Antoinette because I was giving my wealth away.

By Sunday morning, apparently "Pineapple Princess" is all over the news shows. Dad and Mom enter my room. They look serious.

I sigh, sitting on my bed. "I'll take the bad news first."

My mom and dad exchange glances. "Let's not cast this as good or bad, just a change in direction," Mom says.

"Mom," I say. "Don't spin me."

Dad takes a deep breath and sits at the foot of my bed. "What your mother is trying to say is that we're postponing your Hawai'i plans."

I blink. "I'm sorry, are you saying I'm not going to Hawai'i?"

Dad doesn't smile as he nods. I scoff. "But I have that big community service project planned with Senator Sina. I was going to be in charge for once. Like, I'm actually *leading* the event."

I look back and forth between my parents, wondering if they fully understand how terrible this is for me. Senator Sina's charity was going to be a huge component of my college application essays. Mom rubs my arm. "It seems there's some issue with pineapple growers and, well, we don't want Patty to be looked upon negatively in her home state."

"She's canceling because the pineapple growers are upset with me?"

My dad shrugs. "Apparently the pineapple community is very influential."

The ground feels like it's sinking beneath me. "Why can't I just stay at the hotel with Oliver? We have a bunch of activities planned," I say, picturing the escape and freedom we'd enjoy at his private resort.

Mom sighs. "I talked to Ben and we both agreed that maybe a breather between you two would be good."

My jaw drops. "Mr. Darby wants me to take a break from Oliver?" I snicker. But the look in Mom's eyes is totally serious. I guess Oliver's dad wasn't happy about his son being pulled into Pineapplegate with me. And I bet Oliver is happy he didn't ask me to be his girlfriend.

My mind reels. What is happening? How in twenty-four hours has my perfectly planned summer itinerary been trampled and killed like a congressional bill being sent back to committee? I flop back on my bed, staring at the white ceiling. How many other First Kids have looked at that same ceiling in disappointment? I doubt Malia, Chelsea, or Barbara ever messed up. I could see Jenna maybe . . . she seems like fun.

"But the good news," Mom says, perky, "is that instead of staying here at the White House, Tita Karra's invited you to stay with her in Virginia."

"So at least you'll be out of the house," Dad chimes in.

Virginia? With Tita Karra? I shoot up so fast my head spins.

“Wait—so instead of Hawai‘i, you’re shipping me off to Tita Karra’s?” I squint. “Wasn’t she back in the Bay Area?”

Mom and Dad exchange looks.

“You know Karra. She’s working on a new project in some small town . . .” Dad’s voice trails off.

The color drains from my face. “Mystic Hollow,” I say.

Dad brightens. “That’s right. Mystic Hollow. And from the sounds of it, it’s the perfect place for you and Elle to enjoy some good old-fashioned outdoor time for a few weeks. Karra says there’s a lot of activities you two can do: horses, kayaks, campfires.”

“Dad, since when am I into kayaks?”

“It’ll be peaceful; you can catch up on your reading,” he says.

Mom folds her arms across her chest. “Think of it as a retreat, a chance to unplug from all the hustle and bustle of DC.”

My eyes narrow. “Okay, what you mean is that it’s secluded and tucked away from the press.”

“As if that’s a bad thing,” Mom says, her lips pressed thin.

I’m being grounded without them explicitly saying so.

As if being secluded in Mystic Hollow isn’t enough, it’s also where one cranky Gabriel Calabrese resides. After ruining my summer with his ridiculous pizza idea, he’s the last person I want to see this summer, or ever.

CHAPTER 7

"Ice cream? Ice cream always makes things better," Elle says, mostly to herself. We drop our tote bags on the dusty ground at the old barn where the Secret Service has pulled over. The worn, red-painted wood barn looks like it's been there since Abraham Lincoln was president. So long, sandy beaches. Hello, existential crisis, rustic edition.

A couple chickens appear by the barn's door.

"Must be our welcome committee," Elle deadpans. At least she's done with the silent treatment. My shoulders sag like a wilted flower in the summer heat. It's hard to say whether the ride here or the time Dad's parade float broke down, halting a rowdy Saint Patrick's Day parade, was more tense.

I rub my sore back, which was squished for three hours by Elle's backpack, pillow, and panda stuffy as she mashed buttons on her Nintendo Switch, her large AirPods Max headphones on her head, ignoring her loser big sister who got our Hawaiian vacation canceled. All the while, the scene from our car window changed from urban city blocks to suburban neighborhoods to empty golden hillsides with a smattering of trees, and occasional big farmhouses with old wraparound porches and rocking chairs.

Mom said this is Virginia horse country, and sure—it's beautiful. Just not what I've spent months planning for. I'm not great at improvising, which is why the whole Pineapplegate fiasco baffles me. I don't go off script. I *know* I can't order my own pizza. I can't even sleep over at a friend's house without their parents being cleared by the FBI. Hence, no sleepovers. Hawai'i was set. I had a plan for my bucket list. Life was unfolding exactly how I planned. Until I met Gabriel.

I sigh. My bucket list does not have horseback riding or farms. It has beaches and new foods. Picnics and staying up late, all things I envisioned doing near a beach. Not landlocked, and certainly not at a barn that smells like manure or farm animals or both on a grueling summer day.

Agent Shaw paces nearby on his phone, his voice low and annoyed. Nessa stands near our SUV, her eyes shielded by her mirrored Ray-Bans, her head moving side to side as she scans our surroundings. I can only imagine what's going on in their heads: We had swimsuits ready, not cowboy boots.

Suddenly, a loud and rhythmic chugging sound rips through the air.

Elle and I twist to see the source of the noise. If my jaw dropped any lower, Mom would need to send a search party to find it.

A confident and glowing Tita Karra approaches driving a small green tractor, pulling a wagon behind it.

Agent Shaw and Nessa settle when they see it's Tita and not

some rando. I hear Tita's call sign "Razzle" as Shaw's shoulders relax.

With a swift and firm motion, Tita stops the tractor several feet from us. "Long time no see," she jokes from atop the vehicle.

"You can drive a tractor!" Elle exclaims.

Tita chuckles. "Sure! Your mom used to fly helicopters. I can drive a tractor."

I do a double take. Just three days ago Tita was in a fancy ruby Gucci gown, but today her sun hat, jeans, and boots look right at home on her.

Tita opens her arms and motions us in for a group hug. I breathe in her jasmine-and-citrus scent. The jasmine reminds me of my serious mother, but the citrus is playful like my tita.

"You okay?" she asks as I pull back. Her smile remains on her face, but I can see the worry in her eyes.

My mouth twists as I try to hold back my tears. "Honestly, not really," I say.

She nods and pulls me in for a hug again. "I know. I know. This isn't what you wanted," she whispers. I'm thankful for Tita; she's always been a sounding board and ally for me.

"We're going to make the best of it while you're here." She gestures at the wagon. "Let's start with the scenic way to the inn."

"You mean we're not sleeping in the barn?" Elle says dryly.

"If chickens and cows help you sleep at night, I won't stop you," Tita teases. She taps the wagon and motions for us to jump in. "Come on. You're in for a treat. The Mystic Hollow wagon ride is an exclusive attraction in the region."

"When in Rome," I mutter. I thank Shaw for finding wood crates to help us climb onto the high wagon bed. Once aboard, we find hay bales lined up like benches.

In some other dimension there's a version of me who's sitting at the beach drinking from a coconut. This version of me—the one who just had to get a yucky pineapple pizza—is sitting on scratchy dry stalks and overwhelmed by dust and the scent of straw and dirt. At least I'm in a T-shirt and sweats and not something I'd mind getting dirty.

"Hang tight," Tita orders as she locks the back gate of the wagon, then hops onto the driver's seat. The tractor roars to life and the wagon starts moving with a jerk.

Elle yelps with a loud, delighted shriek. I'm relieved my sister looks happy at the moment.

Agents Shaw and Nessa climb back into their SUV and drive behind us. Our tractor trudges along a bumpy dirt path. "Is she trying to hit every rock possible?" I complain to Elle.

She giggles. "All right, Your Highness. Next time we'll ask for the royal carriage."

Soon the farmland changes from dirt and hay bales to an orchard that looks like the perfect place for picking apples when they're in season.

"Who owns this land?" I call over to Tita.

"It used to all belong to the inn," she says. The tractor is loud, but I can still hear the regret in her voice. "But they sold the orchard part a couple years ago."

"That's too bad," I say.

We follow a dirt path into a grove of trees. The shade is a

welcome relief. A creek trickles nearby, and even over the rumble of the tractor, I can hear birds chirping not far away. The trees part, revealing a lush, rolling field—and then I see it.

"Wow." A stately white two-story house rises ahead, with a red roof, twin chimneys, and black-framed windows tucked behind cute old-fashioned shutters. A wide wraparound porch is lined with rocking chairs, and there's even a wicker swing. Iron lanterns dangle from the porch's columns.

Flanking the main house are east and west wings, and down a winding dirt path sits a quaint green-roofed cottage. The entire inn is surrounded by green fields and gorgeous blue-and-purple hills rippling in the distance. It looks like it has welcomed guests for over a hundred years.

A black SUV that must belong to our advance security detail is parked on the mansion's circular driveway.

I glance with delight at a large tree where a well-loved wooden bench swing hangs.

The swing's cushioned seat would be the perfect place to curl up and read a book or maybe stargaze. Stargazing is on my unofficial list.

"What do you think?" Tita asks.

"It's nice," I offer.

Her eyes crinkle. If I were her, I'd take my terse response as a win. The place is beautiful but still not where I had planned to be. No, this mansion represents my summer plans gone wrong.

"I think it's magical," Elle calls out. "A romantic countryside home like Longbourn House in *Pride and Prejudice.*"

Mystic Hollow Inn has a magical vibe, sure, but romance?

Romance was a tropical setting, ocean waves, a brilliant sunset. If Oliver and I are going to start our relationship, that would've been the ideal place to begin. Instead, he's on a ten-hour flight there and I'm here. I glance at my phone and his last messages to me. *Miss you too.* Followed by: *Deep breaths, champ. You got this.*

The large white front door of the inn opens. My breath catches seeing the boy who walks out. Of course. This is my life. Elle leans forward. "Abby? Is that . . ."

"Yes. Elle. It. Is." I pinch the bridge of my nose. I hate how he's even cuter in a white T-shirt and jeans. Gabriel Calabrese stands in front of the inn, hands tucked in his black jeans pockets as he looks warily at our wagon.

This is the perfect storm: the boy who got me in trouble, in the place that ruined my summer plans. With a tight smile on his face, Gabriel strolls to the wagon. "Hey," he says as he opens our wagon's gate.

"Good to see you again, Gabriel," Elle says with a little too much joy as she grabs the hand he offers to help her down. He lowers her like she's no heavier than her favorite panda stuffy.

It's my turn to jump off, and I stare at his outstretched hand that's connected to a very nicely muscular arm. I'm suddenly self-conscious about my gray sweats and baggy SAVE THE WHALES T-shirt.

It's like I gave up even trying. Which, to be fair, I did after spying what I was supposed to wear today—a red-and-yellow tropical flower dress—hanging in my closet this morning.

"Need a hand?" Gabriel asks.

I scoff. Last time this boy helped me, I ended up making a fool of myself on national news. "No thanks. I won't need your assistance." Ever. I don't say that last part out loud.

His brows scrunch but he steps back. I lower my foot to see how far the ground is. Not even on tippy-toe could I reach.

I puff a strand of hair off my forehead and grab the wagon's metal gate, which—is not secured and flings wider. As the door swings, I swing with it. "Whoa!" My legs fly out, dangling like a kid in a chair that's way too big, flailing in midair while I cling on for dear life.

"Abby," Elle says, rushing forward.

As the gate swings back toward the truck, I grab the edge of the wagon to steady myself and somehow, miraculously, lower myself down. I land on the gravel road with a loud thump and catch myself just in time before face-planting.

"I'm fine. I'm good," I say as I wave a hand to stop a worried Agent Shaw's advance.

As I recover, my audience appears in several stages of shock. Agent Shaw seems upset, wondering how he drew the short straw to get the clumsiest member of the First Family. Elle is clutching her belly as she laughs herself silly. And Gabriel has a pained expression.

"Hay naku. You girls are running a full-time campaign to end my sanity," Tita Karra exclaims as she rushes to my side to help steady me.

With as much confidence as I can muster, I toss my long, frazzled hair behind my shoulder. "I'm *fine*."

She shakes her head, then starts for the front door. "Come on, let's get you two checked in."

She glances at Gabriel. "Hoy, godson, can you get their bags?"

I frown. "He doesn't need to do that."

"He does if he wants to get paid." Tita chortles. My blood goes icy. No, no, no, no, no. I watch with horror as Gabriel grabs luggage from our SUV.

"Do you work here?" I cry.

He hauls my bag down from the vehicle with ease. "Nah, I just like hanging here for fun."

I glower at him, ignoring the heat rushing to my cheeks as our eyes meet. He chuckles. "Although watching you fall out of the wagon was pretty funny."

My jaw drops. "I didn't fall out. I just miscalculated a little."

His lips curl into a wicked smile. "Mm-hmm. Bet you help your dad remember his astronaut days."

"Sorry?"

"You seem to have trouble with gravity?"

"Har. Har," I say and glare at him. "And I guess you're the hotel jester?"

"Yeah. And maintenance. And occasionally the front desk. Welcome to my family's business." He cocks his chin at the sign hanging in front of the building.

It says *Mystic Hollow Inn* in dark cursive writing over the logo of a large—

I groan so loud I'm sure Gabriel's ancestors hear me. I gesture at the large pineapple on the inn's sign. "A pineapple? Really?"

"In colonial Virginia, pineapples were a symbol of hospitality."

He laughs triumphantly. "See, Pineapple Princess. There's some Aloha Spirit for you."

I glare at his back as he makes his way inside with my luggage. Tita hollers for us to come inside, and I feel like I'm stumbling into a nightmare—the kind with gross pineapples and a cute boy who should come with a warning label.

CHAPTER 8

Mystic Hollow Inn is brighter and more welcoming than I expected. The foyer walls are painted a cheerful blue, adorned with idyllic countryside scenes and portraits of important-looking people—some smiling, and some who look ready to banish their daughters to a remote location.

A wide wooden staircase is toward the back of the foyer. On either side of the lobby, sitting rooms give modern farmhouse vibes with historic, rustic touches. The cozy seating practically begs for a book and a hot cup of tea. Even the rugs are colorful and inviting.

Behind the small front desk, a gallery of framed photos catches my eye: sun-drenched landscapes and casual candid shots of smiling guests.

Elle giggles as she points out the pineapple-shaped lamps, as well as throw pillows with pineapple designs.

I cover my eyes. Why have the pineapple gods forsaken me?

The stairs creak, and a pretty woman with short dark hair and a classic cream-colored dress gestures at the ceilings as two men in suits follow her. "And we have cameras right here pointed at our front door," she finishes saying.

The woman stops in her tracks when she sees our entourage in the foyer. Her dark eyes widen and I know instantly this pretty woman is Gabriel's mom. She clasps her hands. "Welcome! I was just showing your security detail around."

She looks at Karra. "I thought you'd call when you were on the way."

Karra waves her cell phone. "Only one bar, remember."

Meanwhile her comment sends me fumbling for my own phone to look at my connection. No bars. Not a one.

"Wait. How's the Wi-Fi?" Elle asks, making the same realization. But I collect myself quickly. First Daughters always need to be gracious.

"What my sister means is, thank you for your hospitality," I say warmly.

The woman nods, also seeming to remember herself. "Of course. The Mystic Hollow Inn is honored to have you two join us." She reaches out a hand. "I'm Ruby Calabrese."

She shakes Elle's hand next. "I hope these next few weeks are a relaxing getaway for you two." Her grin is unapologetic. "We are a tech-free retreat, which our guests enjoy as a way to escape the DC hustle."

"As in, no Wi-Fi," Gabriel adds. His bow-shaped lips emphasize a smile that says he finds our situation amusing. I do my best not to glare at him.

Elle grabs my hand tight, and it takes everything in me not to wince from the pain. I had plenty of plans to do non-techy things like reading and working on my college essays, but I wasn't planning on isolating myself from the world either. But I'm sure that's exactly what my parents had in mind. Keep us hidden away from the media and prying eyes.

"Thank you, Ms. Calabrese," I respond.

"Our guests at the inn are like family. Please call me Ruby."

"And I *am* family," Gabriel cracks. "Can I call you Ruby too?"

His mom levels a glare at her son. *Hmm*, another thing he's inherited from her. She shakes her head with a smile. "I'm sure you're already aware of my son's cheery disposition." She brightens. "Though Gabe couldn't stop talking about you and the White House when he returned."

My face warms. Gabriel talked about me with his mother?

I can sense him stiffen nearby. "Mom, it was like a quick chat the following morning," he says between gritted teeth.

Her laugh reminds me of wind chimes. "And that's the equivalent of you having a lot to say." She turns to me. "You need to excuse my son. Like his father, he's a man of few words."

Her expression grows nostalgic and the mood in the room shifts. I glance at Tita, who acknowledges my silent ask for an explanation. There's some family history here that I need to be sensitive about, so I'll want to get the scoop from her ASAP.

"I'll grab the rest of their bags." Gabe grunts and heads outside without looking back.

Ruby hesitates as she looks after her retreating son, but one of our advance team asks her about a gate code and that snaps

Gabriel's mom back to the present. Ruby gives us a brief smile. "I'll let you get settled. Karra knows the way," she says.

I watch Ruby lead the security detail outside, and then it's only Elle, me, and Tita Karra in the foyer. I touch Tita's arm gently. "Did something happen to Gabriel's father?"

She turns and nods to a photo on the wall behind us, next to the front door. Gabriel's family are standing on the inn's front porch, smiling like they're posing for a holiday photo: Gabriel, who's maybe around Elle's age; his mom, Ruby; and a handsome man with brown skin and copper eyes.

Another, smaller framed picture is nearby. It's just of Gabriel's dad with a gold plaque: *In loving memory.*

Elle lets out a soft whimper and Tita squeezes my hand. Sadness creeps into my chest and lingers, recalling the confrontation in the Red Room. No wonder he left so fast after Oliver practically lectured him about his father's expectations. Oliver rubbed in his face that his father was still alive—while Gabriel's wasn't.

A soft hand touches my shoulder. "Let's get you settled in your room," Tita whispers.

I let her lead the way. The walk upstairs to our room is blurry as I wrestle with the sad news. Still, I notice photographs hanging on the staircase walls, not unlike the ones we saw in the lobby with smiling guests from the past. Some look as old as the antique photos in my collection.

A photo taken from behind of a couple on a tree swing at twilight takes my breath away. The sky is in that in-between time as the sun's rays dip below the horizon and the stars begin to take over and shine. In the background, the inn emits a cozy glow, reminding me of a candle at a romantic dinner date. I can't see their faces, but from the way their bodies lean, they look so in love.

The second floor is an inviting hallway with four doors and a large window at the end, allowing in natural light. Karra leads the way. "I know it's a slight change for you all to be in the west wing of the inn," she says, adding air quotes around *west wing*. I offer her a courtesy laugh at her attempt to be cute—back at the White House, my mom's offices are in the West Wing.

She turns a corner and we're standing in another short hallway, which leads to a large wooden door with a sign that says *Blue Ridge Suite*.

True to the rest of the inn, we step into a tastefully decorated sitting room that feels like an upscale hotel room but with historic touches.

The space is a comforting buttermilk color with a cornflower-blue sofa set and decor accents in gold and crystal. Elle gawks at the large marble fireplace, which must make the room extra cozy in the colder months.

I immediately check out the double windows that overlook a stunning mountain vista. I can see why this is the Blue Ridge Suite.

Off the sitting room are two bedrooms.

I claim the room with the king bed and the most natural light by tossing my purse on it, but Elle is more than happy to have the other room, which has a cushioned window bench and large throw pillows.

Tita Karra goes over every detail of the suite's two bedrooms, from the linen count to the brand of bath products. I arch a brow as I put two and two together. "This is the business you're investing in, right?"

My aunt nods. "Yes, I fell in love with the property years ago. And when Ruby called after what happened to Frank, I remembered how much I loved the place."

"Wh-when did you become Gabe's godmother?" I stammer.

"About three years ago." Her eyes shine with sadness. "It all happened around the same time. The accident and then Gabriel's confirmation ceremony." I nod. "It just felt natural for me to be there for my friend, and I was happy to be her son's ninang."

I'm eager to continue our conversation about Gabriel's dad, but a knock on our door draws everyone's attention.

Ruby steps inside, followed by Gabriel with our luggage. "Welcome to our Blue Ridge Suite, Abby and Elle. I hope this space meets your expectations," she says with a sweep of her arms.

"It's perfect." I grin. "You get an official presidential sign of approval."

Ruby walks over to the window. "Actually, George Washington was rumored to have visited the apple orchard nearby." She points into the distance, where Elle and I passed this morning. It reminds me that Tita said Gabriel's family had to sell that piece of land.

An unsettling feeling hits me, and I wonder if Gabriel's family business is in some kind of trouble.

"Are there other guests staying here?"

Ruby's forehead crinkles slightly. I've seen the same expression on Gabriel. "We have one couple here for the Love Package."

Elle waggles her brows. "The Loooove Package."

"It's our Virginia Is for Lovers special," Ruby explains. "They're checking out first thing tomorrow, so they won't disturb you. And then the rest of the time you're here, you'll be our sole guests." Ruby exchanges a look with Tita Karra. The unsaid words between them convey concern. "We're planning for a lot more guests to come July first for our Independence Day Package, but of course you won't be here."

I nod. We're here until the end of June.

Gabriel huffs nearby as he brings the first three of Elle's seven bags into the room. Don't need a thought balloon over his head to know what he's thinking.

Meanwhile, Tita Karra wraps her arms around Elle and me. "Girls, this is going to be the best month ever." As I struggle to breathe, I ask where she's staying.

"Don't worry, I'm not far. My room is in the east wing, with the rest of the family." She squeezes me extra tight. "I've got all kinds of activities and crafts planned. You still like bedazzling accessories and paint by numbers, right?" She clasps her hands. "We're going to have so much fun."

Bedazzling? Paint by numbers? What am I, five? I expect Gabriel's probably savoring this moment so he can tease me later, but the look on his face is quite the opposite and I feel awful. After finding out about his dad—and realizing just how terrible Oliver and I must've come off—I have a gnawing need to fix things. "Let me help. I know my sister has a million bags," I say to Gabe as he heads out the door.

Ruby snaps her head up. "Oh no, dear. Gabe can manage."

He looks at me, a sort of question mark on his face, but I flash my big First Daughter smile. "Oh, I don't mind. I need to stretch my legs anyway after that long car ride." I don't wait for a response and walk out the door.

Heavy footsteps follow and Gabe quickly catches up. "Seriously, I can manage," he says.

"And seriously, I wanted to get some air."

He hesitates. "The last time we ventured away from the crowd, I got you in trouble."

I scoff and stop at the top of the stairs. "You may have ordered the pizza, but I was the one who actually went outside to pick it up."

His silence tells me he's at least seeing my point of view. "Fine, but I'm grabbing your textbook bag. You've got to be the only person who brings the contents of her high school locker on summer vacation."

"How did you know I brought textbooks?"

His brows wrinkle. "You labeled your luggage."

I start down the stairs, glad I'm walking ahead of him, so he doesn't see my red face. "Summer before senior year is important."

"Sure," he says tersely. "Prepping for college applications and senior-year courses."

I glance back at him, nonplussed. "Exactly. You get it."

"Not really."

I nod. "It's cool. Mom has been working to make sure that young people have careers with or without college."

He laughs. "Wow, you're a walking campaign ad."

I wince. "Sorry, guess it's a habit. But seriously, not judging whatever you've got planned after high school."

We're back in the foyer. "You know I'm into photography, right?" he says.

I see red, remembering my photo collection back at the White House. "How can I forget? You ruined my family's photograph arrangement when you rearranged them."

He pretends to be offended. "Wait. Did you say I ruined it?" He points at the photos in the inn's foyer. Many of which I admired when we first walked in. "Most of these are my dad's, but the more contemporary ones are mine," he says.

I nod with appreciation at a rich collection of photographs that capture blue mountains and golden-hued countrysides, along with a diverse range of people—each telling their own story. The ones of the night sky are particularly breathtaking. I glance at a beaming Gabriel. I would be proud of these photos too. All the shots are gorgeous and look expertly composed.

Gabriel continues. "These antique photos were part of my dad's collection." His face softens. "We used to visit countless road shows to look for them. Trust me, I can tell the difference between a daguerreotype and ambrotype, and a couple of your photos were out of order."

My lips purse. "Okay, but the archivist I worked with—"

He arches a brow. "Did they actually see the photos?"

I stand tall. "I showed them to him over a video chat and he reviewed them closely."

He laughs triumphantly. "Over video chat? Your amateur eye

and his digital one made some rookie mistakes. No worries. I won't tell everyone you're not perfect."

"B-but I'm not perfect," I stammer.

He gives me an *oh please* look. "You also alphabetized your luggage."

I squint at him. "It makes it easier to find everything."

Instead of dignifying that with an answer, he opens the front door. I step outside and appreciate the warm breeze and the inn's welcoming porch. I make a mental promise to have a future date with one of the rocking chairs.

"As I was saying," Gabe says. "I'm into photography . . ." His voice trails off, and I can tell he's struggling with what information is safe to share with me.

"Gabe, if there's one thing I know about being a First Kid, it's discretion. You can trust me."

His copper eyes study mine and he nods. "This summer I'm working on putting my portfolio together for a competitive art program."

My eyes widen. "Is that why you were taking photos of the art at the White House?"

He grins. "You noticed that?" I bite my lip. Maybe I noticed more details about him than I care to admit. He continues, "I'm big on light, shadows, and context. Showing important art that's been photographed hundreds of times from a different perspective was a unique challenge."

I recall our dinner conversation with the art philanthropist. "During dinner, you spoke quite a bit with Luca about the art school in Florence?"

I'm delighted seeing his cheeks finally color. "They have an awesome study abroad program there."

"Aha," I say. "You want to go there, don't you?"

"Just for their summer program." He looks shocked. "You're the only person who knows about this."

I tilt my head, surprised and feeling satisfied that Gabriel Calabrese is confiding in me.

He looks behind him like he's checking if anyone is listening. "My mom needs a lot of help with the inn. With my dad gone, all she has is me." My chest tightens as I nod in response. Family obligations. I'm an expert.

We reach the trunk with our bags. Even though I try to grab my bag with the books, Gabe is quick to snatch that one away from me, so instead I grab one of Elle's toiletry bags and her large panda stuffy.

Gabe continues, "I figure a summer program wouldn't be too big a deal, if I can manage to win a scholarship. But if I don't get in, she'll never be the wiser."

I grin encouragingly at him. "You're totally getting in." His silence makes me second-guess my response, so I try again. "Don't worry, I won't tell your mom either."

He nods. "I appreciate it, but actually . . ." His voice trails off again. "I was thinking it might be helpful for my portfolio if I could take some pictures with you in them."

Me? I scoff. "Are you serious?"

Gabe shuffles nervously. "I have a lot of objects and nature shots, but I've been looking for a subject to photograph without the whole town knowing and figuring out I'm applying to art school."

"So, you need someone to photograph who won't spill the beans about your summer plans?" I pinch the bridge of my nose. "Maybe you have a friend you trust?" Or a girlfriend. I don't say that last part aloud.

"Sure, but you photograph well. You have great . . . proportions."

I glare at him. I have great proportions. What am I? A science experiment? Still, I weigh the pros and cons. I've been sent here to get away from prying cameras, but I also respect and understand what it means for someone to chase their dreams. My whole family understands that concept, as children of immigrants and public servants.

I blow a strand of hair off my forehead. "Fine. If we do this, I get final approval of the photos you plan on sharing." He nods and I continue. "And promise. No posting. Because if you do, it won't just be me who's upset—you'll have an entire team of my mom's overcaffeinated PR professionals on your tail." I wave a finger in his face. "You don't want to be on their bad side. I've seen their killer meme skills. It's not pretty."

Gabe breaks into a nervous laugh. "Of course. I'll get your permission before sharing anything anywhere. Besides, I compose my photos from an artist's perspective, not a journalist's. Most of the images will be of your profile or behind." His face reddens. "Not your *behind*. I meant your back. Your entire back. Not just, you know, your *back*. You know what I mean. Artfully composed."

I laugh too. It's satisfying seeing Gabe tongue-tied when he's usually so nonchalant. I hold up my hands for him to stop. "For art. I get it." I think of my own bucket list and my goals to have the perfect teen summer. Gabe's photos would be a great opportunity for me to remember my time here—even if it's just me reading and lounging at the inn. "And for the photos you don't use in your portfolio—the ones where I'm recognizable—I guess I wouldn't mind having those for my own records," I say.

Gabe nods. "You got it. Artsy photos for me. Candid shots for you." I extend my hand, and we shake on it.

When we reach the porch, I pause at the steps. This time it's my turn to get something off my chest. "Before we go in . . . I need to apologize for how things ended that night."

He pauses, Elle's pink duffel bag slung over his shoulder. "What are you talking about? If anything, I should be the one apologizing."

I shake my head. "No. Oliver was out of line, and I didn't stop him."

Gabe scoffs and starts for the door.

"Wait. We didn't know about your father. And Oliver shouldn't have been lecturing about our parents' expectations. It's just—"

"Douchey?" Gabriel supplies.

"Yeah, rude. I'm sorry, and I know Oliver would apologize too if he were here, but he had some family obligations himself in Hawai'i."

A humorless smile stretches across his face. "Because he's in Hawai'i on a family vacation and he left his Pineapple Princess behind."

"He has family obligations in Hawai'i, and I have mine here," I say. "I'll see him again in July."

Gabe faces me. "Exactly, and that's why I should be the one

apologizing for ruining your summer plans. You should be in Hawai'i with Darby and his infinity pool. You don't belong here, Abby."

My arms fold across my chest. "Well, good thing I am. I just agreed to help with your photo portfolio."

His face darkens. "Don't worry about it." He's a flash of pink and sequins from Elle's bags as he disappears inside. But even if Gabe remained on the porch longer, I wouldn't have known what to say in response. He's right, I'm not supposed to be here—it wasn't anything I've planned—but maybe what he really means is he doesn't want me here. And that bothers me more than I care to admit.

The inn's pineapple sign stares me in the face. That cheerful little fruit is supposed to mean "welcome"—yet all I feel is the opposite.

CHAPTER 9

"This is a new low, right?" I mutter to Shaw and Nessa, who stand stone-faced by the barn doors. I'm pretty sure their mirrored sunglasses are less about UV protection and more about hiding the fact that they're dying inside.

We should be listening to the gentle lap of waves, not shoveling a ton of horse droppings as part of Tita Karra's "equestrian education" initiative. Elle and I are the guinea pigs for the horseback riding lessons she wants to add to the inn's revitalization plans. Cleaning up after animals being a necessary part of the program. Who needs the ocean when you've got sweat dripping down your back and hay stuck to your ankles?

I think I prefer yesterday's "vegetable garden education," where we spent all morning learning how to plant heirloom tomatoes at the inn's garden, followed by an afternoon of gathering said crops. We did make a wicked veggie surprise smoothie last night, though.

Elle has done her best waving brochures from the inn's lobby advertising attractions nearby, everything from rafting to museums to even caverns, but Tita Karra has always been quick to point out activities on our property.

When Elle pointed out a flyer for a "Pat's Famous Ice Cream" parlor and asked to go, ice cream was magically delivered to us an hour later, but from a generic brand. I think whoever delivered this ice cream missed the point. Just like I don't want any ordinary brain freeze, I want to go to the store myself, and get my own supersweet and super-caffeinated, ice-chilled mocha latte—the perfect drink for my last high school summer.

I, of course, had plenty to catch up on around the activities Tita planned. For starters, my AP reading list and college essays. But it's hard not to ignore Elle's frustration.

With poor cell phone service, she can't even vent to her friends. I, on the other hand, don't mind. Most of my friendships outside Oliver are built around small group projects. If there's no deadline looming, the conversation fizzles. Small talk isn't my strength.

I wipe sweat off my brow with my wrists because my hands are stuffed into oversized leather gloves. I struggle to lift yet another heavy load.

I blush thinking about Gabriel doing this work. I see where the muscles come from. I've only seen him a few times in the three days since we arrived.

He seems to be working all the time. I caught him a couple times in the kitchen grabbing water or coffee, but our exchanges have been short. Polite. Nothing like the quick-talking, sarcastic boy I met at the state dinner.

Just a few more weeks. Elle and I must last until the end of this month. At least we're not working outside, where the Virginia sun is doing its heat wave thing. Unfortunately, the heat isn't helping with the smell of dirt and manure.

"Does cleaning up after horses count toward your bucket list?" Elle asks, shovel in hand as we work in the barn.

"Sure, it's right there next to going to the dentist," I respond.

Elle pushes dirt around with her shovel. "You know what? I think you should 'fess up to Tita about your last-hurrah-as-a-teenager-let's-find-summer-love unofficial bucket list."

I pause mid-shovel. "It's simply my summer bucket list. And you added 'summer love.' "

"Says the girl who wrote 'first kiss' on that list. Sorry it won't be with Oliver on the beach," she says dreamily.

"What are you saying? I'll be kissing someone else?" My face brightens as I bat away pesky images of a certain boy with a camera.

"I meant Oliver won't be able to kiss you in Hawai'i." Her brows waggle. "Why? Do you want someone else to kiss you?"

"No," I say a little too forcefully. "I made a mistake. A first kiss isn't something you list. It's just something that happens."

Elle snorts. "Not with Miss Perfect. I'm not one bit surprised you'd write it down like a bullet point to be checked off."

I straighten my shoulders and lift my chin. Mom's advice on how to compose oneself. "Elle. Seriously, are we done chatting about hypothetical first kisses? Let's finish this task so we can get out of here."

She guffaws. "Getting out of here is exactly what I'm talking about. Tell Tita about your bucket list."

"I don't think that would help."

"You won't even try," Elle complains.

My fingers clench the wooden handle of my shovel. I'm

uncertain what's worse: admitting to my aunt that I have a list of silly activities I want to do—despite being grounded—or disappointing my sister. "I'll think about it," I say. That's the best I can do right now.

Elle wrinkles her nose. "You know you owe me, right?"

I sigh. *You owe me.* There's three words I've been hearing repeatedly the past three days.

I gesture around the barn. "For what it's worth, I'll add horseback riding back to my list and I can check it off." This was a suggestion Elle made when I began drafting my bucket list.

"On the beach. Horseback riding on *the beach*," Elle emphasizes. She says *beach* with longing. "Why am I being grounded because of your mistake?"

I deflate like a sad balloon. My guilt is alive and well. "I'm so sorry, Elle. I messed up."

"I miss home," Elle says. "And even though she grounded us, I miss Mom too." My stomach lurches. I get that completely. We barely get to see her when we're home, her schedule is so hectic. Elle sighs.

I don't have any response but silently agree. I do owe Elle. And I am the worst sister ever. I deserve to be lifting this heaping pile of manure for the entire month.

A rumble draws my attention to the barn door. A truck passes by, and I catch a glimpse of Gabriel in the driver's seat. I've watched him come and go in that worn green truck. Even though it looks like he's running errands, I envy his freedom.

"Wish we could hitch a ride. I'd die for an ice cream run right now." Elle returns to her pile of muck, reminding me of the sad puppy we once rescued when Mom was campaigning through Georgia.

I purse my lips and slam my shovel into the pile, like I'm planting a flag. I remove my gloves, then throw them forcefully onto the ground.

I'm Elle's big sister, and I owe her one.

Shaw and Nessa don't say they're relieved, but I can sense it when I tell them Elle and I are done and are going to our rooms to clean up.

We take the back entrance of the "manor" so we don't track in any dirt through the pristine front foyer. Elle mutters that Tita Karra will be annoyed we didn't finish our task, but she's not exactly rushing to complete it either.

Our security detail trails us up the back stairs to the second-floor hallway. They're stationed on our floor, while the other two agents stay downstairs, monitoring cameras and screening deliveries. Dressed in plain clothes and driving a nondescript vehicle, they blend in by design.

Shaw and Nessa's black SUV is parked at the back. Unless someone's actively connecting the dots, no one would guess we're here.

And if they did? My bet is the Secret Service would already be watching them.

Fortunately, as my mind races with a scheme, I realize I know enough about our security detail's routine and camera positions to pull off my idea.

Nessa ducks into her hotel room when we're on our floor. With Elle and I in the same suite, only one of them needs to keep an eye on our door, which they'll do in shifts.

Elle does a happy dance around the sitting room. "I cannot wait to wash all this dust off."

I stop her before she closes the bathroom door. "Don't take a shower."

Elle huffs. "Come on. I called dibs first."

"No, that's not what I mean," I hiss. Even though we're in our room, away from Shaw and Nessa, I'm still paranoid they can hear us. I turn on the bathroom fan and look at my watch. "We're getting out of here."

Elle still looks puzzled.

"We're sneaking out."

It takes a beat for her to catch on—then she clamps both hands over her mouth to muffle a squeal. "What? Who *are* you and what have you done with my sister?"

I roll my eyes, but I get it. Even I'm still wrapping my head around this.

Elle bounces on her toes. "How?"

I lift my chin like I'm leading a covert mission. "Wash up and change your clothes quick. We have ten minutes." I look at my watch. "Make that nine."

CHAPTER 10

Elle dashes to her room to grab an outfit. I wash up quickly and try not to overthink what to wear. Instead of grabbing my trusty classic-cut khaki skirt, I go for a pair of cute white jean cutoffs and a pale pink tank top that matches my toenail polish, and practically douse myself in my lilac-and-vanilla-scented body spray. I empty my tote and grab two accessories, which I stash in my crossbody purse before rushing to Elle's room.

My sister's bed is piled with clothes. I nod, acknowledging her decision to wear orange athletic shorts and a matching crop top. She tilts her head as she appraises my outfit. "Dressing up for someone, are we?"

I toss a throw pillow at her head as my response. She laughs and launches it back at me, but I swipe it away. "Focus! Let's go."

"Go where?" Elle asks, but her voice trails off as I climb onto her window bench and unlock the window. She gasps. "Abby? What are you doing?"

I cock an eyebrow at her. "We're getting out of here, kid."

"But we're on the second floor. Abby, you've fallen out of chairs."

I say under my breath, "That was one time, and it was a little kid's chair. I didn't know it was that flimsy."

I slide a leg over the sill and make a show of tapping the roof beneath it. "Honestly, you should be grateful to see how much I care about you." Outside, I confirm the wraparound porch's roof is right under our window. And there's a tree nearby we can climb down.

I don't stick around to hear her response. The faster I do this, the less time I have to talk myself out of it. As my feet land on the porch's roof, it occurs to me that I have no idea how sturdy this structure is, but it's too late now. Elle follows right behind me.

If I wasn't in a rush, I might even enjoy the view better on the porch roof. The purple-and-blue mountains surrounding the inn are even more majestic, if that's possible, and the breeze up here is nice and soothing and smells like leafy woods and fresh grass.

I reach for Elle's hand and lead her toward the large tree near the inn. Elle pulls back. "Why such a rush?" It's not anger but fear and uncertainty in her voice.

I do my best to emulate Dad's confident smile. "We're good to go." I nod back at the hotel. "Right now, Shaw doesn't have a view of us, but when he and Nessa switch places, there's a chance Nessa will see us outside the hall window."

Elle glances back and understands what I mean about the direction of the windows. But she doesn't look completely convinced. "Yeah? And once we reach the ground, how are we going to leave the property?"

I look at my watch. "Because in two minutes Gabriel is going to stop at the back of the house with his truck to drop off supplies."

Elle shakes off her hesitation with a sly smirk. "Paying attention to Gabe's schedule now?"

I give her a tight smile. "He's been doing the same thing every day since we've been here. Not exactly a mystery."

She responds with a smug *mm-hmm*.

Now for the hard part. I lower myself to a seated position and scoot toward the tree branches near the porch roof. I beckon Elle to do the same. "We're about nine feet off the ground and if we grab the lowest branch and shimmy toward the tree trunk it'll be a lower drop from there. Easy."

Easy? Who am I kidding. I haven't played on a jungle gym since the fifth grade. But I am athletic. Daily yoga and dodging reporters count, right? I can do this.

A low roar rumbles from the distance. Gabriel's green truck approaches. I see his silhouette in the driver's seat. He pulls almost directly below us and parks the car. Perfect. Just as I had planned it.

I nod at Elle. "Let's go," I mouth.

I reach for the closest tree branch and am a little startled by how much give I feel. I frantically study another branch a little farther away. I can reach it, but not sure about Elle.

"I'd go with the first option," says a low, familiar voice from the ground. I inhale deeply, peering over the edge of the roof where Gabriel is standing, an amused smile on his lips and both hands in his pockets, looking extra fit in his Levi's and white T-shirt.

The blood drains from my face. "Can you please be quiet," I

hiss. I look around to see if any agents are swarming out the door as we speak.

Gabriel smirks as he mimes zipping his lips. He looks from side to side and then holds up both hands, signaling me to wait.

He rounds the corner of the house and disappears out of sight.

"What is he doing?" Elle asks me.

I shrug in response. As if I know what's going on in that gorgeous head of his?

We don't have to wait long until Gabriel approaches with a ladder and leans it near us.

I don't know whether to laugh or cry.

"How about a ladder, Rapunzel?" he says, gesturing at it.

My face betrays me as it breaks into a grin. "Fine. I will accept your help on behalf of my sister."

I motion for Elle to go first. She steps down quickly, clearly enjoying herself. When Elle is on the ground it's my turn. With one last look over my shoulder to make sure none of the agents have caught on to our scheme, I climb onto the ladder and quickly descend, doing my best to focus on affirmations. I'm not clumsy. I'm an astronaut's daughter. I laugh in the face of danger. After an eternity—or really thirty seconds—my foot touches solid ground.

I turn to find myself face to face with Gabriel, who nods with approval. "Not bad, Pineapple Princess. I had 911 on speed dial waiting for you." I don't dignify him with a response.

Next, we busy ourselves with retrieving the ladder, but he stops me from going with him to return it. "Cameras at the back door, remember." He quickly returns the ladder around the back of the house and emerges again.

"Well, that was fun," Gabriel says. "Didn't think you girls had it in you." He turns to leave.

"Wait. Where are you going?"

"Errands."

"Great." I grab Elle and head for his truck. "We're coming."

He hesitates. "We didn't agree to that. Besides, aren't you grounded?"

I point behind me. "You just helped us climb off a roof."

"Yeah, well, I didn't want anyone breaking a leg. We don't have any money to lawyer up if we go to court."

I don't have time to explain to him about liability. "Please. We'd obviously settle before it ever went to trial." I reach for the passenger door, but he beats me to it. My body flushes as his arm brushes mine. I curse. Is he really blocking the door? "You've already helped us climb down. Leave us here and we'll let our agents know you're involved."

His gaze locks with mine, and I'm rewarded with a crooked smile, dimples and all. "I was just going to say the handle sticks. Gotta jiggle it," he explains. He opens the door with a grand gesture. I quickly slide into the truck's cabin, hopeful he didn't see the color on my cheeks. Elle follows behind me.

His truck's cabin has a single row bench, meaning the three of us will need to cram onto the worn tan seat. It smells surprisingly comforting, like leather and fresh pine trees.

Gabriel slams the door and turns to the house. "Where are you going?" I call from his passenger window.

"Still have errands," he calls over his shoulder.

I curse as I push Elle and myself down so we're not visible from the cabin window. The expression on my little sister's face reminds me of the time she played a prank on a particularly snobbish White House aide. She took a screenshot of his desktop and set it as his wallpaper. She could barely contain herself watching the aide clicking like wild, unable to open anything.

"I'm glad you're finally enjoying yourself," I say to her.

She grins in response.

I shift my leg, which has bumped into something hard inside a canvas bag that has to be Gabe's camera. It's no surprise he carries one around with him, although this is much larger than the one he brought to the White House.

We hear two thunks in the cab before Gabriel opens the driver's side and smoothly hops in. I hold my breath as the truck drives away from the inn. Elle is doing the same. You'd think we just pulled off some great heist like robbing a casino or something.

Gabriel reaches for his radio—it's an old-school one with a dial and meter for the stations. A mix of guitars, drums, and strings blasts over his speakers. I recognize it's from the '90s. Figures he'd be retro.

Several minutes pass before I can't stand the crick developing in my leg. I do my best to avoid the camera bag on the floor. "Is the coast clear?" I ask.

Elle doesn't wait for an answer as she struggles onto her elbows. "I don't care. Your big head is making my back hurt," she complains, pushing me aside.

"My head isn't big," I protest.

"I don't know about that. If you sit up, Shaw could probably spot your head all the way from the house," she cracks.

"Haha," I deadpan, and lift my body up to take a seat.

"Seat belts," Gabriel chides.

We oblige and settle into our bench. We're silent as the music changes into a poppy rock sound. "I like this," I say.

Gabriel laughs. "Of course you do, this is the All-American Rejects."

"How fitting," I say sarcastically. "After Pineapplegate and losing my dream vacation that's exactly how I feel. Like a reject."

He arches a brow. "And now, here I am helping you and your kid sister escape your prison. I mean, the inn."

Elle folds her arms across her chest. "I'm an innocent bystander in this whole mess."

Gabriel scoffs. "More like collateral damage."

We're driving down a simple two-lane street lined with trees and brush. The entrance we would've come in if Tita Karra hadn't decided to offer us a wagon ride. Since I'm in the middle seat, I lean over Elle to roll down the window and breathe in the fresh summer air. I lift my face toward the blue sky to soak in the sunrays poking through the trees. "Freedom," I sigh to myself.

I catch Gabriel staring at me. He quickly turns away to focus on the road.

"Something you want to say?" I ask.

"I'm just surprised you two would even attempt running off."

I look him up and down. "Didn't seem hard for you to help us climb off that roof?"

He chuckles. "Trust me, I've navigated that roof for many years."

"So why judge us?" I ask.

"You two are supposed to stay on the property. Tita Karra has made that clear."

"But why do you care?" I press.

He gives me an awkward look. "Because when I'm grounded it's by Ruby Calabrese. When you're grounded it's by the president of the United States. Has a little more weight to it."

I sigh. "She's still just a mom at the end of the day."

"And commander in chief," he adds.

"Both can be true at the same time."

"For you, sure," he says. He doesn't finish his sentence, but I know what he's thinking. There seem to be two kinds of people: those who want to know me to get close to my mom, and those who are too scared of me because of my mom. It's why I'm so close to Oliver. He gets it.

From the worried expression on his face, Gabe is in the second camp: too scared. At least I know where we stand. We'll never be friends, but for the time being we can act friendly.

"Thank you for getting us out," I offer. "We were getting a little bit of cabin fever."

"Well, as I said, I have to run some errands," he says, nodding at the large bags in the truck bed behind him.

Elle scrunches her nose. "What you got in there? Skeletons of bad guests?"

Gabe smirks. "More like the skeletons our grounded guests

want to keep hidden," he jokes. "I'm going to drop these linens with the cleaners in town."

"In town." Elle perks up. "Can we stop by Pat's Famous Ice Cream?"

He does a double take. "How do you know about Pat's?"

"From the flyers in the inn's lobby. Abby and I have collected a few of them to figure out what we can do for her summer bucket list."

Gabe perks up. "You have a summer bucket list?"

Elle nods. "She does. And it's full of actual fun—"

"Elle. That's enough," I snap. I can't believe my sister. If I wasn't going to share my bucket list with Tita Karra, our *family*, why would she think I'd spill it to Gabriel?

She throws up her arms. "Seriously, Abby? How can you finish your bucket list if we're stuck at the inn. Why can't you share—"

"Please stop," I say sternly to Elle. She glares at me, then digs into her purse and pulls out her giant headphones, signaling she's done with me. Without a word she dials up the volume on her phone and disappears into whatever the Enzo-emo pop song of the day is. She's sitting next to me, but she might as well be on Mars.

Gabriel's smirk gets under my skin. "You enjoying your front row tickets to the Elle and Abby show?" I snap.

"I didn't say anything," he says, but his amused chuckle says otherwise.

Sighing, I whip out my phone and show him my checklist app. "This is my summer bucket list."

His hand tightens on the wheel. "Abby, you don't have to share if you don't want to."

I shake my head. "You told me about your summer goals. So," I exhale. "I can tell you about mine."

His copper eyes glimmer as they lock onto mine, and I do my best to not be distracted by them. "Fair," he responds.

I take a deep breath. "This is the last summer I have as a high school student. My summer before college will be spent with college prep and traveling the world volunteering."

His brows lift like that's not so bad.

I look at my hands. "I know. I'm so grateful for all the privileges and opportunities I have. I'm fully aware of how lucky I am."

"Stop," he says. "I wasn't judging. You didn't ask for your life, Abby. And everyone should get the chance to enjoy their summer break." He looks in his rearview mirror and then pulls over to the side of the road.

"What are you doing?" I demand.

He puts the truck in park and smiles. "Giving you my full attention."

I glance at Elle, who makes a point of holding her phone closer to her face. "We're going to stretch our legs a moment," I say. She barely acknowledges me. I sigh. I'll have to get on her good side later.

Gabe opens his door, and I climb out after him. We head to the back of his truck. He opens the truck bed's door and we sit side by side like we're tailgating. I show him my phone and he bends to get a better look. "Sorry, can you make the font bigger?"

I sigh and hand Gabe my phone with my checklist app. His lips move as he reads my list aloud. "Art lessons, team sports, cooking . . . Obviously not the Hawai'i stuff."

"Obviously."

He laughs. "Do something 'nature-y'? I'm glad you're not above made-up words."

I flush. "What I mean is enjoy the great outdoors."

"Uh-huh." He types on my screen.

"What are you doing?" I demand.

"Making improvements."

He shows me the phone and my mouth twitches as I read his edits to several of my bullets. "You changed 'community events' to 'parties'?" I exclaim.

"Hold on, I've got more edits." He taps my screen, but instead of typing, his eyes widen. My pulse spikes like I said the wrong thing on the campaign trail. He must've accidentally swiped and seen my "unofficial list"—and my "first kiss" goal!

I groan as I cover my face with my hand, but through my fingers I see his reaction. His Adam's apple visibly bobs as he swallows.

"You weren't supposed to see that page," I whimper.

He nods slowly in agreement. "First kiss and date stuff is probably best with your boyfriend."

I lower my hands and stare at him. He must mean Oliver. I bite my lip. He's probably right. Didn't I write those bullets with Oliver in mind, to do while the two of us were in Hawai'i? It sounded like the perfect romantic plan for Abigail's predictable life, or at least it used to.

But now that my summer plans have been ruined and I'm

sitting next to this boy who makes my body tingle in spite of myself—the only thing I'm certain of is how uncertain I am.

I close my eyes. The best thing to do now is stick to the facts. "I'm not allowed to have a boyfriend until I'm in my senior year, but"—I laugh nervously—"according to Elle I'm technically a senior since I've completed junior year, so . . ."

"So, you and Oliver?"

I stammer as Gabe's copper eyes lock onto mine. "Oliver's my best friend. And . . ." My voice trails off as my brain wrestles with how to respond. All signs point to Oliver and me heading in that direction, and no matter how exciting Gabe may be, we're parting ways in a few weeks. I can't even . . . I shouldn't even entertain anything happening between us. "You're right. Those items should be with my—"

Gabriel cuts me off as he hands me my phone. "No worries. You don't need to explain. Your list is good." His voice is friendly, but flat. He heads back to the truck's cabin, and I follow right behind.

If awkwardness had a soundtrack, it'd be playing at full volume. I glance at my sister as I buckle up. She's still not acknowledging me, but her body seems to have stiffened. Gabe, on the other side of me, is also at peak awk.

I stare down the empty road in front of me, and for some reason I start to laugh. I have no idea where it goes, and I'm in a truck with a boy who I just met, after doing something I never thought I'd do—climb out of a second-floor window and escape my security detail. And despite all the unfamiliarity of this situation, a thrill goes down my spine at having done something for myself for once.

Maybe my summer plans aren't completely ruined—just different.

Elle squints at me. "What's so funny?"

"Don't worry about it. I have an idea," I say.

Gabe lifts his brows as I continue. "I help you with your photo portfolio as your subject with good proportions," I tease, using his words when he shared his art school dream. "And you help me with my bucket list." I clap my hands. It's the perfect idea.

Gabe pauses as he considers. "Your list has things that would require you to leave the inn. How are we going to do all these activities when you're grounded? Would I have to fetch a ladder for you every time?"

I realize spending time with me has always been difficult because of my constant Secret Service babysitters, but this summer I'm up for the challenge. "We've slipped away once. We can do it again."

Gabe takes a deep breath. I'm relieved when he nods in agreement. "All right. Being able to leave the inn will obviously provide me more photo opportunities." He rolls his eyes. "And you'll probably start alphabetizing our refrigerator if we don't get you out of the house. So, Abigail Cary-Alzona. Deal me in." He rewards me with a dazzling smile.

"Agreed," I say.

I smile at him, and for the second time since I've arrived at Mystic Hollow, we shake hands—and I do my best not to react to the jolt of energy I feel from his touch. I take a mental snapshot of this moment: the warmth of the summer breeze, the cute boy in dark jeans and a white T-shirt, and his sun-drenched smile.

"All right. We're officially launching Operation Bucket List," Elle says.

I gawk at my sister. "You've been listening the entire time?"

She scrunches her nose. "I've got a vested interest. I need to get out of the house too."

I shake my head at her but smile. "Fine. We have the rest of the month to complete our mission and experience a regular teenage summer." But as Gabriel pulls back onto the road, I can't help reminding myself that after our time here, I'll be back in DC with Oliver and my carefully planned life.

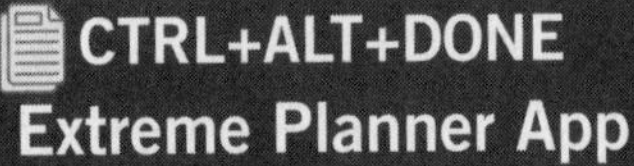

CTRL+ALT+DONE
Extreme Planner App

<u>Gabe's Edits</u>* Abby's Personal Summer Endeavors List

- ❑ ~~1. Add senior year schedule to academic planner~~ ***(Seriously? How many planners do you have?)***
- ❑ 2. Complete senior year AP English summer reading ***(I'm surprised you're not done with this j/k)***
- ❑ 3. Demonstrate "character and commitment" ***(Does anyone really question this???)***
  - ❑ 3a. ~~Volunteer with Pod Patrol: dolphin rescue group~~
  - ❑ 3b. ~~Lead Hawaiian community service project with Senator Sina~~
- ❑ 4. "Gain new perspectives"
  - ❑ 4a. Travel (~~Hawai'i!~~ Italy!) ***(Ciao, Hawai'i)***
  - ❑ 4b. Broaden culinary palate ***(the Pike Special is a cultural phenomenon)***
  - ❑ 4c. Shop local ***(Downtown shops, especially Marge's stores)***
- ❑ 5. Enriching activities outside of academics to be "well-rounded"
  - ❑ 5a. ~~Community events~~ ***<u>Parties</u>*** 

- ❑ 5b. ~~Cooking class~~ ***Homecooked meal***
- ❑ 5c. ~~Art lessons~~ ***Paintball?***
- ❑ 5d. ~~Team sports~~ ***Again, paintball?***
- ❑ 5e. Do something nature-y ***(Lots of options)***

CHAPTER 11

The tree-lined lane widens, and the scenery shifts. The sprawling farmhouses give way to cute homes, then to clusters of quiet neighborhoods. We round a corner and a cheerful red-and-blue sign comes into view: *Welcome to Mystic Hollow.*

Gabriel pulls into what must be Mystic Hollow's downtown. An adorable quintessential main street of redbrick buildings, each crowned with colorful awnings shading whimsical little shops. They all face a quaint town square at the heart of it all.

Elle and I have seen plenty of places like this while on the campaign trail across the country, but this town is especially charming.

I watch as a couple girls about my age leave one of the shops carrying chic mint-green shopping bags. #Wishthatwasme.

Mystic Hollow's picturesque downtown could easily be the backdrop of one of Elle's feel-good rom-coms—the kind where someone trips into a meet-cute and a cupcake at the same time, and the resolution only happens after a huge misunderstanding and magical lighting. Real life? I never.

The town square and surrounding park glow with easy summer vibes. Green benches warmed by the sun line the square while towering oak trees cast slow-moving shadows.

At the center of the square, a large white gazebo with a red roof and surrounded by flowerbeds bursting with cheerful zinnias and marigolds is the perfect setting for live music and dancing. On the other end, a sunlit fountain bubbles cheerfully. I imagine how refreshing it would feel sitting nearby as the fountain sprays its cool mist in the summer air.

Elle coos at the cute boutique shops housed within worn brick buildings, each with attractive displays like pastel soaps, bespoke jewelry, and lovingly crafted home goods.

American flags and colorful rainbow Pride banners ripple from tall, old-fashioned streetlamps, each one announcing events like FARMERS' MARKET or FOUNDER'S DAY CELEBRATION in happy fonts.

It's the kind of vibrant downtown my parents would love—brimming with small businesses, neighborly warmth, and a strong sense of community.

Elle jumps in her seat as she points at a shop on the corner. "That's it. I recognize the green-and-white awning!"

Gabe nods. "The one and only Pat's Famous Ice Cream."

"We have to stop!" Elle pleads.

"On it." Gabe makes a turn into a small parking lot behind the shops and parks in a space. I'm relieved to see there are only a couple cars, but then it is midmorning on a weekday.

"Let's make this quick," I say. I open my purse and retrieve two baseball hats. Elle wrinkles her nose. I wave it at her. "Come on, you know we shouldn't draw attention." Especially after sneaking out of the inn. I hand her the lavender hat while I pop on one of Dad's old ones.

"We did it," Elle says as we step out of the car.

"I told you I'd pay you back," I respond. She beams at me, and I can't help laughing.

"We're going to be in so much trouble," she whispers.

"I know. But we're already grounded, so?" I shrug. My voice may be confident but inside I'm a pool of nerves. I've never done anything like this before. First, the pineapple pizza scandal. Next, I sneak away from my security detail. But if Elle notices how I'm really feeling, she doesn't say so.

Gabe walks from his side of the truck to meet us. He's wearing sunglasses and has his camera bag slung around his shoulders.

"Remember, I get to approve the photos," I say pointedly.

He smirks. "I don't know. I think I'm in the clear. With those hats, no one will ever recognize you." He fails to hide the fact that he's laughing at us.

I squint at him and point at his sunglasses. "May I borrow those?"

He frowns but removes his Ray-Bans and places them in my outstretched hand.

I slide them on and look at my reflection in his truck's window. I'm pleased with what I see. Abby Cary-Alzona incognito mode.

Elle leans over. Her lashes flutter in that I'm-the-baby-so-you-have-to-listen-to-me way that's plagued our relationship since always. “How about you and Gabe go get the ice cream. I’ll sit on a bench over there.” She points to a bench by the fountain.

I frown at my sister. “But ice cream was your idea.”

Elle shrugs. “There’s only one pair of sunglasses. Besides”—she holds up her phone—“I get service here! Bring me back a bubble-gum waffle bowl with rainbow sprinkles, would you?”

I roll my eyes. “Disgusting, but fine.”

Gabe motions toward the sidewalk, holding up his camera. “Shall we?”

I cast one last glance at my sister, who’s clearly abandoned me. By this time, I should be used to being alone with Gabriel, but the fluttering in my belly says otherwise.

CHAPTER 12

Gabe glances my way with that quiet smile of his but doesn't say a word. I swear on Hamilton's *Federalist Papers*, I don't find the curves of his mouth attractive. His face just has nice symmetry and interesting bone structure. It's a scientific observation, that's all. In fact, I'll ask Mom's science adviser about it next time I see her.

I'll also be asking how walking next to Gabe can somehow feel completely familiar and ridiculously exciting at the same time. Is there a study on that? Because I have questions. I try to focus on the cute store window displays we pass, making mental notes of where to buy gifts for my family. I spy a quirky candle shop called the Wick and Whimsy. Mom is a huge fan of scented candles. You can even tell her moods based on the scents—read extra hugs on eucalyptus days.

As we pass by, I admire a trendy retro diner that spills onto the sidewalk with outdoor seating and espresso-colored umbrellas. Gabe nods. "That's Mike's Biscuits n' Burgers. It's a popular hangout." Based on how the air smells like buttery biscuits and salty fries, I can see why.

As Gabriel's pace slows down, I recognize the green awning for Pat's Famous Ice Cream. Up close, I appreciate the lively window display with old-fashioned golden letters of the parlor's name alongside paintings of towering sundaes. A green Tripadvisor Certificate of Excellence sticker glints near the door, along with other top local ratings, and flyers sit behind a glass display.

An OFFICIAL FOUNDER'S DAY DANCE SPONSOR flyer catches my eye with a cartoon sketch of the town square. Another flyer promoting the "Fourth of July Jubilee" sits right beside it. I exclaim, recognizing a photo of Mystic Hollow Inn surrounded by carnival booths and fanfare on the flyer. "Does the inn host the jubilee?" I ask, pointing at the flyer.

Gabriel's reflection appears in the glass beside me, his brows tight. "Yes," he says with a clipped inhale. "It's been a tradition for decades. My family's hosted it since my grandparents bought the property."

I squint at him. "It's only a couple weeks away; why am I just hearing about this?"

He shrugs. "We had to remake the flyer after some changes to festival sponsors."

Something in his voice makes me pause. I remember the hushed conversation between his mom and Tita Karra about bookings—or the lack of them.

Before I can press further, Gabriel brushes past me and swings open the parlor's door. With a flourish he ushers me inside. I pause at the flyer, wanting to ask more, but it's clear he's ready to move on.

Inside, the sugary smell of ice cream makes my mouth

water. The shop is tastefully designed in mint green and ivory, with charming paintings of ice cream cones adorning the gold-accented walls.

Nearby, a mother and son sit together enjoying a gleaming bowl of rainbow-colored ice cream, sprinkles, whipped cream—and gummy bears. My heart leaps. My dad would love the vibe of this place. He's a certified ice cream fiend.

Toward the back of the parlor is something I wasn't expecting: an open doorway to what looks like a diner, complete with red booths and a jukebox. Gabriel must see my puzzled look because he explains Pat's Famous Ice Cream is connected to Mike's Biscuits n' Burgers. It's Mystic Hollow's version of a "food hall," except the same family owns both establishments. I nod, knowing my mom would love the entrepreneurial spirit of this shop.

A man with a soft face and wide grin wearing a white triangle cap talks to a couple in business attire. He hands the woman a golden waffle cone decadently topped with scoops of vanilla, mint chocolate chip, and strawberry. I grin. Now that cone is speaking my language. I spin around, taking in the scene. Despite the chill in the air, the shop makes me feel warm and cozy like a childhood memory I never want to forget. The click of Gabriel's camera draws my attention. My brows lift as I glance at him.

He flushes. "Sorry. The look of quiet joy on your face—I wanted to capture that." He holds up his camera in explanation. I gasp, unable to recall anyone ever wanting to take "quiet" pictures of me. It's usually me doing something official—or unofficial and not flattering. #Pineapplegate. I'm glad to give him material for his portfolio, and bonus, this is the perfect summer memory for me.

I smile and pretend to turn up my nose. "You have a gift, Jack. You see people." Gabe laughs at my *Titanic* reference. I'm glad he understood it.

A loud cooing noise interrupts us. "If it isn't Gabriel Calabrese and his significant other." The ice cream attendant approaches and leans over a frosted ice cream case as he winks at us. Despite the chill in the air, I practically sizzle from embarrassment. Did he get "significant other" vibes from us?

Meanwhile, Gabriel lowers his camera, his face and ears a crimson red. "Pat. No," he says. His eyes dart to mine; he's clearly mortified and wishing he could teleport himself to a deserted island.

"I was talking about Gabe's camera," Pat says with a hearty guffaw. He grins at me, his eyes full of amusement as he ribs him. "He doesn't go anywhere without that thing."

Gabe sighs. "Abby, this is Pat. He's famous for his ice cream—not his jokes." He jerks a thumb in his direction.

Smiling, I reach out, and he wraps my hand in a firm but friendly handshake. I hold my breath, waiting for the recognition in his eyes, but the twinkle in his gaze never changes. I sigh with relief—it feels incredible not to be recognized. But then, I'm sure the idea that the First Daughter would be at his ice cream parlor on a random weekday wearing a NASA baseball cap would never occur to Pat. It would've never occurred to me, if it weren't for Gabe helping me escape.

The warm chime of bells jingles as the parlor's door swings open.

Pat waves a friendly goodbye at the couple with the triple-scoop ice cream cone. Their forced grins—like their suits—feel out of place. It might've been a chilly exit, except for the unexpected hop in their step as they moved aside to avoid a feisty-looking older woman entering the parlor.

She flashes them a glare that's the very definition of looking down your nose. The couple scurry away.

The woman huffs as she marches toward us. Her dress is as loud as her energy—head-to-toe florals, bright lipstick, and bangles that jingle with every step.

Gabe and Pat shoot each other a look as the woman waggles a finger at Pat. "I can't believe you gave them ice cream," she exclaims.

Pat bristles. "I assume you understand the concept of giving customers what they pay for?"

The woman guffaws. "You also have the right to refuse service."

Pat throws his hands up. As the two bicker about rules, Gabe leans close to my ear. "Marge is the president of our town's small business advisory board council and the Main Street Council, and one of the town's busiest entrepreneurs," he says.

"I'm all about female entrepreneurs. I was raised by one," I whisper back. "I even like her fashion sense." And it's true. I live in a world of neutrals back in DC, so Marge's bright colors are refreshing.

Gabe continues with a glint in his eyes. "The fact that she's dating Mayor Lee is also the town's worst-kept secret."

I cover my mouth. "Oh no, it's a scandal?"

He shakes his head. "Not at all. Mayor Lee has been a widower for over a decade. Most folks think Marge doesn't like mixing business with pleasure. I prefer to think she's a self-made woman and doesn't want her relationship with the mayor to distract people from her own success."

"I can respect that," I whisper back.

Gabe nods. "Me too. But her connections make her one of the town's busybodies," he warns, "so be careful."

My response is cut short, as Marge and Pat abruptly go silent. Their attention focuses on Gabriel. "Tell him, or I will," Marge says, hands on hips.

I exchange glances with Gabe. This doesn't sound good.

With a heavy sigh, Pat meets Gabriel's expectant gaze. "Those two customers are from the resort." He says the word *resort* like it leaves a bad taste in his mouth.

Gabriel's eyes narrow. "I guess they're part of this town now."

"I was going to give your mom a call," Marge says as an apologetic look crosses her face. "They stopped by my shop to ask if I'd bring my boba tea truck to their property for the Fourth."

"And they wanted my ice cream cart," Pat admits.

Gabriel does a double take. "You're joking."

Marge shakes her head. "Wish I was. They said they were going to hold some festivities that day."

Gabriel frowns. "What festivities? Mystic Hollow Inn holds the town's annual Fourth of July Jubilee."

Pat nods vigorously. "That's what I said. I told 'em, nope, Pat's Famous Ice Cream is booked. But thought you would want to know. They might be asking other businesses to work their event."

Gabriel's knuckles are practically white as he grips his camera.

Marge gives him a heartfelt smile. "Your mom's inn has been a special topic at our council meetings. We're all rooting for you."

Pat looks at Gabriel and then me. "Come on. Ice cream always makes things better."

Marge huffs. "I think these two need something extra special. Give him the Pike."

Pat's eyes widen, then he gives a small salute. "You got it." He opens a back door and shouts an order to folks in the kitchen.

Marge sighs. "I swear you can hear Pat on the other side of town." Gabe and I exchange a look. The woman turns her attention onto me. I stiffen as she gives me a once-over. "Look at me prattling away all rude-like. Are you going to introduce me to your friend?" The twinkle in her eyes is genuine and kind.

Gabe clears his throat. "This is Abby. She's a guest at the inn, and I'm showing her around town." I silently thank him for skipping the whole president's daughter backstory.

"How delightful. Y'know, I've been developing a walking tour for visitors. Maybe you two—" Marge frowns as her pocket vibrates. "Oh shoot. I need to take this." She fumbles for her phone and steps away.

Pat thumps his counter, signaling his return. "One Pike Special." He hands Gabriel a white paper bag, already half see-through with grease. A warm, salty smell hits my nose like a hug from a deep fryer.

My eyes widen. "Fried food?"

Pat beams. "Perks of my family owning the diner next door. We share the same kitchen." He nods at the ice cream case. "This will go great with your ice cream. What'll you have?"

Intrigued, I order Elle's waffle bowl with bubble-gum ice cream—yuck—and my order of Neapolitan (all the classic flavors, vanilla, chocolate, and strawberry, in one scoop). I can already picture Elle's face when she gets her scoops. I know I can really use a couple brownie points when it comes to my sister. As we head out, we run into an animated Marge as she paces on her phone. She waves goodbye, but not before telling Gabe his mom's council presentation needs to be moved again. Gabe nods, his face once again grim.

I wait until we're away from Pat's parlor before asking Gabriel my burning questions. "Is the inn in some kind of trouble?"

His stride slows and my arm hairs prickle. "You don't have to talk about it if you don't want to," I say nervously. My mom has always been better at reading people; I hope I didn't offend him.

Gabe stares at his ice cream cone a moment before answering. "No, it's fine." He looks around and beelines for a nearby bench. He sits down and I take the unspoken invitation to join him.

"A big fancy resort opened nearby about a year ago and has been attracting guests away from our property." He stares at his camera. "Summer is the hardest—we can't compete with a resort that has a golf course, infinity pools designed for Instagram, and five-star dining."

"How about Wi-Fi," I say, and immediately regret it.

He rolls his eyes. "Of course." He rakes a hand through his already unruly hair. "My mom is struggling more than she lets on. If the jubilee doesn't bring in more guests, we're in trouble." His voice trails off.

His eyes dim. "If we can't turn things around, the inn's at risk."

My stomach lurches and my ice cream suddenly feels less appetizing. "Here I am upset my summer plans are ruined. Meanwhile, you and your mom could lose your business."

"Abby, don't feel bad about wanting a real summer," I hear him say, but my brain has already started churning. "You've done everything for your family. And for the country. That's huge."

He moves closer, tone soft but sure. "I want you to have the best summer ever. And I want to help you get it. Especially if this is your last chance."

I exhale. His sincerity wraps around me like a warm blanket on a cold night.

"I appreciate that. I just didn't realize how much the inn is weighing on you too."

He stares at his hands. "Very much so."

I suck in a deep breath. "What exactly happens at your jubilee?"

He looks to the sky. "What *happened* may be more accurate. Since my dad passed away, the festival hasn't been the same."

"I'm sorry," I say, and mean it.

He smiles in appreciation. "It used to be huge—barbecue, dancing, live music, and a ton of arts and crafts booths from businesses all over. Our inn hosts the festival during the day, while Grand Meadows, our region's equestrian center, hosts the fireworks."

I tap my chin. "So basically it's like a county fair?" Elle and I have been to countless fairs during Mom's campaigns.

He pauses in thought. "I guess so, but a much smaller one."

I nod vigorously as my idea fully forms. "Hear me out," I say.

He smirks. "I feel like what you're about to say is going to add to the prison time I'll be sentenced to for helping you leave the inn."

I ignore his teasing. "We needed a way for me to leave the inn to work on my bucket list and your photos."

"I thought we were going to play the theme music to *Mission: Impossible* and sneak out every day," Gabriel deadpans.

"Did you really think we were going to trick Shaw and Nessa for the rest of the month?" I laugh. "I mean, Shaw I might be able to sweet-talk. He's got a weakness for chocolate. But Nessa—"

"Is very good at her job," Gabriel says, cutting me off.

"Right, Nessa is—"

"Right behind you."

"We found Rapunzel." I jump as the familiar stern voice startles me.

"Oh no!" I screech as both ice cream cups fall out of my hands and splat onto the sidewalk.

Nessa and Shaw look almost apologetic. Almost. The disapproval on their faces is more evident. If having them sneak up behind me is surprising, what's even more shocking is seeing them in casual attire.

If I weren't in hot water, I'd probably burst out laughing at the sight of Shaw in a tan blazer and salmon-pink shorts. So preppy.

Nessa, thankfully, looks low-key in olive-green athletic shorts and a track jacket.

"Abby, how could you drop my ice cream?" Elle yells from the back seat of a white X5 idling behind the agents.

Across the street, a black SUV that looks like the one we rode in here from DC is parked. Yup. We're busted.

My blood chills as Tita Karra steps out of the driver's seat of the white car. She is the more easygoing sister, but right now, lips pressed together and forehead clenched into a V, she's channeling Mom's fury. I blink, wondering if it's possible to be grounded while being grounded.

"Get in the car," she orders.

"It's not her fault," Gabriel says but is quickly shut down by my tita's glare.

"Go home, godson," she hisses.

Gabriel faces me. His eyes search mine like he's asking for permission. "I'll be okay," I say in my most reassuring voice.

A few people in the park start to notice us. A boy my age with wild reddish hair cups his hands around his mouth and calls out, "What'd you do this time, Calabrese?"

Gabriel groans. "Kyle *turd-breath* Schwab."

"Turd-breath," I repeat. If I weren't in trouble, I'd probably be snort-laughing.

Shaw lets out a pointed grunt—that's our cue.

"Meet us at home," Tita orders Gabriel.

Before I hop into her car, I squeeze his shoulders. "I have a plan," I say to him, hoping he doesn't hear the worry in my voice.

His brows lift, clearly not convinced, as he avoids Shaw's glare. "Abby," Tita Karra warns, muttering Tagalog curse words under her breath. I hop into her SUV and roll down my window to say goodbye to Gabriel.

His gaze meets mine and he looks strangely amused. Before I can ask him what's so funny he raises his camera and takes a photo of me.

"I'll call that shot 'the moment before two teenagers are exiled to Area 51 for life,'" he says.

CHAPTER 13

Tita Karra's knuckles are white as she grips her steering wheel. I glance at Elle, who's furiously texting on her phone like she'll never see her friends again.

"Chill, Elle," I mutter.

"Easy for you to say. You do fine with no technology. All I'll have is paper, pencil, and shame."

"Maybe not even that," Tita warns. My eyes widen. She wouldn't take my books . . . would she?

Peering over my shoulder, I see Shaw's SUV tailing us. If I squint, I can see Gabriel's worn green truck next in line.

My entourage wheels us back to our dungeon. My stomach flutters—not with dread, but with the smallest kernel of hope. Maybe my idea will work. But first, I need Tita Karra on my side.

I lean forward. "Tita?"

She doesn't respond, but her dark eyes flick up to the rearview mirror, catching mine.

"Does my mom know what we did?" The car goes silent as Elle stops tapping and waits for the response.

Tita sighs. "Not yet. Your father is on a plane and your mom's in a classified briefing for another hour, but Shaw has notified his superiors of the incident."

Basically, I have an hour before Shaw's boss tells Mom what happened. An hour to convince Tita about my idea.

We pull into the oak tree–lined road that leads to Mystic Hollow Inn. The large old house looks even more enchanting as it appears suddenly from behind the trees.

A figure waits on the front porch. It's Gabriel's mom, and as we get closer, the worry on her face is obvious. Guilt hits me hard and I feel a pain in the back of my throat. This is worse than the time I was nine and watched a scary movie with Senator Smith's son, who peed his pants right before a major rally. I was supposed to be the big kid taking care of everyone. Instead, I freaked out my charges. Eight years later, I'm still irresponsible. I snuck out of the house and am getting not only myself in trouble but also Elle.

I look at my watch. I have forty-five minutes before Mom knows.

Ruby rushes to our car. "Is everyone okay?"

My face is probably the color of Ruby's red sundress. "Yes, we're good," I say, trying to project a calm demeanor.

"Our ice cream isn't," Elle mutters. She's right, of course. I dropped our ice cream when we were caught. I assume Gabe got rid of my Pike Special too. Kinda sad I'll never know what it was.

Gabriel's truck pulls up and I watch as his mom's face transforms from concern to fury. My stomach lurches. No, no, no. He can't get in trouble because of me. Before she says anything to Gabriel, I jump in. "Your son is so talented, Ms. Calabrese," I say in my most gracious First Daughter tone.

Her face whitens. “You mean at helping you escape.”

“No, no!” I clasp my hands. “Gabriel was helping me figure out community project ideas for me to work on this summer. My mother desires that Elle and I volunteer whenever we can. She believes it not only helps my fellow citizens but also teaches us crucial life and work skills.”

Ruby blinks at me. Tita Karra stands firm with arms crossed, but her silence tells me she’s listening. I don’t look at Gabriel but can feel his eyes on me. I inhale deeply and smile my perfect finishing-school smile.

“As you know, this summer I was supposed to be in Hawaiʻi helping a local community project with Senator Sina’s staff. But . . .” My voice trails off as the image of a stupid pineapple pizza pops into my mind. I chase it away quickly. “But a turn of events changed my itinerary and now I find myself here at your lovely, historic, and charming inn. And I just learned your son is a courteous and informative guide.” I look at Gabriel now and raise my eyebrows, signaling him to play along.

He squints, then I watch as his face melts into a wholly manufactured smile. “Thank you, Ms. Cary-Alzona. The pleasure is all mine,” he says.

Ruby’s shoulders ease and I seize the moment. “In particular, Mr. Calabrese introduced me to a town tradition I am wildly excited to support.” I dial my voice to full sunny optimism, impersonating one of Mom’s perky social secretaries. “It checks all my mother’s boxes—small businesses, the arts, community building, and bonus! It’s patriotic.” I flash my brightest smile. “It’s the Mystic Hollow Inn’s annual Fourth of July Jubilee!”

The silence that follows is so thick only the birds dare fill it. At last Ruby speaks. "You want to volunteer for the jubilee?"

I nod enthusiastically. "Exactly. If you'll have me. Gabriel was showing me around town to meet some of the vendors. The jubilee is exactly the kind of relationship building my parents are hoping I'll take on." I think of Pat and his ice cream cart. Not *technically* a lie.

Ruby glances at Tita. "We could use all the help we can get, but I'm not sure having you on board planning our festival is allowed?"

Tita considers. "Anything official would have to be cleared by the White House." My stomach sinks, knowing if that happens the chances of my idea working are as good as Mom's favorite baseball team making the World Series.

"However," Tita Karra adds. "If Abby is working behind the scenes, is not at all connected or visible, and keeps a low profile—I think that would be fine."

Ruby and Tita Karra exchange meaningful looks. I hold my breath as the two step aside to discuss. I wring my hands, wondering if I should pitch my case further, but Ruby and Tita break off their conversation.

I freeze as Ruby offers me her hand. "You've made a strong case for yourself, Ms. Cary-Alzona. We're glad to have you on board."

My jaw drops and I find myself pumping Ruby's hand and wrapping my arms around Tita. She shakes her head, letting me know she's still angry at me, but she also squeezes my elbow, letting me know she's not *100 percent* mad.

Meanwhile, Elle does her version of a victory dance. "We've

got this," Elle chimes in. "Plus, I've got a lock on the young peeps demographic."

Tita levels us with a look that could melt icebergs. "All fine and great. But no more sneaking out. From now on, everything goes through us *and* your security detail. Do I make myself clear?"

We all nod like bobbleheads. No one wants to end up permanently on Shaw's bad side.

Gabe lifts his camera. "How about an unofficial committee photo?"

Ruby grins. "You've seen how good he is, right? He's even shot a couple weddings here."

Tita claps a hand on his shoulder. "Impressive. How many inns have their very own photographer on staff?"

I catch Gabriel's face waver, and I recall he hasn't told anyone about his desire to go to art school.

Gabriel captures a shot, and then after some cajoling, I get Shaw to take a photo so Gabriel can also be in the picture. The two of us are somehow pushed to the front and middle of the shot, standing side by side. I try not to blush at how personal this all feels.

After we finish our photo, Ruby claps her hands, her face transforming into the hotel manager I met on the first day. "Okay, back to work. Why don't we let the girls get cleaned up? Gabriel, I need your help with some flowers that have to be picked up at Ms. Hirono's shop."

He doesn't say *see you later* aloud, but his smile at me is practically a promise. The butterflies in my belly aren't just fluttering—

they're full-on uprising. As he hops back into his truck, I feel a hand on my shoulder. Tita Karra has an amused smile.

I look at her hopefully. "You'll explain to Mom this was all a big misunderstanding?"

"Indeed, dear niece."

I clasp my hands. "Thank you for covering for us."

She sighs. "I've watched you and that boy work so hard. Last summer all you did was campaign to help your mother win her reelection. You both deserve some downtime—and to freeze your brains with frozen coffee lattes."

My eyes widen. "How did you know about the lattes?" I guess right away as Elle scurries inside the inn with a giggle. I turn to my tita. "Elle told you about my bucket list."

She shrugs. "She gave me some highlights when I caught her at the park."

I nod. Elle was right. I should've told Tita Karra about my list. My aunt turns serious. "Listen, I mean it when I say your participation must be behind the scenes."

"I know. I know. The last thing we need is some misunderstanding like what happened with the pizza."

"Not just that," Tita says, pinching the bridge of her nose. "You need to know that there's a resort that has recently opened up—"

"I heard about it downtown."

My aunt looks me dead in the eyes. "That resort is owned by Oliver's family."

I stare at Tita before coming to my senses. "Wait. The competing resort is owned by Darby International?"

My stomach flips. If that's true, then no wonder Gabe is losing customers. Oliver's uncle pours a lot of money into marketing for his luxury properties. And that's why Gabe was so snarky with Oliver. Oliver's family is hurting his mom's business. And now, they're sponsoring a daytime activity to compete with Gabe's festival.

I moan as I cover my face with my hands. "Helping a family-owned business is usually a good thing," I say, mostly to myself. "Besides, I don't work for the Darby family."

Tita Karra shrugs. "I know. But after your mother asked me that you keep a low profile, do we really want to draw any of her attention by possibly antagonizing her vice president's family?"

"No, of course not," I say. "But there's nothing to worry about. I promise to stay behind the scenes."

Tita doesn't budge. "Promise me—no headlines. And make sure no one you work with is the type to sell out to the press."

I press my lips together. "Got it. All the usual rules. Elle, Shaw, and Nessa—we all know the drill."

Tita Karra nods, then pulls me in for a side hug. "Good. Here's to Operation Bucket List."

CHAPTER 14

The next day, it's after lunch when Gabriel returns from his errands.

"Hard at work, I see," he muses from the doorway of his mother's office, looking gorgeous as usual in shorts and a white V-neck T-shirt. I look up briefly, then force myself to stop staring and return to the news clippings I was reading. Elle, of course, has no issues with addressing him.

"Abby and I have been doing some research on the previous Mystic Hollow jubilees," Elle declares. She sits beside me, going through printouts of old flyers and newspapers.

Gabriel folds his arms. "Mom gave you internet access. She must really trust you."

"And why wouldn't she?" I say with some sass. Turns out the inn *does* have access to the internet. But it's in Ruby's office, a DSL line that is strictly for the owners of the inn.

I've already come up with some ideas about how to attract attention to the festival. "There are some booths here that look like they were popular back in the day," I say. "There was a midway with games for kids."

Gabriel grins. "Yeah, I remember those. Unfortunately, the local business that used to run those games closed and we never found anyone to bring them back. And it just sort of dropped off."

"Family activities are always a draw," I say, mostly to myself as I write down *games* on my brainstorming list.

I tap my chin. "What would be great is if we could come up with some kind of theme or special occasion?"

"The Fourth isn't special enough?" Gabriel asks, deadpan.

"I mean like . . . is this the twentieth anniversary of the festival? Or the thirtieth for the inn?"

His mouth twists. "Nope, inn's been around about forty-six years and the festival's on year thirty-nine."

I snap my fingers. "So close to a milestone. Just missed the forty-fifth and just shy of the big four-oh."

He sighs. "And the festival's in just a few weeks."

I flash him my most confident grin. "Plenty of time. I've seen major events get pulled off far faster."

"Right," he says, "but you would also have a whole team and, I dunno, the resources of the White House at your disposal?"

I purse my lips. He's not wrong, especially these days, but it wasn't always like that. "Back in the day, grassroots volunteers and small staff were the bread and butter of my mom's operations. Plus"—I wink, recalling advice from the campaign—"it's not what you have, it's who you know."

Elle giggles. "And what they got."

I high-five Elle, who's on point. While we're no longer in "campaign mode," one of my mom's staff who practically babysat us over the years, Erin, has always been an email or text away whenever we need advice. I'm eagerly awaiting their response now.

"Speaking of who you know, I have a tip that might help you," Gabriel says. "An old baseball teammate of mine is having a 'community event' this afternoon that has 'bucket list' item all over it."

I laugh. "What kind of community event?"

He smirks and leans forward. "Let's find out."

★ ★ ★

"Isn't that the guy you called turd-breath?" I ask when Gabriel tells me the party's host is Kyle Schwab.

"It's a term of endearment," Gabriel says. I can't quite tell if he's serious or not. Gabe clearly isn't a fan of Kyle, so I appreciate him taking me to this party anyway.

I sit in his truck, listening to the hum of his rock music but not really paying attention. Five minutes into our drive and I haven't said a word except "I'm buckled" and "blast the AC."

I see him looking at me from the corner of my eye. "Are you okay?"

"Yes," I begin to say. "I don't know. I guess I'm a little nervous."

He guffaws. "You're joking. Don't you meet new people all the time?"

"Yes, but that doesn't mean I'm not nervous when I do."

"Seriously? You seem so confident, all the time."

"No, that's Elle. She's more like our dad." I shake my head, thinking about my kid sister, who opted to do "retail therapy" with my tita this afternoon.

But before taking off, she made sure to help me pick out my white eyelet two-piece swimsuit, which I wear under a gauzy pink cover-up dress. The floppy sun hat on my lap completes my look. "Remember, you're hot teenage Abby, not boring First Daughter Abby," Elle chided as I walked out of our suite.

The look on Gabriel's face and the stammer in his voice was well worth Elle's nagging as I met him at the bottom of the steps.

I sneak a glance at Gabriel, appreciating how good he looks: stylish tousled hair, Ray-Bans, white T-shirt, and teal swim trunks.

It took serious negotiating to get clearance for Gabriel to drive me solo, with Shaw and Nessa trailing behind. But hey—there was precedent. I cited Susan Ford, the First Daughter who once got picked up for a date at the White House. And bonus, Gabe's already passed more background checks than some cabinet members.

I savor the rare freedom and hang my arm out the window. Warm air rushes over my fingers as we cruise past roadside farmstands packed with green vegetables and colorful fruit. In the distance, golden hills dotted with trees, a farmhouse, and grazing cows. This is a welcome change of pace for me.

"You have nothing to worry about," Gabriel says, eyes on the road. "Kyle and his party crew are goofballs, but harmless."

The mention of Kyle and goofballs reminds me of a question I had. "Why 'turd-breath'?"

Gabriel chuckles. "Boys being dumb," he says. "During

Little League practice one day, he showed everyone a white rock he found."

"White rock?"

"It was a petrified dog turd."

I cringe. "Ugh!"

"When we pointed that out, he didn't believe us until he sniffed it, and, well." He laughs.

"Do you still play baseball?"

His eyes go flat. "No. Don't have a lot of free time these days."

"That's too bad. I never joined any sports teams," I say.

He arches a brow. "Right. Hence the bucket list item for team sports. Aren't you, like, Ivy-bound? Aren't sports necessary for your résumé or whatever?"

I smile ruefully. "Closest thing I do is occasional doubles tennis with Oliver."

Gabe goes quiet and my face reddens. I'm fully aware of the possible innuendo of my statement. In fact, I hadn't thought much about Oliver these past few days. Just a couple texts of me explaining the lack of cell phone service here and him saying the same as he does some hiking trip across the islands.

"Not a golf club?" Gabe says in what is probably an attempt to lighten the mood. "I figured you have meetings with elite country-club types."

"Oh yeah," I say. "Just as elite as you and your hoity-toity equestrian types. Owning horses means you're rich, right?"

"Touché," Gabriel says. "Is hoity-toity like 'nature-y'? An AP English word, right?" I side-eye him for his reference to my bucket list.

My retort is cut short when a white truck suddenly appears

next to us, but instead of zooming past—which isn't hard because Shaw insists Gabriel drive the speed limit—it keeps pace with us.

I groan as the teens in the truck recognize us. They look about our age. I force a strained smile and slide lower in my seat.

"Seriously?" Gabriel exclaims, shooting them a glare. He motions for them to drive ahead, but they're still gawking.

Then Shaw's voice crackles over the loudspeaker from the SUV behind us. "Keep moving," he barks, in full Secret Service mode. He pulls his large black truck directly behind the white pickup to let them know he's serious.

The truck's driver looks stricken as he hits the gas.

Gabriel says quietly, "Sorry about that. They go to school with me and should know better."

"It's okay. I'm used to it." And it's true. I suck in a deep breath. "I guess word has spread I'm here?"

Gabriel looks pained. "Must be. I had to tell Kyle about the Secret Service coming to secure the party location, and naturally that led to questions and his motormouth."

Gabriel looks my way with concern in his eyes that sends goose bumps up my arm. "They all know they're not allowed to publicize your presence, Abby. And I'll make sure everyone remembers when we get there." The edge in his voice is serious.

"Thank you. I'm sorry for all the trouble."

He grows quiet. "We only have a month together and already I feel like I'm in a bubble. My life will go back to normal, but how you do this your entire life . . ." His voice trails off.

"This is my normal" is all I can think to say. He looks at me with sympathy, and I don't blame him. We come from two different worlds.

His "only a month" remark also irks me. Is he already counting the days for me to return home?

We turn off the main road onto a gravel one that goes into a wooded area. I breathe in the fresh, cooler air. It smells like damp dirt and fallen foliage. I love how the sunlight filters through the canopy like little lasers of light.

I glance at Gabe, warmth blooming in my chest. It's nice sharing a new experience with him. He must feel it too—he glances over, and for a brief moment, our smiles meet in perfect sync.

The trees start to thin out and I notice a sign that I wasn't expecting. "Mystic Hollow Lake?" I blink. "I thought we were going to your friend's house for a pool party?"

Gabe laughs. "I said 'swim party,' and Kyle's family has a lake house. Your bucket list said you wanted to relax at the beach, right?"

My confusion turns to shock as the lake comes into view. A small, rocky shoreline blends into patches of sand, where groups of teens are lounging in beach chairs or splashing in the water. Several of them turn our way and lift their red cups in greeting, hollering their welcome like we're celebrities.

All of a sudden I'm not so sure about this. I'm used to being around my peers in the context of a school project or homework. But just hanging out, with no agenda? My stomach roils as I try to think of things to say.

"You'll be fine. They greet everyone coming down the road like that, see?" Gabe says as he nods at Shaw's car behind us. He's right—the same people shout at the SUV, then immediately back off. Shaw's scowl will do that to people. But seeing that still doesn't calm my nerves.

"I don't have a script for high school parties," I whisper to Gabe.

His brows furrow. "Abby, you don't need a script for parties. That's the whole point."

I shake my head. "You don't understand. If people talk to me I'll default to asking them questions instead of answering any of theirs." It's a tactic I've learned from Mom's staff.

Gabe places his hand on mine, jolting me. "Don't overthink this. Just be yourself." I nod. I wish it were that easy.

"And, hey, if it gets bad, we can hang out in Kyle's library and alphabetize his family's books," he says with a smile. I know he's teasing, but it's sweet he knows that would calm me.

Kyle's lake house is a nice two-story wooden home nestled among tall trees with a small pier. It's the kind of place that says "hit pause" and "take a breath."

Gabe parks on the side where several cars and trucks are already parked, facing a row of trees. Shaw's black SUV pulls up behind us.

Shaw and Nessa hop out of their vehicle. He comes up to Gabriel's window and thumps it. Gabriel rolls it down and we listen to Shaw's instructions for us to wait in the car as he sweeps the area.

Gabriel gives a thumbs-up in response. If Shaw senses any attitude, he doesn't let on. Meanwhile, Nessa stands next to my window. Even though my detail is dressed down, their polos and long khaki pants still look formal.

"I bet Kyle is regretting inviting me," I say quietly.

Gabe laughs. "No. I think he's feeling the opposite of regret. He'll be gloating about this the rest of his life." His voice lowers. "What about you?"

"No regrets. I'm just mentally preparing myself for a function with my peers."

His laugh is hearty. "A function with your peers? Is that what you call a party," he teases.

The loud thump on my window doesn't help with my rattling nerves. Nessa leans in, sunglasses lowered on her nose so we can see her very serious gaze. "All clear." She opens my door to let me out of the vehicle.

"Rapunzel and Rascal are en route to the front door," Nessa says into her earpiece.

"Rascal," I say, laughing at Gabe's Secret Service call sign. I look at Gabe, who doesn't seem amused.

Nessa does her best to hide her smirk. "Wasn't my call."

I've barely set foot out of Gabe's truck when a boy with damp reddish hair and flamingo swim trunks greets us. "You made it!" he says. I can't help returning his smile. Kyle definitely has a goofy energy to him.

Gabriel responds with a low-energy " 'Sup" before turning his attention to me. "Abby, this is the party host, Kyle . . . Schwab." I pick up on his pause after he says Kyle's first name, clearly reminding himself not to say "turd-breath."

"Abby Cary-Alzona!" Kyle exclaims. "What's up! I can't believe the First Daughter is here at my humble abode." He goes in for a hug, but Nessa's cough would make anyone think twice.

"Right," Kyle says nervously. "How 'bout a quick tour." He motions me inside the house. I appreciate the invite. I'm not ready to face the group of teens hanging at the beach.

Inside, Kyle's house is inviting and open, with a cozy, rustic vibe. He points out the bathroom and then we go straight to the kitchen, which faces the house's living and dining room and large floor-to-ceiling windows.

The view of the lake is gorgeous. I notice maybe two or three other homes farther away with their own piers, but really there aren't many houses out here.

I've never seen such a spread of snack-food goodness as the one on the kitchen island. I smell everything from dill to honey BBQ.

Except for a few partygoers lingering on Kyle's deck, I'm relieved it's not too busy here. "You can drop your backpack if you want," Kyle says, nodding at my bag. I hug it close. I always bring a couple of books; you never know when you'll need a fictional friend. Kyle continues his tour. "And I can hook you up with a couple more-quality snacks or drinks. Something better than what the herd's picked over," he adds, eyeing the half-empty bowl of Cheetos like it personally offended him.

I'm about to decline when two girls nearly topple a bottle of ginger ale while barreling toward me. "Abby! Abby! You're *actually* here!" one of them squeals. Or maybe both of them. It's hard to tell—they're practically bounding in unison. Once they've stopped jumping, I realize they're the girls from the white truck who gawked at us on the road. And they're twins.

"We loved your dress at the Italian state dinner," Twin One with the single braid says.

"It was vintage Atelier Versace, right?" Twin Two with the double braid adds. Her sister continues before I can confirm.

"We're so sorry about the whole pineapple thing."

"Yeah, for the record. We agree. Pineapple on pizza is, like, so gross."

"So gross," the other agrees.

"Is Oliver going to come visit too?" The girls giggle. "We'd love to meet him. You two are so—"

Gabriel fake coughs loudly. "Okay, Billie and Jaisha. Maybe Abby could use some space?"

I sigh inwardly, relieved to avoid gossip about me and Oliver.

The twins focus their attention on Gabriel, or rather his camera. I've gotten so used to seeing him with his black-and-red camera strap I forgot he's carrying it around. "Hoping to scoop another hot story for the paper with that?" Billie asks.

"Is our photojournalist back in action?" Jaisha adds.

She's addressing him but looking at me.

Gabriel is visibly agitated. "No. I don't work for the paper anymore, remember?"

I frown. Gabriel said he was interested in art photography. I'm shocked he used to work at his school's paper. I look to him for an explanation, but he's suddenly busy opening bottles at the drinks station.

The girls stare after him. "That's too bad."

"Not really," Gabriel says.

I'd love to know more about this newspaper business, but I also don't like seeing Gabriel uncomfortable. "It's nice to meet you," I say to the twins. "I love your outfits. Very cowgirl core," I add.

"Oh my gosh, you're so sweet," says Billie, the one with the single braid, swishing her fringe skirt.

"You're not a stuck-up pineapple princess at all," Jaisha adds. "You're such a nice person."

"See you soon," I tell the twins. They practically squeal as they head back outside.

"Newspaper?" I ask Gabriel.

"Freshman and sophomore year, for a hot second." I give him a once-over. I knew he had media vibes to him, so that must be it. His days with the school paper. "I was the paper's staff photographer and I took a lot of photos for Kyle and the twins' stories." From his tone, I can tell that's a sore spot for him.

"What's your poison, Abby?" Kyle shouts from across the room at me. He sweeps a magnanimous arm across the table full of bottles and cans.

"You want to poison me?" I ask.

Kyle's face falls. "No. Not literally poison. It's a figure of speech. I—"

I cackle. "I'm joking. I'm sorry. I'm so used to hanging with this one." I nod at Gabriel.

Kyle looks from me to Gabriel, then back to me. The strange look on his face turns into a goofy smile. "I get it. I love messing with Gabe too. It's fun getting him worked up."

Gabriel rolls his eyes. Kyle hands me an Arnold Palmer—iced tea and lemonade—in a red Solo cup. I hesitate and whisper to Gabe, "This is just iced tea, right? It's not like every teen movie where the good girl gets in trouble . . ." I feel heat creep up my neck. I sound like such a prude. "Not that I'm a good girl. I mean, I try to be, but—"

Gabriel holds up a hand and laughs. "Relax! You're hilarious," he says more to himself. "First, good thing this isn't a movie, and second, I'm not going to let you get into any trouble, Abby." His eyes search mine and my heart flutters. He arches a brow and offers me his hand. "You wanna go to a real party?" I laugh at his *Titanic* quote.

A speaker blasts Sia as we exit the lake house onto Kyle's porch. A set of stairs leads to the beach below. And beyond that, a group of Kyle's friends lounge in colorful beach chairs sunbathing, chatting, and living it up. I smile as a couple folks in the lake splash water on each other. I shut my eyes, enjoying a cool breeze, warm sunlight, and the smell of water and freedom.

A flood of energy like an electrical current passes through me. #Summervibes. "This is exactly what I was hoping for," I say to Gabriel. He lowers his camera. I didn't even notice him taking photos.

He returns my smile. "I told you I'd help you with your list."

We stop at a lounge chair, and my eyes widen at the large inflatable pineapple on it. Kyle's laugh is high pitched as he throws the pool toy aside. "Sorry, someone has a bad sense of humor. But this is the chair I reserved for you."

"You didn't have to do that," I insist, but my protest is

short-lived as I spot a somber-faced Shaw near Kyle's house. Arms crossed, mirrored sunglasses, and a stone's throw away. "This tracks. I'm in direct line of sight of my real babysitters," I say.

Kyle shrugs. "For the record, we were going to save you a chair anyway."

"Thanks, but I don't want any special treatment." I lower myself onto the chaise and take in the scene. I'm here. I'm at a full-blown summer party sans parents or any authority figures—except Nessa and Shaw, but they'll do their best to blend in and not meddle.

"Kyle, Gabe," someone shouts across the way. "Come help us settle this bet."

Gabriel is visibly agitated. "They need both of us?"

"Duty calls, my friend," Kyle says, clapping his back. He mimics a bow in my direction. "Make yourself at home."

Home? This place is nothing like 1600 Pennsylvania Avenue, in a good way. Across from me, a couple girls lounge with their eyes closed, sun-soaked and content. Inspired, I peel off my pink cover-up. Elle swore this white two-piece was peak "it girl," but today, I'm just a regular American teenager hanging out at a summer party.

I sink into the lounge chair, the cushion soft against my back, the sun bathing me from head to toe. This is it. Bucket list item, hang out at the beach for as long as I want. Check.

I twist to get some sun on my back, and am awarded with an unexpected view. A very hot, nonchalant Gabriel without his white T-shirt is heading back in my direction. I force myself to look away, even though I know that image is now permanently etched into my brain.

And I notice I'm not the only one who's staring. Gabriel has some fans.

No, nope. I banish any pesky thoughts away. Think of Oliver. Good old Oliver Darby. My bestie and soon to be more. I'm sure of it. As soon as I see Oliver again, all will be right with the world.

"Abby?" Kyle is waving a hand near my face.

I blink. "Sorry?"

"Come join us!" I look where he's pointing, and it's a group nearby dancing and grinding on the sand not far from someone's Bluetooth speakers.

"Dude. Let her be," Gabriel says with a warning look that kind of irks me. Why shouldn't I dance? Sure, the buttoned-up, perfectly poised Abby would sit it out.

But this is Bucket List Summer Abby. And she says: *Why not?*

"Sounds fun," I say, ignoring Gabriel's concerned expression. Soon I'm holding my drink in the air and moving to the beat as a bunch of people circle around.

My eyes close, and I let the music take control, my body bouncing along without overthinking it. Several folks shout, "Go, Abby!" and some crowd around, dancing alongside me.

I laugh from the exhilaration of doing something spontaneous for once. I check out Gabriel a couple times and am a bit disappointed to see him sitting on his lounge chair, sunglasses on and fiddling with his camera. Not paying any attention to me. It's fine. As Pat at the ice cream parlor said, his camera is his significant other.

As the song dips into the next, a bunch of people run into the lake. Billie and Jaisha leap into cannonballs, calling me to join them.

I laugh and follow right behind. I shriek with delight as the lake's chilly water surrounds my body. A welcome relief from the summer heat.

I swim a bit to where I have to tiptoe to stay above the water. I hear some splashing and see Gabriel joining me.

"Shaw doesn't look like he's enjoying the water," Gabriel warns. I see my agent standing knee-deep in the lake holding a life preserver.

I sigh. As much as I'd love to stay out here, how embarrassing would it be to have my Secret Service agent nearby, floating on his own plastic flamingo life preserver?

Gabriel reads my mind and motions me to follow him. Clumsy-rella I am, I slip on a rock on the lake bottom and take a little dive into the water.

Gabriel helps me out. "I'm fine," I say, quickly wiping the water off my face. He offers me his hand. I ignore the jolt that thrums through my body as he leads me out of the lake. I hold on to his hand a little longer than necessary while I regain my footing when we're back at the shore.

"Thanks," I say. "I'm having the best time ev—" I cover my mouth as I'm hit by a fit of coughs.

He frowns. "Are you okay?"

I gasp. "I inhaled some lake water."

"Let me get you a drink." He doesn't wait for a response before he jogs toward a watercooler. I watch him. For someone I barely know, he's surprisingly super attentive.

I take my time walking back to my beach chair, letting my feet kick up the lake water and feeling the sand between my toes. I relish the heat of the sun warming my skin, contrasted by cool water dripping from my swimsuit.

In the distance, a soothing beat from someone's speakers hums in the air. I feel my body relax. This is what summer should feel like.

I stop mid-step as I notice a swift movement from the corner of my eye. My body tingles with warning.

A boy crouches behind one of the lounge chairs, cradling something in his arms. My eyes widen as he turns in my direction.

"Ooof!" I yelp as I'm pushed down and hit the sand hard.

"Stay down," Nessa hisses into my ear. Not like I have a choice as her body covers mine.

I turn just in time to see Shaw yelling at a boy.

"It's a toy," he insists. "It's just a game." I follow the boy's gaze and see water guns in the sand.

Nessa grips my arm and hauls me to my feet. "We're leaving."

"But they're just toys," I protest.

Doesn't matter. Her tone says this isn't up for debate.

In the distance, an angry Gabriel yells at a guilty-looking Kyle before walking toward me. His expression is so furious he looks like he could burst into flames. "They're playing Assassin," he says. "It's a silly game where players are assigned targets and use toy water guns to take them out."

"But my agents would've swept the place," I say.

He points at Kyle. "Turd-breath has water guns that look like foam pool tubes, which security must have missed, and I think the Millers at the next house over brought some water guns too. Kyle should've suspended the game today."

I'm barely listening. My stomach lurches, seeing the terror and confusion on everyone's faces as Shaw and the rest of the

Secret Service agents who've now arrived on scene yell at them to keep back and be quiet.

Guilt fills my chest as Gabe's classmates freak out. It's not fun having massive superhuman-sized agents barking orders at you. "Let's get out of here," I say to Nessa.

I ruined Kyle's party. This is why I shouldn't have friends.

CHAPTER 15

I'm sitting in my room drying my hair when I hear a knock on the suite's front door. It must be Ruby, who very thoughtfully offered to bring me hot tea after the incident at Kyle's lake house. Gabe's mom must've felt bad for me. Instead of me glowing with triumph from my first real summer party, I arrived back at the inn sopping wet and red with embarrassment like I'd done a belly flop gone wrong.

I pad barefoot into the sitting room, and aside from Elle's Doritos bags dominating the coffee table, I appreciate the calming vibe of the room as the afternoon sunlight pours through the windows. If not for my silly bucket list, I would've stayed here curled up with a book. That version of Abigail would be dry and cozy. I fling open the door.

My hand flies involuntarily to my chest when I find Gabe at the doorway, looking like guilt, regret, and sadness are all fighting for space on his face. I run a hand through my damp hair, feeling self-conscious in my worn tank top and shorts.

"Room service," he says.

Before I can respond, he rolls a cart to my door. Atop the cart is a teapot, a white paper bag, and a waffle cone with chocolate chip ice cream.

"I remember someone saying ice cream makes everything better," he says.

It feels like a whole minute before I register what's happening and step back to let him into my suite. As Gabe sets the items on the coffee table, I notice the Pat's Famous Ice Cream logo on the bag, the telltale signs of grease, and the smell of fried goodness.

A light bulb clicks in my head. "Is that the Pike Special?"

"Yeah. Since our first attempt was a bust," he says, lips quirked.

I let out a soft, breathy gasp recalling how we got caught by my agents before we could try the special treat. It was an unfortunate loss, but it eventually led me to convincing Gabriel and his mom to let me help with their Fourth of July festival.

Gabe pulls out a box of hot, salty, delicious fries. I salivate at the sight. Ceremoniously, he takes a golden fry and dips it into his ice cream. My eyes widen. "You dip your fries in ice cream?"

He holds up the fry box and motions me to grab one. "Here's to checking off 'broaden culinary palate' on your bucket list."

I bite my lip. Literally a minute ago I was ready to trash that list, but as I watch his eyes close as he chews, I'm reconsidering that decision.

"Come on, Abby," Gabe says in between bites. "You know these golden fries are calling your name."

I laugh and take my own bite. I relish the crunch of the fry and moan as the hot salt and sweet ice cream mix. "Soooo good.

Who knew two opposite sides of the food spectrum could work so well together?"

"The Pike Special is a national treasure, right?" He grabs another fry.

We sit silently side by side as we wolf down the food. Gabriel is the first to finally talk. "I've never heard you so quiet."

"I know." I lick some ice cream off the side of my mouth and notice he's still in his swim trunks. Ashamed, I realize Gabe must've gone straight to Pat's instead of coming home and taking a hot shower like me. "I feel bad. You ran out to get this treat for me and I ruined Kyle's party."

Gabriel throws his head back and laughs. "No way. I'll take any excuse to get the Pike. And second, you pretty much made Mystic Hollow High School's best party ever."

"But in a bad way," I say.

"Abby. I promise everyone is having the best day ever. Kyle's probably mad because he can't report it in the paper."

He runs a hand through his hair. "I'm the one who should apologize. I should've remembered Kyle's stupid game. I let him have it after the party—I told him how important it was for you to have a fun and relaxing summer for once."

I freeze. "Wait, you didn't mention my bucket list, right? Because I don't want people to know about that."

"I didn't." He pauses. "But if I did, would it be that bad? I think it shows you're kind of normal. Isn't that what you want?"

"Does it say I'm normal? Or how sad I am? And how everything on my list makes it look like I'm a spoiled brat? Or a sheltered kid?" I put my head in my hands. "And I don't want people's pity."

I realize I'm babbling, but I can't help myself. I'm a mess.

Gabriel squeezes my arm. He looks into my eyes and holds my gaze. "Abby, it's going to be okay." He inhales deeply and encourages me to do the same.

I stare at his shoulders and suddenly wish I could lean my head there. We're so close on the couch. If I just moved . . .

"Speaking of your list," Gabriel says, suddenly making me jump. "Do you want to tick off another item?"

I frown. "I think I've officially hit my bucket list limit for today."

He nudges my shoulder. "Come on, Pineapple Princess. Meet me after sunset." His grin is impossible to read—equal parts mystery and mischief. "You won't regret it."

It's a beautiful evening outside, with a crescent moon and grass fluttering in the breeze.

Though honestly, most of my attention is on the boy in a green T-shirt, khakis, and a black backpack as I follow him out the back door of the inn.

"I wouldn't normally do a shot like this so close to the inn, but since it gets your babysitters off our tail, it's worth it," Gabriel says.

He walks purposefully and I follow briskly to keep up with him. My heart is hammering in my head being alone with him at night, though I'm sure Shaw and Nessa are nearby, keeping tabs. My shadows always following me.

I stare above. "I can see so many more stars here than in DC."

Gabriel nods at the sky. "Exactly. I've been practicing my astrophotography, and this night sky is perfect."

"Astro what?"

His laugh is soft. "I'll explain when we get there."

"There" turns out to be the small building behind the inn. I tilt my head to study the cute structure. Of course, I've noticed it before, but didn't think much of it after Tita explained it was a guesthouse that was being renovated. "What is this place?"

Gabriel opens the door of the building and ushers me in. "It's our Honeymoon Cottage."

I stop at the door as he says this. Glad it's dark or he could see my bright red cheeks. "Honeymoon?"

He guffaws. "Oh no, we're not hanging in the honeymoon suite. Just up there." He points at the ceiling.

"Sorry?"

He flicks on a small lamp, illuminating a tidy construction zone with a bunch of lumber and tiles on the floor. He goes to the back of the cottage and from the ceiling pulls down a door, revealing a ladder.

I point at the ladder with a shaky finger. "You want me to climb that to the roof?"

"None of your dad's astronaut stuff rubbed off on you, huh?"

I narrow my eyes at him and grab the ladder's rails with a huff. Regular Abigail would take a pass. Summertime Abby is up to the challenge. Minutes later we're standing on the roof of the Honeymoon Cottage.

After a few questionable shingles move about loosely, I laugh at how light and free I feel being up here. The moon's light and stars twinkle in greeting. "I'm king of the world," I shout.

"Okay, Leonardo. Maybe not too close to the edge," Gabriel warns.

I frown. I'm practically standing on the middle of the roof. "Not too close to the edge," I say, mimicking Gabe's raspy voice.

Gabe's laugh is infectious. "Really, I sound like Batman underwater?"

I laugh. "You want me to do Batman underwater?" I do my best to imitate a low growl but making it bubbly-sounding.

He laughs. "You're brilliant."

I grin ear to ear. It's nice to be appreciated for a hidden talent I've only ever shared with Elle.

Gabe gets to work setting up a tarp for us to sit on and unpacking his bag. Dark Knight he is not, but he has his fair share of gadgets. He points one of the lenses toward the moon.

"Are you taking photos of the sky?" I ask.

He nods. "I'm photographing the stars. Astrophotography, get it."

I look up. "I don't know much about photography, but taking photos at night is super difficult, right?"

"One of the hardest fields of photography," he murmurs, doing something with his camera lens.

"So why?"

He pauses and looks up. The moonlight is reflected in his eyes as his gaze holds mine. "Guess I like a challenge."

Again, I'm grateful for the dark to hide my blush.

Gabriel continues. "It's for my art school portfolio. I want to show them my range of ability, and if I show them pro-level astrophotography shots . . ." His voice trails off like he's envisioning finding gold at the end of the rainbow.

"I want to capture shots of the planets, the Milky Way, and eventually a meteor shower for my portfolio. I figure a bit more practice and I'll be capable of getting the shots I want. A portrait shot with the Milky Way in the background would be epic. Like a portrait framed by the cosmos."

My mind jumps to the couple on the bench swing on the inn's staircase. That photo was also at night. "The photo of the couple on the inn's swing must've been difficult."

Gabriel looks up. "You noticed that?"

"Of course, it's gorgeous. Did you take it?"

"No, that was my dad's work. He took that photo of my grandparents," he says with a bittersweet smile.

My hand flies to my heart. "That's so sweet. Your dad was super talented."

"He is—was." His voice lowers as he corrects himself.

My chest tightens. "Is that why you're reluctant to tell your mom about the summer program?"

He stares up at the sky. "It's always been about the family business for her. She calls photography a hobby. And after my dad died, I stopped mentioning it. I think it kind of upsets her."

"I'm sorry. Must be hard."

He nods. "I can't be a burden on my mom. I'm going to stay here in Mystic Hollow and help the business, but I just want to study abroad, at least for a semester."

“So, the art school is kind of your bucket list item?” I say with a tiny smile.

He chuckles in agreement, but any response he has must be cut short as the sky brightens. Gabe’s face lights up. “The clouds covering the moon have moved,” he says. He lifts his camera and goes straight to work-mode.

As he shoots well into the night, I know I’ve crossed stargazing off my bucket list at least a dozen times, but I also can’t help thinking about that other item on my list, go on my first date. Does this count?

I don’t know what’s going on between us, but whatever I’m feeling, I think this is just the beginning. And I can’t imagine ever forgetting this evening, even long after this summer ends and Gabe and I go our separate ways.

The sunlight streaming through my windows is extra bright when my eyes flutter open. I’m momentarily confused; I usually never sleep in. I wiggle in my warm down comforter, stretching my arms and relishing not having to rush out of bed.

A smile plays on my lips as I recall last night. What started out as pictures of the sky turned into a portrait shoot of me under the stars as Gabriel practiced adjusting his lens to take night shots. Nothing happened, of course, but being the focus of his photos made the butterflies in my belly work overtime. And that’s coming from me, who’s been photographed a million times.

When I make it downstairs, I see Ruby clearing up the breakfast table and Gabriel loading the dishwasher.

I'm relieved Ruby doesn't notice me right away. Because Gabriel—bathed in golden morning sunlight—honestly takes my breath away. It should be illegal to look that good both day *and* night.

When our eyes meet, there's this charge. Like a secret passed wordlessly between us.

Before I can finish apologizing for being late to breakfast, Ruby cuts me off. "Honey, I have a teenager, I know how it goes." She nods at the fridge with a warm smile. "There's food in there, or you can head into town with Gabriel."

It's subtle, but I notice Gabriel pause at the sink before resuming rinsing the dish he's holding.

If Ruby notices anything between us, she doesn't give it away. I clear my throat. "Sure. I'll head to town with Gabe."

"Sounds good, Mom—" he says at the same time. His laugh makes me take a mental note to pack sunglasses, because that gorgeous face of his is blinding.

As soon as Gabriel and I hit the road, Shaw's SUV is following right behind. We pass by some landmarks and homes that are starting to feel familiar and head toward downtown Mystic Hollow. I roll my window down and inhale the smell of fresh-baked bread as we pass by a bakery. Across the way in the town's square, I notice a few joggers and even a group doing a yoga class by the gazebo. It's a nice sight. Yoga in DC is people twisting to avoid each other at our crowded metro train stations.

"A little too early for a Pike Special," I joke as Gabe parks by Pat's parlor.

"That sounds like a dare," he says, opening his door.

"You're not serious—" I begin, but he laughs and motions for me to follow him. "No, but I do have another bucket list item for you."

I grab my baseball cap and sunglasses and get into incognito mode before he leads me down the block, past Mystic Hollow's cute storefronts.

I try to keep my distance, but walking side by side on the sidewalk makes it awfully hard to not bump into him. And my hand practically aches whenever it brushes against his. I sneak a glance at his face and catch him looking quickly away like I caught him staring. "We're almost there," he says.

We stop in front of a cute café with yellow-painted bricks and blue tables and chairs. I swoon seeing the café's name. "Latte Love? That's adorable! And bonus, 'shop local' is also on my list." Though, that's one bucket list item I won't have trouble fulfilling at Mystic Hollow's cute stores.

Gabriel motions me to the front door. "By the way, you've already met Marge, the café's owner."

I grin, remembering the woman in the colorful dress Gabe called the town's busybody.

Gabe continues, "She sells a summer iced frappé orange mocha something something that is known for—"

"Brain freezes!" I say, my eyes lighting up.

His eyes sparkle. "Does that sound like the perfect whipped cream–smothered summer drink to you?"

I do a little shimmy. "It's exactly what I had in mind for my bucket list."

He tilts his head and motions me to follow him inside. I'm as giddy as Charlie entering the chocolate factory, and he's Wonka—the Timothée version, of course.

The café has a steady stream of customers, and we dodge one exiting with a large crinkly bag of goodies and a pretty purple boba tea. The scent of sugary fried sweets makes me happy dance. I know an iced-coffee-induced brain freeze is my bucket list goal today, but there are a lot of other temptations: pastel frosted doughnuts, flaky sugar-dusted pastries, and jewel-toned macarons that remind me of the gem collection at the Natural History Museum. "What's your favorite?"

"I don't eat this stuff," he says.

I gasp. "Says the boy who dips fries in his ice cream?"

"That was for the sake of your bucket list," he says. "I took one for the team."

"Or maybe you're more boring than I am," I tease. He breaks into a gorgeous grin that makes my knees wobble like the jelly filling in a doughnut.

"Oh, my word," says an excited voice. "Is that Gabriel Calabrese gracing my 'sugar-induced coma' store?" I recognize Marge immediately as she makes finger quotes around *sugar-induced coma*, which sounds like something Gabe would say.

His grin is tight-lipped as he greets her. "Abby, you remember Marge."

"Of course. I was just telling Gabe how excited I am to visit your shop. And your café is adorable. You're clearly an accomplished entrepreneur with a good eye for design. I love your dress."

Marge twirls in her flowy emerald-and-rose-pink dress and winks. "I have others like this at my boutique. Gabriel can take you." She leans close so she practically whispers. "I'm glad you made it. I figured they'd keep you holed up in the inn. It would be such a pity for you to not visit our town."

I must look as stricken as I feel on the inside. Of course Marge would know who I am. "Gabe has permission to show me around a bit," I say.

She makes a motion like she's zipping up her lips in a your-secret-is-safe-with-me way, which is a relief. She smiles knowingly at Gabe. "And you couldn't find a better guide. He's probably taken photos of every inch of this town, and of course being part of the town's hospitality industry practically makes him an ambassador for Mystic Hollow." Her eyes alight. "Hey. Do you think your mom would be into—"

Gabriel speaks up quickly. "Marge, thanks again for talking to the business council about sponsoring the inn's jubilee this year." I exhale, glad to have Gabe interrupt. Once people start discussing Mom, those conversations tend to take a while.

Marge's body shifts back and she smiles resolutely. "You can tell Ruby a few folks still want to run the numbers, but you have my support wrangling those last-minute holdouts."

I grin. Coalition building—now *that's* a language I grew up around.

She continues, "I know that new resort's been poaching some of your usual business. It's tough." Gabe looks like he's holding back choice words. Marge places a hand on his shoulder. "But I've got a good feeling about this year. Your jubilee's going to shine. And who knows, some of those resort guests just might wander over looking for the real heart of Mystic Hollow."

"We would prefer that those guests stay at our inn," Gabe says. Marge squeezes Gabe's shoulder encouragingly, and not for the first time I wonder how much trouble his family business is in.

The front doors of the café swing open as a large group of women in sundresses enters. "Ah, excuse me, that's my bridal shower party here for high tea. You two order whatever you all want." She nods at one of the store clerks. "Gabe, we can make you a Worm Cup just like the old days," she teases. "He used to insist on only green worms too, so high-maintenance."

Gabe's face reddens from embarrassment. "I'm good." I join Marge as she cackles.

"Let's check off that bucket list item," he insists. As he orders our drinks, I spy with envy on the bridal party seated at a festive long table. If I were having a party, my guests would be vetted carefully with staff input and security checks, but these women all look like they're just hanging out with a group of friends and zero expectations.

"Here you go," Gabe says. My eyes widen as he hands me a huge cup that looks part milkshake, part coffee magic with a fluffy puff of whipped cream dusted with orange sprinkles, and an orange-striped paper straw.

"Like it?" Gabe asks, a pleased smile on his lips.

"Are you kidding me? This drink is so cute, it needs its own profile and a filter named after it."

He chuckles. "Speaking of social media, how about we sit outside?" I catch his gaze at the women behind us. My pulse quickens seeing some of them whispering and looking our way. Agreed. I prefer to not end up on anyone's feed.

Outside, we grab a table with an umbrella located on the far side of the café, away from the window with the bridal party. At a nearby bench, I see Nessa reading a newspaper and Shaw holding his phone in his lap, but not actually looking at the phone. Even they must be enjoying the nice weather and the chance to breathe a bit in civilian clothes, though the hunter-green windbreaker makes Shaw look a bit like the Hulk.

Gabriel is looking pleased with himself as we place our drinks on the table, and he adjusts his camera.

My face flushes. All kinds of emotions are running through me—excitement, anxiety, and anticipation—and it's not just because of my beautiful iced coffee concoction.

"Ready," he says, angling his camera at me and the frappé. "The trick is to slurp fast."

I nod and take a deep breath as he counts down from ten like a rocket about to launch. On "liftoff" I take a long, hurried sip.

I savor the rich, smooth, and sweet chocolate mixed with coffee and a refreshing citrus burst of flavor. And then I wince as a dull pain makes my forehead tighten and I see stars. "Brain freeze!" I laugh and hiss as my hand rubs my forehead. Why do people like that feeling?

His camera clicks. "That's another one off the list and a strong contender for my portfolio." He laughs as he twists his lips and wrinkles his nose in what I think is a poor attempt at imitating my expression.

"Making fun of my pain?" I chide, but my retort is cut short as I notice Shaw talking to a woman by the café's entrance. His back is to me, but I know the drill—he's kindly asking her to give me some privacy. The woman doesn't look happy, and I notice she isn't the only one waving their phone cameras in my direction. I shove my sunglasses back on.

Gabriel sees the commotion and curses under his breath. "Wow, it must really suck sometimes being you."

"I'm not complaining," I say, trying to keep my tone neutral and even.

He waggles his brows as he offers me the crook of his arm. "Come on."

I hesitate, feeling everyone's eyes on me, but Gabe's smile is so goofy and inviting I can't help following his lead. I slide my arm into his.

"Where are we going?"

He flashes a crooked grin. "I think you could use some art lessons."

I let out a breath, half laugh, half surrender. "Lead the way."

CHAPTER 16

I'm all nerves as the maroon-and-silver sign proclaiming *Mystic Hollow High* comes into view in front of the brick building at the end of a tree-lined street.

"No way—is this your school?"

"In all its glory," he jokes. The worn large brick building is idyllic, with green ivy creeping up the sides and tall windows glinting in the sunlight. Sitting beside Gabe, I can't help imagining what it might feel like driving to school with him. The fuzzies I'd feel walking with him as we passed weathered brick walls and entered through the large double doors. I imagine school bells echoing down long hallways and lockers shutting with satisfying clangs as we rush to class. Gabe walking me to first period.

"Don't worry, we're not going inside," Gabe says, interrupting my daydream.

I'm slightly disappointed. It might've been nice to see somewhere Gabe has obviously spent a lot of time. Kind of like looking through old photos to learn more about someone.

He drives around the front of the building, and soon we're approaching the school's athletic fields.

As he approaches the football stadium, I tilt my head. "I don't think you're familiar with how 'art lessons' work," I say as he parks near the field. "There's usually a classroom, and easels?"

"Keep an open mind," he says as he hops out his door, comes around, and opens mine.

As my sneakers kick up dust from the track surrounding the football field, I imagine how exciting it must be here on a game night. The bleachers full of rowdy students and the field illuminated by Friday-night lights. I get another pesky vision, this time of Gabe and me hanging out during a game. I laugh nervously because of course this fantasy hits me as we walk behind the bleachers. I start to wonder if Gabe ever spent any time under the bleachers with someone special.

I feel Gabe's eyes on me and I wonder if he's thinking the same thing.

He clears his throat. "Do you like your clothes?"

My body flushes. What is he thinking? I glance at my shorts and a tank top from a NASA center. "Did I miss some kind of dress code instructions?"

He smirks. "Dress code? Really? I'm asking because if your clothes get ruined during your art lessons, would you be upset?"

I study him, not sure I like where this is going. "These clothes aren't special, but if we're painting I prefer an apron." Gabe only laughs in response.

As we turn the corner, I see a few people sitting on the bleachers. Immediately I spot the twins, Billie and Jaisha, from Kyle's lake house, along with a couple others I vaguely recognize from the party.

"They're here," Billie exclaims as soon as she spots us.

"Gabe, why didn't you respond to my text?" Jaisha demands. Both are dressed in identical maroon basketball shorts and gray tank tops. "I'm glad I told Kyle to bring extra balloons."

"We were going to need extras anyway with how bad your aim is," Billie retorts. The folks behind them laugh.

Everyone is wearing some kind of athletic apparel. My Spidey sense tingles. Whatever is going on, it involves balloons, "art," and a football field.

Meanwhile, Gabe takes his backpack off and pulls some camera equipment out. Jaisha shakes her head. "There Gabe goes. Setting up his camera equipment everywhere and anywhere but can't take photos for the school paper anymore."

Gabe doesn't miss a beat. "What can I say, I use my photography for art, not gossip." He winks at me and my stomach flutters.

"Ignore her," Billie says, giving her sister a dirty look. "She's annoyed Kyle was selected to be editor next year."

Jaisha huffs. "Seriously, he covers the state championships, and I handle all the school funding controversy, and Kyle gets editor in chief? At least with Gabe, our paper had some serious news coverage."

Serious news coverage? I turn to Gabe for an explanation, but he seems more interested in his equipment. I make a mental note to ask him about it later when we're alone.

"Where is Kyle, anyway?" Billie asks, looking around. "He said he was just going to his car. Should've been back by now."

I jump back as something small and fast flies through the air. It lands with a *thump* on Gabe's chest.

Gabe curses as a bright green splotch appears on his white T-shirt. My hand flies to my mouth as my horror turns to laughter. He looks like he was just slimed.

"See, it's just paint," a whiny voice says. Kyle holds a bright green bag as he approaches alongside a displeased Shaw and Nessa. This explains why Kyle was running late. He was getting a dressing-down from my security detail.

I swipe a finger through the green goop on Gabriel's shirt. It feels like a cross between paint and slime.

"It's milk paint," Kyle says with pride. "And the water balloons are made of seaweed. Everything is eco-friendly." He holds up the little green golf ball–sized spheres that wiggle like water balloons.

"It checks out," Nessa barks before striding off the field. Shaw gives Kyle one last warning look and then joins Nessa on the sidelines.

I tap Gabriel's shoulder and point at the bright green splat across his chest. "So this is your idea of 'art'? It looks like a smoothie exploded on you."

"Art is in the eye of the beholder," he says smugly.

Kyle bellows so hard his curly hair wobbles like red Jell-O. "It did feel pretty good pelting Gab-a-saurus."

Gabe's face turns several shades of red.

"Gab-a-saurus?" I echo.

"I went through a dinosaur period when I was young," he mutters. He glares at Kyle. "That was a cheap shot, bro."

Kyle shrugs. "I needed to demonstrate that the balloons aren't a danger."

Gabe huffs. "Funny. I'm about to show you how dangerous they can be." Several folks ooh and aah at the challenge.

"Ohh, are you going to get Jurassic on me?" Kyle says, mimicking a T. rex's small arms.

"You're going back to the Stone Age," I say, and cover my mouth. Gabe and the rest of the folks cackle. "Nice one," Gabe says, offering me a high five. "Should've added 'throw some shade' to that bucket list of yours," he whispers conspiratorily to me.

"Okay, okay, I know when to concede," Kyle announces. He rubs his hands as he addresses the group. "I'm sorry to report that our game of Assassin—an innocent party game where we secretly target one another—is over. So our grand prize—the best table in senior quad—is still up for grabs. That's right, a prime table for you and your buddies to claim bragging rights and bask in legendary lunchtime status."

Prime seats and bragging rights—is that something Gabe's into?

"I couldn't care less about the table," Gabe says to me like he's reading my mind. "Kyle's dumb game does check off two things on your list: art lessons and a team sport. If I do win, I'll let anyone sit at that dumb table."

"Even me," I say playfully.

He makes a face. "Abby, you wouldn't have to ask."

"Listen up," Kyle shouts. "The game is Last One Standing." He holds up two sacks full of golf ball–sized water balloons. One bag filled with the green balloons like the one that splattered Gabriel and the other bag with blue balloons. "And these are our weapons."

He counts everyone. "Perfect, there are twelve of us, so we'll have three rounds. Starting with two teams of six and eventually down to the final round and the last three players standing. The goal: eliminate opposing players by landing a paintball hit *directly* on their torso. Only frontal hits count—no back, arms, or legs. If you're tagged square in the chest or stomach, you're out. And hits to the head are forbidden. The team that eliminates all the players of the opposite team first wins, and those players advance to the next round."

My cheeks flush as Kyle announces that I'm his first pick. I try to play it cool, but inside, I'm a little stunned—and weirdly flattered. Not missing a beat, Gabriel insists that he join the team with me. Billie and Jaisha are next since the other players didn't want to have to deal with being able to tell them apart. Our sixth player is a guy built like a bulldog, stocky and intense. Gabe leans over and whispers, "He was the best slugger on his baseball team." And I believe him. He looks like someone who could knock a water balloon into the next ZIP code. I'm relieved he won't be pelting any water balloons at me.

Kyle and the Bulldog get a couple buckets by the bleachers and set them on opposite sides of the football field. "We're the Blue Team," Kyle shouts. "If you're hit with a green splat on your chest it means you're out."

Gabriel grumbles as he looks at his T-shirt, which already has a green splat on it from when Kyle hit him earlier. I look away quickly when I see him begin to remove his shirt. How am I going to be able to concentrate with that body running around?

Kyle rolls his eyes. "Here comes Gabe the Babe," he teases. He claps and yells for everyone to line up at the fifty-yard line. I turn to follow Kyle but hear Gabe calling my name. He walks beside me. His copper eyes look concerned. "This is honestly a lot more intense than I thought it would be," he says. "Billie said 'water balloon fight with paint.' I didn't think it would be the Hunger Games. Seriously, if you want to bail, we can. No judgment."

I sigh. "Regular Abigail would probably prefer to watch than play, but Operation Bucket List Abby says, I volunteer as tribute."

Gabe snorts at my impersonation. "Then may the odds favor us, or however it goes . . ."

As our two teams line up at the fifty-yard line to face off against one another, the air is charged with tension and my heart pounds in my chest. This might be even more nerve-racking than debate competitions—at least those I've prepped for. A water balloon fight? I don't have the faintest idea.

The player across from me is a girl who looks like she's captain of the rugby team. One hip-check from her and I'll be sent back to the Reagan Administration.

She gives me a curt "hey." I try not to melt into a puddle. I play tennis, do yoga; I don't do these physical group things. I manage to squeak a "hello" back and then force myself to stop my usual small-talk pleasantries. The game is Last One Standing, not Miss Congeniality.

Another large presence settles besides me. Gabe leans close. "As soon as the game starts we'll need to grab as many balloons as possible while avoiding getting hit in the chest." I follow his gaze toward the bucket of balloons at the twenty-yard line as an idea forms in my head.

Kyle yells, "Game on!"

A rush of adrenaline surges through me as I grab Gabe's hand. "Here's the plan. We stick together. I'll stand in front of your chest as you throw and you'll block my chest as I throw."

Gabe laughs. "Abby, our backs are going to get pelted!"

"I know, but at least we won't be eliminated."

We reach the bucket and load up on water balloons.

"Three o'clock!" I yell at Gabe as Rugby Girl comes barreling toward us with water balloons in hand.

In a move that Shaw would appreciate, Gabe throws himself in front of me in time to block a balloon. It pelts him hard on his arm. Another one goes whizzing by both our bodies.

As Gabe blocks my body I peek out and launch a water balloon. It's a direct hit on Rugby Girl's chest. She looks at the green splat in shock.

I launch another water balloon at a boy and pelt him ten yards away.

Gabriel looks at me. "Wait, the girl who trips over her own shoes is an amazing shot."

I eliminate another player. "Right? I've gone to so many county fairs on the campaign trail and played those hit-the-target games, I guess I am a pretty good shot."

Gabe laughs. He looks behind to make sure we're all clear and then bends so his lips are inches from mine.

My body quivers as he lifts his fingers to my face, gently streaking green under each eye. I'm positive my face is full-on campaign-poster red from his touch. "That's your war paint, FDOTUS," he says with satisfaction. "Here's the strategy. I'm your human shield. You take the shots."

Our eyes lock, and for a heartbeat, the rest of the world blurs. It's just us.

"What happens if we have to eliminate each other?" I ask.

He grins, warm and unshakable. "Then I hope you let me sit at your table."

CHAPTER 17

"Victory tastes sweeter than my orange mocha," I say, resting my head on Gabe's car's seat. It's late afternoon and I love the hue of the sun and how it tints the high school's athletic fields, the weathered bricks of the campus, and especially Gabe's hair and skin with a golden outline.

Watching him, I feel warm, happy, and safe. "Thank you for helping me with my bucket list. I had an amazing time with—" I catch myself. I was about to say *you*. My cheeks warm. "I had an amazing time hanging out with everyone."

His lip twitches. "Same. Can we confidently check off 'art lessons' and 'team sports' from your list?"

I open my app and ceremoniously put a check next to the two items and turn to him. "Good job, partner. We're making some serious progress on my list."

He makes a show of rubbing his back. "I think I'm going to need sandpaper to get all this paint off." I beam. Thanks to our strategy, I was shielded for most of the game, whereas Gabe took the hits for us.

"At least my portfolio's shaping up," Gabe says, tapping the camera gear beside him on the trunk bench. "You, in war paint, pelting people like a war goddess? That's money. They should give me a college scholarship off that footage alone."

Apparently, he had set up a camcorder to record part of the game.

I laugh, the image flashing in my mind—me nailing Kyle square in the chest and the surprised and angry look on his face. Nothing has ever felt so satisfying.

I cover my face with my hands. "Oh my goodness. If the press got ahold of that video."

"This is officially top secret." As Gabe pretends to hold his camera possessively like he's carrying the nuclear codes, I suddenly remember my talk with the twins about his time at the newspaper. "Speaking of material . . . what happened with you and your school newspaper?"

The smile on his face wanes. "I was on staff freshman year. I was interested in photojournalism. I broke a big story about a bully."

"A bully? Sounds important and helpful. I think journalists are brave, especially when they catch the bad guys."

"I got some important people in trouble." He runs a hand through his hair. "Everyone was happy—no, *happy* is not the right word. Everyone was impressed and said I could have a future as a photojournalist. But I didn't like the limelight. I didn't like the idea of investigating other people's dirt." He stops and looks out the window. "And then shortly after, my dad got in that accident. And I just stopped."

“I’m sorry,” I say. I feel bad having triggered unhappy memories for him. I take a deep breath. “Thanks for sharing that with me.”

“I realized I prefer being behind the camera as an artist, not a journalist.” He exhales. “I don’t know if that makes any sense. It’s just, my heart wasn’t into the news. I wanted to tell my own stories through art.”

“I’d rather be behind the camera too.”

His eyes hold my gaze and his lip quirks. “Hold that pose.” He reaches for his phone and takes a picture of me. He shows me his screen and it’s me still with war paint under my eyes and my cheeks flushed from running on the field, the afternoon sky a golden hue. “I’m going to use that as my contact photo for you,” he tells me. “Abigail Cary-Alzona and her authentic self—thoughtful, strong, and beaut—” He stops mid-sentence. “And in beast mode.”

I exhale. Was he going to say *beautiful*? Am I glad he stopped himself or disappointed? Either way the tension has turned to full-blown awk. I fake cough. “How about some selfies?”

He looks relieved to change topics and slides next to me, holding up his camera. We laugh and take a few, including one where we make duck lips at the camera.

“Now *those* are the money shots,” he says. We grow silent, as we must both realize at the same time how close we are. His arm is wrapped around me and I’m leaning against that strong chest of his. Not even an inch closer and we’d be in prime make-out territory. My heart races as I stare at his mouth, not far from my own. Am I about to check off another bucket list item?

Gabe clears his throat. The sound snaps me back to reality and I scoot away. "I have a few errands. Festival stuff," I mumble.

"Me too," he says, turning on his ignition. "How is festival stuff going?"

Meanwhile, my heart pounds. Were we about to kiss? And maybe more confusing, did we both want to? "I'm making progress. Found a potential sponsor. You know me, I'm checking off my list."

"Right, great."

"Progress. Progress. Progress," I say too loud and too quickly.

He turns onto the main road. I try not to stare at the unreadable emotions on his face. Is he upset? Is he glad we didn't kiss?

He glances nervously in my direction. "I know you've got a million things going on, but I've got another idea for Operation Bucket List. Tonight. If you're in."

His gaze holds mine and my heart thumps as I nod before I can talk myself out of it.

But even as I smile, the question hums beneath the surface. What *are* we, exactly? Acquaintances? Friends? Something more? How could it be more when the clock is ticking down—when I know I'm leaving at the end of the month?

Whatever this is . . . it's fleeting.

And maybe that's what makes it so impossible to ignore.

CHAPTER 18

My bed is buried under a rainbow of shopping bags. Elle's still riding the high of her shopping locally downtown with Tita Karra. If there's one thing the Alzona girls like, it's a good deal. Meanwhile, my Depop habit is becoming a full-blown personality trait.

"These are *super* cozy." Elle smirks as she hands me a lacy number that screams anything but "comfort."

"Why do you keep suggesting that I wear dresses? He said dress cozy. I think this outfit is fine," I say, gesturing at my nineties-retro pink tie-dyed cotton shorts and matching crop sweatshirt.

Elle wrinkles her nose. "He already saw you in athleisure wear today. Do you want him to call you *beautiful* tonight or stick to *beast*?" My palms suddenly feel clammy. Why did I tell her about our conversation? Now my sister is convinced tonight's bucket list activity is a date.

Elle gestures at her own outfit, which is like mine except she has on a matching turquoise set with a cute teddy bear eating a taco on hers. "Pajamas," she insists.

"Fine." I grab the dress and slip it on. This lacy spaghetti-strap number is at least stretchy, but it would never be labeled cozy. As I leave the room, Elle chases after me holding a blinged-up sandal, but I draw a line in the sand as I slip my feet into my white sneakers and walk out of our suite's door.

As I head to the living room where Gabriel asked to meet, my insides tingle with anticipation, wondering what his plan is.

Although there are no other guests at the inn, the house feels warm and inviting. A place where a lot of happy memories have happened. The photographs that line the walls with smiling faces help paint that image. As I head down the stairs, I stop again to admire the photograph of the couple on the tree swing. The one Gabriel's father took of his grandparents.

My thoughts go to my collection of family photos in the White House. There's something so safe and comforting knowing about the people who came before you. It's like a mini pep talk from my ancestors.

I lean in so close my breath fogs the glass as I study the photograph. The way the moonlight illuminates the sky, stars scattered like confetti, the way the shadows emphasize the private moment of the couple . . . it's stunning. No wonder Gabriel wants to learn how to capture something like this.

When I get downstairs, the living room is empty—no Gabriel in sight. I settle on one of the couches. Everything in this room feels like a perfectly curated Instagram post.

Several minutes pass and I'm wondering if I'm early or late. I'm even second-guessing if Gabriel asked to meet at all. Or what if he is having second thoughts? After a couple days with me, he's dealt with multiple Secret Service run-ins, a water balloon attack, and having to keep me from being recognized by the public—I'm sure it hasn't been fun. I glance by the living room's entrance where Shaw is standing and wonder if he feels bad for me.

Footsteps creak down the staircase, and I hear my sister chirping along with another person—Ruby. They pause as soon as they see me, both of them looking nice and comfy in their pajamas complete with fuzzy slippers.

"Hey, Abby, joining us for game night?" Ruby asks, her gaze sliding down my outfit. Heat creeps up my neck. *Game night?* Was that Gabriel's plan for this evening? He said to wear something cozy.

Footsteps thud down the stairs, and Gabe appears. He's in a T-shirt and track pants and looks flushed. "Sorry, we had a leaky faucet and—" He stops mid-sentence when he sees me. "Wow."

I fidget under the sudden spotlight, tugging at the hem of my dress. Across the room, Elle beams like the world's most unrepentant matchmaker.

Gabe runs a hand through his hair, clearly scrambling. "You, uh . . . you look really nice, Abby."

I want to run upstairs and not come back down. Tita appears from another doorway wearing a white robe and blue jammies. She cackles when she sees me. "Ah yes, your mother had her diva moments too when she was your age, Abby. She'll deny it, but I've got photos." Normally I'd find that amusing, but right now I feel like the butt of a joke.

"I'm sorry. I misunderstood this evening's dress protocol. I'll go change."

"Nonsense," Tita Karra says. She hands me the fluffy robe she was wearing, which I graciously accept.

Ruby smiles. "Abby, dear, you do you. In this house, we want you to be yourself." She lifts a knowing brow and heads toward the family room. Elle skips after her, linking arms with Tita.

Now it's just me and Gabe. "I figured game night would satisfy your 'stay up all night' bucket list item," he explains. "But I could change, if you had other ideas."

The way his voice lowered when he said "other ideas" gives me goose bumps. I laugh nervously. "Game night sounds perfect."

He stretches an inviting hand. "After you."

In the family room, I immediately spot the iconic Monopoly box on the coffee table. A rush of excitement courses through me. "This night is mine," I declare.

Gabriel laughs. "No way. You're way too nice. You're going to be eaten alive."

I fix a glare on him. "You have no idea who you're dealing with."

"I look forward to it." He nods toward the kitchen. "First, I have another quick bucket list item for you. Follow me."

On the kitchen counter is a jar of marinara, a big bag of shredded mozzarella, and a lump of pizza dough. "Here's your cooking class item—we're gonna pop a homemade pizza in the oven." He puts air quotes around *homemade*. I double over laughing.

"What," he asks.

"You, me, and pizza. Not a good idea," I say.

He leans close. "Well, maybe we should have made one together the first time around," he says. My cheeks burn as he gathers more ingredients from the fridge.

I hip-check him when he says he found the pineapple.

Gabe turns out to be an excellent teacher—doubling every portion I add like I'm rationing toppings in a crisis. In ten minutes flat, our masterpiece is in the oven. By the time we return to the family room, Ruby, Tita, and Elle have set up the game and claimed the comfiest spots.

I beat Gabe at paper rock scissors for the race car game piece. Apparently, it's both of our go-tos. Elle gets the Scottish terrier. Ruby's go-to is the same as Mom's—the top hat. Gabriel winds up with the thimble.

The game is intense. Tita knocks out Ruby and Elle fast. When I knock out Tita, it leaves me and Gabriel. He's leading in property owned, while I lead with the cash pile.

"I'm taking pity on you, since race cars are so much cooler than thimbles," I mutter as he collects rent from me after I land on his B&O Railroad.

"Joke's on you, bunch of Monopoly grand champions use the humble thimble," he says.

The phone rings, making me jump. Maybe I've gotten used to no service; hearing a landline is always a surprise here.

Tita Karra hops up, stretching her arms. "I'll get it. Going to the kitchen to grab us some snacks anyway."

"Doritos? I'm starving," Elle asks.

I sigh, since she ate most of the pizza Gabe and I made.

Ruby's shoulders slump, and I notice her eyes look glassy. "I might need some tea," she adds. I study Gabe's mom, who looks burned out. Running a business takes a lot of time and energy. My mom had the same vibe before she became a senator. Gabe takes a photo of his mom as she stretches, which makes her laugh. "Do not print that," she warns.

"Are you kidding? I'm going to frame it and put it next to the check-in desk," he jokes. She tosses a throw pillow at him.

I laugh. "I love the photos in this house, especially the one of Gabe's grandparents on the swing." Ruby nods, a nostalgic look on her face. "Gabe's father was an amazing photographer." I pause. Would now be a good time to highlight her son's own skill? I sneak a glance at Gabe and see the same sad look. Maybe not the best time, so I change topics. "What's the oldest photo on the walls?"

Ruby taps her chin. "Good question. The oldest ones of the inn are probably fifty years old. That's when my grandparents bought the house."

My face scrunches as I think about Ruby's comment. An idea sparks. "Are you saying your family has owned this house for fifty years?"

"Yes, they officially bought the house fifty years come July. It took them a few years to open the inn," Ruby explains with pride.

I turn to Elle, who immediately understands what I'm thinking. She offers me a fist bump. I return it and we make "boom" sounds. "Fiftieth-Anniversary Jubilee," Elle says.

I grin. "It's always nice to tie in a milestone to make an event special. For your jubilee we can celebrate the fifty years your family has owned the property." My mind racing with how to celebrate and promote this milestone.

Ruby claps her hands. "That's a great idea. It's our thirty-ninth year of hosting the jubilee, but fiftieth year of owning the house has a better ring to it."

Gabe raises his Sprite can. "Seriously, you're next-level brilliant."

"Well, maybe hold that thought." Tita Karra stands at the doorway, looking like she just landed on "Chance" on the Monopoly board.

"Your mother is on the phone, Abby," Tita Karra says. I freeze. Lately, we've been trading texts, especially when it's after 23:00.

The room falls silent. I flash my best reassuring smile. "I'm sure Mom isn't calling with some earth-shattering announcement for America. She's just checking in on me as mothers do." Even I don't buy the fake confidence in my voice.

★ ★ ★

I grab the receiver from Tita Karra's hand and make my way toward the library. Even though I can't see her, I can feel my mom's presence on the other side of the phone. "Hi, honey."

"Hey, Mom. Anything important happen today?"

I can feel her smiling on the other side. It's an inside joke now that she's the "most powerful person in the world."

"Oh, you know, the usual. Some kids in Congress were acting up again. I had a stern talk with a couple bullies from the business community. And I received a nice briefing about art education initiatives from our country's most talented artists."

"Cool. I got my first brain freeze today."

"That's nice. Sounds like you're collecting firsts during your visit." I hold my breath as she continues. "Including reaching out to my campaign staff about a festival?"

I cringe. "What did Tita tell you?"

"I want to hear from you."

My insides feel like jelly. Maybe I shouldn't have used Mom's contacts for assistance, but at the end of the day I'm just asking for advice. And it's all volunteer work. That's the point I should emphasize. And then I will spin this, so everything ends on a positive note.

Mom speaks up. "Before you begin, don't bother trying to spin this in a way that ends on a positive note."

My nose scrunches. I can't get away with anything with her.

"I can already see the face you're making. Believe me, I know how you think. You're my daughter, after all." I've heard that line so many times, it's one of my go-to Mom impersonations.

"Fine. If you know what I'm thinking then you know that I'm doing nothing wrong. In fact, I'm helping a small business. Something that you champion."

"I do champion small businesses," she says. "But when I hear from colleagues that you're helping a business that might be competing with one of the Darbys' hotels, I expect to hear this kind of news from you, and not a campaign worker."

My stomach flips. "Mom, it's not like the Calabreses' inn poses any threat to the Darby family. I'm pretty sure they spend more on toilet paper than what the inn makes in a year."

I imagine her pinching the bridge of her nose. "It's not that, honey, it's the optics."

"Which is what? FDOTUS is volunteering at a Fourth of July festival, which has nothing to do with the Darbys' hotel."

She sighs. "And don't think for a moment I don't know that you are using this activity to be able to leave the inn."

I cringe. Freedom to work through my bucket list is part of the arrangement Gabe and I made, but I don't tell her that. "Mom, I'm not trying to game being grounded. I really do think volunteering in a small community is a good thing. It's one of the ideas you used to campaign on."

I picture her massaging her forehead as she considers her words. "I think what you're doing to help Tita Karra's friends in the end is worthwhile."

She agrees with me. I'll take the win. "But this doesn't mean you have free rein," she adds. "Remember, you are to stay out of the media. No drawing attention. And you will return on July first to resume your duties as First Daughter. Which I think you know means you won't be able to participate in the jubilee on the Fourth."

"I get it, Mom. Manage my expectations and all that." I knew I wouldn't be able to go, but some small part of me had hoped. Her saying it out loud feels like a gut punch.

Her exhale is slow and heavy. I know she has a lot going on, on top of parenting. The last thing I want to do is make things worse for her.

"Oliver will be back at the White House's Independence Day Gala." I hear levity in my mom's voice, and I wonder if she's already assuming we're together.

"Great," I say. I wonder how he's doing—not that it's hard to guess. He's so predictable. I could probably script his day. It's been tough not being able to call or text with no reception out here. But if I'm being honest, I wasn't exactly checking for bars at the lake party. Or in town. Or really, any time I did have reception.

"You'll be seeing him soon enough," my mom reassures me. "In the meanwhile, I'll be interested to hear what you come up with for this jubilee event."

I feel myself brighten. "You'll be proud to hear I've learned some tips from Erin. We just realized that the inn has been owned by Gabriel's family for fifty years."

"That's something to work with," Mom says.

"I know. I just need to think about how to recognize fifty years."

She pauses on the other side of the phone. "How about something to do with fifty states? With the Fourth of July as a theme, what better way to celebrate the country?"

"Mom, that's brilliant."

She laughs. "Now if only me and my staff can figure out our Independence Day messaging. I want to highlight something important about our economic priorities." She pauses and I can tell she's slipping into her thoughts.

"Mom, you're doing an excellent job," I say.

She pauses. "As a mother?"

I laugh. "Yes, as mom in chief *and* president."

She chuckles, and I wish I could hug her through the phone. I wish we had more moments like this. Most conversations lately have been quick texts, nothing more.

She praises me and my sister before signing off. "Wish I didn't have to go, honey. I can't wait to see you at the Independence Day Gala."

We hang up and for the first time, I feel truly torn—between my life in DC with Oliver and this unexpected new world in Mystic Hollow, and a certain boy who's leading the charge for Operation Bucket List and maybe even my heart.

CHAPTER 19

"Fifty flowers? Every state has a flower," Elle says, practically jumping out of her chair. I jot her idea down in my designated festival-planning journal. My colored pens and markers are scattered across the inn's coffee table for our emergency post-breakfast brainstorming session.

Gabe paces back and forth; apparently he likes to think on his feet.

Elle keeps going. "Birds? Doesn't every state have a bird?"

"I'm not sure how we would get fifty birds sent here." I chew on a pen cap. "Maybe we could ask our friends from the National Audubon Society to help us locate the birds," I say.

Gabe laughs to himself. "I just had this image of the sky darkening from a flock of deadly birds."

"I bet hosting fireworks is expensive and needs all kinds of insurance and legal agreements," I say, channeling one of Mom's lawyers. "Still, if we expanded the jubilee to nighttime fireworks, that would be a huge draw. I bet you'd get more guests checking into the hotel."

Gabe sighs. "Yes, but it's tradition—the owner of Grand

Meadows always hosts the fireworks. We handle the barbecue and festival during the day."

Elle scoffs. "Pretty sure that new resort doesn't care about tradition, since they're also trying to host the daytime Fourth of July crowd."

"She's got a point," I say.

Elle triumphantly grabs a toaster pastry off the table. "These freshly made Pop-Tarts are the best."

"They're from our local bakery, Pie Hard," Gabe says.

I gasp. "That's brilliant."

He shrugs. "I guess? The owner really loves cheesy action movies."

I laugh. "Not the *Die Hard* movie reference. Pie! Elle and I have traveled to pretty much all fifty states, and each has a signature pie."

"Our dad loves pie," Elle adds. "He loves to eat them. Bake them. He'd probably take a bath in them if possible."

I clap my hands. "My point is, we could have a baking competition where entrants submit pies from each state. And we'd have a panel of celebrity chefs to judge the entries."

Elle's eyes grow wide. "We can ask the bakers to submit two pies, one for the contest and one for a cakewalk."

Gabe grins. "Sweet. Nothing gets people more motivated than a competition. But why get celebrity chefs when we have you two?"

I bite my lip, and he answers for me. "Because you won't be here for the jubilee."

My sister murmurs "bummer" under her breath. I shake my

head, not ready to dampen the mood. "We'll find someone great." I rub my hands together like an old-school villain. "I may know a few people who know people."

"A local judge would be good too," Elle says. "Give us some street cred."

"Kids? Are you here?" Gabriel's mom enters the family room looking very dressed-to-impress. "There you are. I've got some encouraging news, but I'm going to need your help." I look at her expectantly. "Marge has invited us to the business council's annual barbecue."

Gabriel sits up. "Does that mean they've decided to be a key sponsor of the jubilee?"

"I hope so," Ruby replies. "Only problem is that I have a meeting with the bank. So, I'm going to need you to go in advance to represent the inn. I will arrive when my meeting is done."

I raise my hand. "Can Elle and I join the advance team?"

Gabriel's mom laughs. "I was already counting on you girls helping Gabriel. I can tell you make a great team."

As soon as Ruby is out of the room, Elle strikes a mock cheerleader pose. "Go, Team AbbyGabby."

I shoot her a look, hoping it conceals my red cheeks. Back to business. "Maybe we offer Marge a spot as a local judge for the pie contest? Could sweeten the deal?"

Gabe, cheeks flushing in rare sync with mine, nods. "Abby, I think you'll be the one to sweeten the deal."

It's the perfect day for a barbecue. Blue sky, warm breeze, and for once in my life, nothing on my agenda. I find myself skipping my khaki shorts in favor of a cute cornflower-blue maxi dress—it's my prairie princess look. I complete my outfit with white sunglasses and sandals.

Gabriel is waiting on the porch. He's in his classic 501s but has switched his white T-shirt with a brick-red V-neck. The color looks great on him. He stands as soon as he sees us, a smile on his face that is downright swoonworthy.

"You look great," he says.

"And that color looks good on you," I say, forcing myself to focus on his eyes.

"What about me?" Elle twirls in her yellow jumpsuit like a model on a runway. "I call this outfit *third-wheel core*," Elle whispers to me. I elbow her as she snickers.

We hop into Gabe's truck. Shaw and Nessa are already in their car behind us. The drive is pleasant, including a Taylor Swift lip sync contest, which Elle, of course, wins.

Shortly, Gabe pulls his truck into a parking spot near a shaded picnic area. I appreciate the sight of several tables covered in a red-checked tablecloth and the smell of sweet, tangy barbecue sauce in the air. "Does this check off 'picnic' on your list?" Gabe asks.

"Nope," Elle says before I can respond. "That item specifically stipulated a fun picnic with friends. This counts as work." I keep my mouth shut. She isn't wrong, but I don't like that she's shamelessly hinting to Gabe to take me out. I'll have to talk to her later about minding her own business. Gabe, meanwhile, looks untroubled by Elle's meddling.

A crowd of people surrounds tables loaded with barbecue staples—potato salad, coleslaw, chips, baked beans, and soft rolls. I've been to plenty of events like this, campaigning with my family and with Oliver's, but it's different with just Gabe and Elle by my side. The freedom and excitement is new.

The three of us walk toward the crowd, but I'm so self-conscious of Gabriel beside me it's hard to focus on anything else.

The barbecue's host finds us right away. Marge greets us wearing a GRILLS JUST WANNA HAVE FUN apron and a huge grin. "There they are. My guests of honor, Abigail and Eleanor Cary-Alzona." She barely waits for my response before grabbing my hand and shaking it wildly. "Abby, I hear you've been doing a great job helping out with the jubilee. The entire Mystic Hollow community really appreciates all your hard work and leadership."

My face reddens. It's nice to receive a compliment without my mother attached. "When I told Vince you were coming to my barbecue, we just about fainted." She looks around, I assume for her secret partner and the town's mayor, Vince Lee.

We follow her line of sight to where a man in a matching apron is talking to another in a business suit. Marge rolls her eyes. "Those pesky resort people are chasing us even here."

Gabriel's eyes narrow. "They're such a big corporation. Why do they need Marge and the business council to sponsor their event?"

I grimace. "Because the Darbys know the value of local support."

Marge nods. "Just so you know, the resort's offering deals to all the small businesses in town, and they're not only offering space but money too. Not surprising considering how they practically bribed Sunshine Farms off their land."

Gabriel mutters under his breath.

"Vince and I were tempted," Marge adds. "But both our businesses are going to stick with tradition, and the rest of the business council agrees!" she exclaims.

Elle does a happy dance. Gabe and I grin at one another.

"Especially now that you've brought some star power," she says, grinning at me and Elle.

I stiffen. "Marge, you should know that Elle and I won't actually be at the jubilee. We're expected home at the end of the month."

Marge nods. "That's too bad. We would love to have you here, but our commitment doesn't change. Gabe's family has been here for this town. And now that we know we're not offending the vice president's family, we're good." Marge looks behind us. "Where's your mother, Gabriel? We should set up a meeting to discuss the details soon."

"Kicking down doors and taking names," Gabe says. "But she'll be here soon."

As Elle gushes to Marge about the midway games and the need for a local judge for the pie competition, I catch Gabriel's eye. I can feel both relief and nerves vibrating off him. Getting the business council to sponsor the jubilee was a huge win, allowing us to pay for some of the attractions we wanted to have, but the revelation that the Darbys' resort is still actively chasing down local sponsors for their competing event is not welcome news.

Marge waves wildly at another family. "I had better get back to my guests. Please make yourselves at home." She shakes my hand one last time. "And don't worry, your Secret Service detail made it clear that you're to keep a low profile at this event. My friends and employees will respect your privacy. We're all such huge fans."

I exhale as soon as we're out of earshot. "Looks like we can report to your mom that we've achieved our primary objective, sponsorship from the council." Gabe's silence is palpable. "And gotten some unfortunate but not insurmountable intel," I add. "Oliver's uncle is the CEO of Darby International, but I'm sure I can ask Oliver to talk to him about not stealing your sponsors."

Gabe makes a sour face. "Please don't. I don't want you to get tangled in this situation."

"But I could try to reach Oliver and . . ." My voice trails off. A few feet away, a crowd of people gesture for us to join them. A pleasant-faced woman holds plates for us while others in the group smile and whisper with one another. Maybe they're talking about the food but the grins on their faces suggest otherwise. I sigh. We'll have to discuss the Oliver situation later when we're out of earshot. Plus, my stomach's clearly shouting it's time to eat.

We head toward the food, which is divided into stations. Gabriel and I are at the hamburger table. I grab a bun and pepper jack cheese to put on my burger. I tease Gabriel about his blue cheese choice. He thinks my mayo selection is disgusting. And I give him a lecture about mustard. The next station is sides. Potato chips and French onion dip for him, Tostitos and guacamole for me.

As we near the dessert station, Gabriel leans in. "This isn't on your bucket list, but it should be," he says. He gestures at small round pancakes. "Virginia ham biscuits."

My eyes widen. "You had me at *biscuit.*"

We balance our plates as we navigate through the crowd, but

I barely make it two steps before I'm stopped—again. And again. After the fifth photo and third handshake, Gabe grabs my plate to help. "Mayo and crushed chips on your dress is not a good look," he says. Finally, we escape to an empty bench under a tree, away from the crowd.

I sit on our bench, suddenly self-conscious about the two of us being alone. My sister is talking it up with some other kids near the lemonade. She's waving her arms around and I know she's telling another one of her wild stories. Nessa is nearby. I spot Shaw about twenty feet away from us, standing under a tree.

Gabe is wolfing down his burger. He appears completely oblivious about being alone with me. I guess I'm the only one having feels at the moment.

I take a bite of my burger and enjoy the smoky taste. But my appetite is low. "Great barbecue," I say.

Gabe puts his plate down and wipes his mouth with a napkin. "Yeah, Marge knows how to throw a party."

"Does she?"

"She leads the committee that hosts the town's annual Founder's Day Dance."

"Oh," I say brightly. "I remember seeing the flyer for that dance. It's soon, right?"

Gabriel nods. "Yep. Mystic Hollow may be small, but we sure like to throw a bunch of parties." He sighs. "Locals go all out: string lights everywhere, live bands, food trucks . . . that's why it's hard for us to be asking for help with our jubilee. Most businesses try to sponsor one major thing during the year. My family has the Fourth."

I fiddle with my napkin, somehow nervous to ask him my next question. "Are you going to the dance? I mean, are you volunteering?"

He arches a brow. "I don't know. I do recall something about dancing on your bucket list," he teases.

"Oh. Yeah, I totally forgot about that." I throw in a nervous laugh. Dancing under the stars *is* on my list.

A familiar voice calls Gabe's name. It's Ruby. She and Marge are motioning for us to come back to the barbecue tables. She wants Gabe to set up a group photo. The man I saw earlier with the barbecue apron shakes my hand and introduces himself as Mayor Lee—he's quieter and the opposite of Marge, which I kind of like for her. Bonus, Mayor Lee is friendly and casual. Most officials see meeting me as an opportunity to give my mom a message. His welcome is another bonus for Mystic Hollow. After Gabe sets up his camera with a timer, Marge moves him to stand next to me.

After pictures, Ruby pulls us aside, a grin stretched across her face. "Great job, you two. Marge has said she and Mayor Lee and the rest of the Main Street Makers Business Council are going to be key sponsors. We're going to meet on Monday to discuss." She claps a hand on her son's shoulder, positively radiating excitement. "We just heard that Grand Meadows won't be able to host the Independence Day fireworks show." My brows furrow, recalling the equestrian center hosts the region's evening fireworks show, while Gabe's inn hosts the daytime activities.

Gabe grimaces. "Do you mean their fireworks show is canceled?"

Ruby shakes her head, a smile on her face. "Grand Meadows

already paid for the pyrotechnicians; they just need a new location. I'm thinking the inn."

Gabe's brows lift. "If we host the fireworks, we'll draw a huge crowd."

Ruby winks. "That's right. That could solve a lot of problems for us. I'm talking with the business council and mayor about switching the fireworks to our location, and so far they sound on board." She wraps an arm around my shoulders. "You girls are my Fourth of July good luck charms."

I smile. "We're trying."

"And they're modest," she says, placing her hands over her heart.

I've been so distracted by our conversation with Gabriel's family, it's only now that I finally notice the crowd that has gathered around Elle and me.

No one is being rude or anything, but there are a lot of phones pointed in our direction. I notice Shaw creeping forward.

I plaster on one of my First Daughter smiles. Elle does the same. "We should go, Abby. Tita Karra is taking me to get my nails done." She grins. "You don't have to join us. I know you don't have the patience, especially when I get neon orange on my toes." She smirks, her eyes in Gabe's direction.

I roll my eyes at my sister just as Gabriel leans in with that dashing smile. "Want to get out of here?"

"Y-yes," I stammer. As I'm staring into those copper eyes of his, my hand finds his and I follow him out of the crowd. He drops my hand once I'm clear, but I can't help the tingle in my fingers, wishing they were still intertwined with his.

CHAPTER 20

Gabe is quiet as I go over the details of the jubilee in his passenger seat. His eyes focus on the road, but every now and then I catch him grinning at me and making my insides flutter like I'm watching Election Day returns.

I swipe through my text messages. "Fantastic. Our White House florist has said a display with all the state flowers is doable and will send their ideas for us to design them here. You may need to pay the cost of shipping for some of the flowers we can't find locally."

He hesitates. "You sure we're not taking advantage of your mom's position, right?"

I nudge my shoulder into his. "Concerned about ethics, are you?"

He lifts his brows. "Um, yes."

"Good. You'd fit right in with my mom's advisers."

"You mean she'd like me?"

I hesitate, maybe reading more into that question than I should. Does it matter to him if my mom likes him? Does it matter to me? I look away. "This isn't an official event. And so long as you're paying for everything, or items are being donated and people are volunteering their time, I don't see the harm in asking for suggestions."

If he noticed I dodged his question about my mom, he doesn't let on. "You're amazing. I don't know how my mom and I can ever come close to repaying you."

"No way. We had a deal, remember? I'm not helping you out of the goodness of my heart," I tease.

He feigns shock. "That's right. Operation Bucket List is still a thing."

"And you better make good on your end of the deal."

I'm rewarded with his perfect smile. "In fact, I'm taking us somewhere to conquer another item on your list."

"Conquer and annihilate. That's my approach to lists too," I joke.

"I feel bad for any list you write."

I glance out the window, watching the green fields stretch flat, then rise into gentle slopes. He makes an unexpected turn and we're winding up a mountain road. I'm silent as I take in the view between the trees. As we go higher, the roofs and trees below get smaller and smaller, like paint splattered across a canvas.

"I think this is a two-bucket-list-items day," I muse, my pesky brain wandering to "first kiss" on my list.

"Two items," Gabriel says, and whistles. "Okay. Will do my best."

"Speaking of your best, how's your portfolio work going?"

I'm not sure he heard my question as he pulls his truck into a dusty area that appears to be a parking lot and stops the truck.

I'm awestruck by the vista overlooking the valley below. This vantage point makes the mountain scenery near the hotel look tiny in comparison.

"We're not even at the spot I was going to take you. This is just the parking lot," Gabriel says. I'm speechless as I take in a view that makes me think of the lyrics "for purple mountain majesties."

"It's golden hour. A photographer's favorite natural light," Gabe says. He grabs his camera from its case. "Since you asked about my portfolio, I figured I can try to capture some more photos while we're up here," he says, answering the question I forgot I had asked.

"It's a stunning place to do—" I hear Gabriel's camera click. I smile at him as he lowers his camera. "Sorry, the light was . . . perfect." I blush. Something tells me he wasn't just talking about the light.

I hop out of the truck and give Shaw the briefest wave as his SUV pulls into the parking lot a few feet away from us. "Sorry, you know my babysitters," I say wryly. Though I'm not sure why I need to apologize. It's not like we need the privacy, right? We're not here on a date.

My sandals crunch on the rocky dirt as I wander. I close my eyes and feel the cool mountain air against my face and take in the clean scent of trees, dirt, and grass.

Gabriel gestures for me to follow him. We trek around some large rocks and to an area that leads up a small dirt path that disappears into a patch of trees.

Beyond the trees, I'm blown away by the scene. It's like *The*

Sound of Music, a grassy meadow on a hilltop. Gabriel was right; the parking lot wasn't the view. Stretches and stretches of blue-and-purple mountains spread before us in all directions. The afternoon sun casts a warm glow everywhere it hits. The sun tends to take its sweet time to set in the summer, but the world is starting to slow down too—unlike the racing of my heart.

He grins. "Almost there," he says.

"This isn't the spot?"

"No. But I love coming up to this meadow. Especially at night. This is where I want to capture my astrophotography shots for my portfolio."

I nod. "The Milky Way, right?"

He looks pleased that I remember. "It's going to be gorgeous at night. No light pollution here. Just me, alone—with the stars." He turns so I can just see his profile. "You're actually the only person I've ever taken up here."

Gabriel sharing this place with me feels so special. "I'm honored," I tell him. We pause as we stand in the grass, admiring the golden valley below. Finally, he motions for me to follow him to another group of trees and rocks.

"Think you can manage climbing up these rocks?" he asks.

I look at my strappy flat sandals. "Sure," I say, taking a wobbly step up.

Gabriel grabs my hand. "Careful."

I stare at my hand in his and can't quite work out how both exhilarating and familiar his touch is. I stare up at his face, and his eyes are warm and comforting. "I got you."

"Thanks," I blurt out, letting him lead me up a few more steps.

Soon we're at the top. After stepping past a few trees, I understand why he led me up here. The view is Ansel Adams–worthy.

"Here's a great place for portraits," he says, channeling his tour guide tone.

"Portraits? This place is poetry."

"This is Shenandoah Valley," Gabriel explains. "And the Blue Ridges in the back."

"No wonder you come here. Who wouldn't be inspired?"

Gabriel chuckles. I hear a few clicks as he takes photos. But his camera isn't pointed at the mountains; it's pointing at me. I throw my hands on my hips and give him my best serious model pose.

Gabriel clicks more photos and grins as I make a pouty face. "Work it," he teases.

"The First Daughter of the United States is only styled by the best." I point at my clothes. "Depop and a local DC boutique." I point at him. "What about you? Levi's 501s?"

"Oh, looking at my butt, are you?" My cheeks heat as he twists, pretending to look at his Levi's tag on the back of his jeans. He lowers his camera and laughs. "I'm joking. They're 517s."

"Trendy."

"Classic."

I tilt my head as he adjusts his lens. He isn't using his digital camera. He has a vintage-looking one. "Was that your dad's?"

"Yeah." I hear the tenderness in his voice. "He liked old cameras as much as he liked hunting for old photographs."

"The camera must be over fifty years old."

"They made them to last back then." He holds up the camera

and I walk so we're side by side. "This camera took pictures on the moon's surface," he muses.

I gasp. "What?"

"No, not this exact camera." He laughs. "But same brand." He turns the device slowly in his hands, letting the light catch its vintage frame. It's unlike the modern cameras I've seen on the campaign trail—no touchscreen, no obvious lens.

To take photos, he looks down into a small viewer instead of holding it up to his eye. And no flash? "How does it work?" I ask.

Gabriel smirks. "Want to try?" I nod and he hands me the camera like he's handing me a baby. "The trick with these is patience and trusting your gut," he says.

I peer into the viewer, holding the camera uncertainly. "Is this right?" My fingers stumble as I try to place them, and I feel him a step behind me, his arms hovering just above mine. Close, but not touching.

"Mind if I show you?" he asks gently.

His hands cover mine and guide my fingers to where to place them on the camera. He's closer now. The heat from his body radiating against my back and his musky, mint-and-smoky-wood scent make me tingle with anticipation.

I only need to back up an inch and I'd be in his arms. I'm doing my best to concentrate on his words but also losing myself in his presence.

"How about taking a shot of the mountains?" he asks, bringing me back to our lesson.

"Yes."

"The trick is capturing the light just right."

I'm tickled by the view. "It feels like I'm looking at a canvas rather than peeping behind a lens or holding my phone up."

Gabriel nods. "It does feel more artistic."

His hand guides mine again and I feel the camera's shutter button. "And press here when it feels just right for you," Gabriel says. My mind goes blank. We're talking about taking a photo, right?

I tilt the camera and watch as the shadows and sunlight play across the trees and spill over the mountain ridges. I gasp and take the shot. A thrill zips through me, and I can't help but squeal, joy bubbling over like adrenaline.

"Very good," Gabriel says. I feel his breath tickling my ear. "You'll remember this moment when you look at this photo." I turn around and meet his grinning face. I'll remember this moment, but not just because of my photo.

My heart races. We are toe to toe. Only one of us needs to lean an inch forward to close the gap. His eyes study mine with a glow in them I haven't seen before.

I lick my lips and his eyes drop to my mouth—heat floods through me, sharp and unfamiliar, making my blood burn with an intense, unfamiliar heat. "My bucket list," I whisper, the words catching.

His gaze snaps back to mine, startled. "Sorry?"

"My bucket list." My voice cracks. What am I doing? This is more confusing than the Electoral College. More dramatic than a presidential debate stage.

"You said we'd knock out two items," I whisper. His eyes dart all over my face like he's trying to read me.

I lean forward. My lips hover over his. "We can check off watch sunset and—"

Gabriel's hands wrap around my waist. I murmur with delight as I tiptoe up to kiss him.

I'm warm and safe as our lips touch. Happy and exhilarated. A firework exploding into a thousand sparks. He's right. I'll always remember this moment. The moment I kissed a boy for the very first time.

A loud buzz accompanied by a vibration makes me jump. Of all the places and times, I have phone reception.

Gabriel takes a step back. I know instantly the moment is gone. "I'm sorry," he says, his face pale.

"No, I'm so sorry," I say, annoyed my phone won't stop buzzing. As I fumble to silence it, my phone falls to the ground. Gabe and I bend down to pick it up at the same time. My eyes widen when I see the screen with Oliver's name with a text message: *Miss you* along with a wave, a dolphin, and multiple heart emojis.

I glance at Gabe, who must've seen Oliver's text, but so what? Oliver is not the boy I'm kissing. Gabe steps back, raking his fingers through his thick hair. Then he steps away and packs his camera back in the case like we didn't just have the most mind-blowing kiss ever.

"I think I got some good candidates for my portfolio," Gabe says, not making eye contact with me.

"That's great," I say, confused by his sudden aloofness. "And I think we can check off three bucket list items." I giggle nervously.

"Three," he asks. "I only count one."

I frown. "No. Three. We're watching the sun set, we've hiked somewhere 'nature-y,' and—" I stammer trying to not shout, *Hello?! We just had the most epic kiss.*

He looks up. The cold distance in his eyes throws me off. "I'd hardly call this a hike. And, well . . ." He pauses. "That third item we can just consider practice for the real one."

I stiffen. "What?"

He acts like he doesn't hear me. "It was practice. For the real one . . . with your boyfriend."

My blood goes cold. "My boyfriend?" I shake my head. "If you're talking about Oliver, he's not— We're not together." Gabe's expression has relaxed into his familiar max chill vibe.

He shrugs as if nothing even happened. "It's fine, Abby. We had a deal and I'm glad I'm able to help you with your list." He turns back to the path.

If that's the game he wants to play, then fine. "Still counts as two in my book," I say, pretending to check something off in the air. "The sunset alone earns a gold star," I say, catching up with him.

He shakes his head. "I can't in good conscience count this as a real hike."

Just like he can't count our kiss as a real kiss.

He gestures for me to follow him down the trail and offers his hand to help me balance down the path. Our eyes meet and his darken for a second.

I ignore his offer and step past him. Risking a fall feels safer than risking that kind of contact.

Silence settles between us, thick as the trees. I'm disappointed when Gabriel turns away, and he doesn't look at me again until we're back at the inn.

CHAPTER 21

Elle sits across from me as I lie on the couch, going over what will from here on be known as "the photo shoot" with her. She fidgets with her friendship bracelet as she listens to me discuss everything from how he held my hand up the hilltop and then the awkwardness back when we left.

"So, he's willing to do 'practice kisses' with you?" She makes finger quotes around *practice*. "What's the problem?"

"He called our kiss practice for the one I do with my boyfriend, and in his eyes, that's Oliver." I take a deep breath. "He's acting like our kiss didn't mean anything."

Elle is quiet. Unusually quiet. I squint at her. "What are you not telling me?"

She winces. "So . . . he asked if you and Oliver were a thing."

I sit up. "What did you say?"

She shrugs. "I said you two are besties and he checks off all the items on your perfect boyfriend list."

I throw my hands up. "Elle! I don't have a perfect boyfriend list."

"I've known you all my life and your tastes are super predictable." She crosses her arms. "And I never said he was your boyfriend—just that he checks off all the boxes." Guilt flashes across her face. "I should've clarified, Abby. I was hangry, and then Tita Karra barged in with her chicken adobo. The whole convo just went sideways from there."

I rub my forehead. "This whole time he's assumed me and Oliver were official."

Elle sits next to me. "I'm sorry, but nothing I said to him was a lie." She leans her head on my shoulder and bats her lashes. "You should talk to him. Tell him how you feel."

I sag against her. I did tell Gabriel that Oliver and I aren't official, but Oliver's text message during our hike didn't help. But even if Oliver and I aren't together, the idea that I could be with Gabriel feels impossible. And I bet he feels the same way. "How can I date Gabriel if we don't see each other every day? It's already hard enough for me to get out of the house."

Elle sighs. "Maybe love isn't always easy and convenient?"

My jaw drops. "Love?" Suddenly, me having a heart-to-heart about *love* with a girl who used to kiss frogs hoping they would turn into princes is too much even for me. "This convo's over."

I retreat to my room and crumple onto my bed. In two weeks, I'm heading back to DC. Gabriel is staying here in Virginia, three hours away. Two if Shaw is driving, but not all of us come with a Secret Service escort.

Oliver makes sense. We go to the same school, my parents like him, he's polite and smart, we laugh at the same jokes, he understands my life and the world I live in, and he's objectively cute. Plus, he's clearly into me. And when I'm back to DC, we'll be dancing under the stars at the White House Independence Day Gala.

Gabriel will be here in Mystic Hollow.

I hear a little knock on my door. Elle pokes her head in, looking convincingly apologetic. "Cookie?" she asks.

I nod at her peace offering and she flops down beside me. "Sorry for being a butthead. I really like Gabriel, but it's your love life, not mine."

I wrap an arm around her shoulders. "I like him too." I tap her knee. "But like he said—that kiss was just practice . . . It didn't mean anything."

She looks like she wants to argue, but I also see doubt in her eyes. Doubt that mirrors my own, but I won't let her suspect I feel the same. "We've still got time here, so let's not be all awkward about it."

Elle nods as I continue. "Let's make these next days count. We'll plan the best jubilee ever and make some memories this town will never forget." Of course, my kiss with Gabe is something I could never forget if I tried.

I rock in my boots. I've had them for almost a week, the length of time the sporting goods store said my hiking boots would take to begin to break in.

It's also been a week since that kiss with Gabriel. The kiss that meant nothing.

I've spent a lot of time on the jubilee the past few days—working with the florists and organizing the pie competition. We have more than fifty entries, and each state has at least one baker. From Maryland's Baltimore bomb pie to Indiana's Hoosier sugar cream pie to Alaskan salmon pie, we have our bases covered and mouths watering.

Elle thinks I've been avoiding spending time with Gabriel.

It's not *not* true. But he's also been busy. We have that in common. Diving headfirst into our tasks for the jubilee.

With Elle off somewhere, I'm left in the suite alone. In the White House I'm surrounded by staff. Here at Mystic Hollow Inn, I'm by my lonesome. No one to give me a hard time that I'm still in my pajamas or tell me what I should be doing.

It's the perfect time to take my boots for a test walk. The stairs are a little hard to navigate. I teeter down and almost slip. My hand reaches for the rail, and I catch myself with a little yelp.

My gaze comes directly into line of sight of the photo of the couple in the tree swing. My heart warms seeing Gabriel's grandparents. They look so at home with one another.

My head is swarming with thoughts about Gabriel's secret career plans, and the true love between Gabriel's grandparents, intermixed with images of my own parents. How lucky these women were to find the perfect match. I bet Gabe's grandma didn't make a list of qualities for her future husband.

As I reach the first floor, the sound of classical music comes from the direction of the kitchen. It's the waltz. A dance that is now synonymous with my life in DC.

I rock to the beat in my new hiking boots, swaying with an

imaginary partner. Eyes closed, I picture being swept away in the White House ballroom. One of President Ford's daughters was married in that room. Another First Daughter held her prom in that very room. Someday, maybe . . .

"Nice footwork," a voice says from the door.

I keep my eyes closed a beat longer than necessary, if only to try to recover my composure. Of course, this is totally and unequivocally embarrassing, being caught dancing alone.

A hot and sweaty Gabriel leans in the doorway with an amused smile. His workout clothes, red basketball shorts and a sleeveless black top, emphasize his trim waist and broad shoulders.

His hair is damp and face flushed from his morning run. I clear my throat. "I was just making sure my new boots fit properly."

"Really? Looks like you were auditioning for *Dancing with the Stars*."

"Funny," I say, and because sometimes humor is a good way to deflect, I curtsy in my boots and my purple pajamas. "I'm gonna crush it."

He studies me, then steps forward, hands outstretched. "Not with that box step."

We haven't been alone since the photo shoot. My pulse quickens as he reaches for my hand. I already know he's a great dancer—our state dinner waltz proved that. But somehow, the prospect of dancing with him now, in the early morning, in my pajamas, feels even more exhilarating. More intimate.

Deep breaths, Abby. No big deal. Or as Dad says, fake it till you make it. I lift my chin, pretending he doesn't affect me, and slip my hands into his.

Gabriel pulls me close. I'm transported to our kiss on the hilltop. The one we filed under "bucket list" and nothing more. But part of me wonders . . . would one more practice round really hurt?

"Your technique is satisfactory," I say coldly.

"Maybe I've been rehearsing in case the First Daughter of the United States needed a dance partner."

"A *practice* dance partner," I say, my voice breathy.

His eyes darken into that same passion-filled shade they were after our kiss. "Maybe you and me practicing isn't such a bad idea."

My heart races as our bodies inch closer. And then he hisses as my heavy hiking boot accidentally lands on his toes. "I'm so sorry!"

He grimaces and laughs at the same time. "You were saying who needed lessons?"

"I do, clearly," I say, turning all shades of red.

"You know what?" He winces. "I think you've broken in those boots."

★ ★ ★

"Is this nature-y enough?" Gabriel teases, pulling into a dirt parking lot near a sign that says *Mt. Mystic Hollow Nature Trails*. In the distance, I note dense woods and hilly terrain and predict I'll need a few Band-Aids this afternoon. Still, this was on my bucket list and I'm here to conquer that list. I take a deep breath. "Very nature-y."

I notice a few teens hop out of another car nearby. I do a double take, realizing it's Kyle, Billie, and Jaisha, dressed for a hike. Did Gabe invite them to join us?

"What are you guys doing here?" Gabe asks.

Kyle makes a face. "It's a free country. We can't hike the same park as you?"

Gabe leans in so only I can hear. "I was comparing notes on local trails with Billie and I guess they took it as an invitation."

"No need to explain," I say, trying to hide my disappointment. After our kiss, I'm guessing Gabe probably doesn't want to be alone with me. "Besides, I brought my own entourage."

I jerk a thumb toward Shaw and Nessa, both wearing hiking gear. Another team of agents in an unmarked van is parked nearby, serving as base camp, while Nessa and Shaw will go into the woods with us.

"What's with the colors?" Elle asks, pointing at a sign with trail names.

"Each trail is assigned a color," Gabriel explains. "As we walk along, we should see markers with the trail's color along the way to let us know we're on the right path."

I study a nearby sign that lets us know this is an official state park. My finger hovers over each trail and description. I smirk at the trail named *Old Tinker*. "This one has the highest difficulty level."

"We're going to stick with the Red Apple trail," Gabriel says firmly.

"Boring," Kyle says. "Come on, Calabrese, take her through the Tinker. That's where we're going."

Gabe throws his head back and laughs. "Then we're definitely not hiking the Tinker." He shifts his backpack. I don't know what exactly he has in there, but it looks heavy. I assume it's more camera gear. He steps forward and motions me and Elle to follow him. "Okay, FDOTUSes, let's get nature-y."

"Nature-y," Kyle cracks.

"I think it's adorable they've got their own inside jokes," Jaisha says. "Care to comment if you and Oliver have jokes like that?"

My face warms as Gabe gives Jaisha a warning look, but it's not necessary. Billie loops an arm around her twin and steers her away. "Someone needs a shot of endorphins." She points at her sister, then waves goodbye.

"Ignore Jaisha. She can't turn off her inner reporter," Gabe grumbles. He nods for us to follow him into the woods, which I'm more than happy to escape to.

The temperature difference is abrupt as soon as we're among the trees. The stifling summer humidity is more tolerable under the shade with a light breeze. I close my eyes and appreciate the twittering of the birds and the musky wood and moss smells.

"This is what freedom smells like," I say.

Gabriel already has his camera in hand. I pose with my arms wide, framing the trail, as he takes a picture of me. As we walk farther into the woods, I'm very aware of how quiet it is, save Elle's occasional yelp as she captures shots of birds and deer sightings for her feed. She's been skipping ahead as Gabriel and I hang back at a comfortable pace.

I don't hear them, but I know Shaw and Nessa are close behind. And somewhere else in this park are Kyle and the twins. "Was Kyle acting funny to you?" I ask.

"Funny is Kyle's default," he says.

"Do you all do this often?" I press, not sure why the whole situation feels . . . off.

Gabe flashes a grin. "Absolutely. Last month I was guiding a Polynesian princess through these woods." He shrugs. "Except *she* was able to take the Tinker trail."

I playfully smack his arm. He laughs and I grin back. Our eyes meet and I'm glad we're finally joking around again. Things have been so tense since the practice kiss. "Sorry. Seems like we've both been so busy the past few days," I say.

He sighs, resigned. "Yes, but also my mom—she hasn't confided in me or anything, but I think things are pretty bad with the inn."

"How bad?"

"Like shut-the-doors-forever kind of bad."

I try to make eye contact with him, but he's suddenly interested in the moss too. "I'm so sorry. I know my tita is trying to help, but she represents a group of investors and they all have to agree on the projects they support."

"First it was the pandemic and now it's this new resort," he says. "Business has been brutal."

I stiffen. The new resort being one of Oliver's family properties. "I'm so sorry. I still can't believe the Darbys would do that."

Gabe shakes his head. "I'm sure it's not your boy's daddy making this call."

I clear my throat. "Oliver is not 'my boy.' We've been friends all our lives and I can talk to him about your situation—" I stop my thought, seeing Gabe's sharp look.

"I'd prefer you not do that," he says through gritted teeth.

I want to argue, but the look in his eyes stops me in my tracks. Maybe Ruby would feel different, but I don't want to press Gabe further since it clearly makes him uncomfortable. "Maybe there's resources for small businesses. I'm sure we can think of something."

He shakes his head. "Thanks. Tita Karra is investigating that for us." I nod. Of course she would.

We walk silently. "Seems working on the jubilee has been keeping you busy too," he says. "I'm sorry that we haven't made much progress on your bucket list, but today, I think we might be able to check off two items." He winks as he taps his backpack. "Come on." He heads left and steps into brush off the trail.

"You know you're going off the trail," I say, conjuring one of my tita's tsking sounds.

"You know I grew up in the area," he responds. A jolt of anticipation passes through me as he hollers for Elle to come back to us.

We trek up a large stone until we're at the very tip. We're about seven feet from the ground below. Rocks jut out and I give Gabe a wide-eyed look at his suggestion that we climb down.

It's honestly not that high, but still high enough to twist an ankle or sustain a minor injury if we fall. "I've done this millions of times," Gabriel says as if reading my mind. He crouches. "I'll go first, then help guide you down. Watch what I do." He goes first and I do exactly as he directs me, including the part where I let him lift me down, relishing the quick but firm grasp of his hands on my waist.

Shaw has caught up and won't let Elle do even half of what I did to climb down, which is easy for him since he's six foot four.

Gabriel leads us through another group of trees, and I hear the water before we see it. We arrive at a sandy, pebble-covered bank of a peaceful river. The water moves lazily underneath the pale blue sky and drooping tree limbs. The riverbank across from us could be easily accessed by hopping over stones or perhaps even with a cool, refreshing swim. The air smells like warm mud and a bouquet of wildflowers. Even the heat is soft here.

"Do you like it?" Gabriel asks, his intense copper eyes searching mine.

My face tips toward the sun and I listen to the trickle of the small river. Time doesn't move here. It just sways. DC hustle and bustle this is not. "I love it."

"Picnic was on your list, right?" He taps his backpack, and now I know what he has inside. He gestures for me to follow him. There's a patch of grass and some logs not far away where we can set up. My feet wobble on the uneven riverbank, but tripping isn't the only reason I reach for his hand. He adjusts his grip, lacing our fingers together as he guides me around rocks and roots. His touch feels effortless, like it belongs here—like it belongs *with* me.

He picks a patch of grass near a log with a great view of the river and produces a red-checkered blanket from his backpack. Next, he retrieves a cooler. He winks. "And now for the pièce de résistance." I groan unintentionally as he pulls out peanut butter and Oreos, the two foods I told him I'd have at picnics when we first met.

"Oh, no way!" Elle, who I forgot was with us, hoots with

delight as she reaches for a cookie. She heads toward a huge boulder not far away. "Where are you going?" I call after her.

"I have reception here," she calls over her shoulder. Gabe asks her to join us, but I know better than to disturb Elle when she's living her best life.

Our picnic spread is exactly how I envisioned it when I wrote my summer bucket list: fancy cheeses, salami, bread, butter, honey, and a fruit tray. A bottle of sparkling cider to top it all off. And bonus, it's like we're at a beach near a river. Of course, not what I pictured when I imagined this picnic is the gorgeous boy sharing the meal with me. No. I don't think I could've ever dreamed of Gabriel Calabrese.

After our meal, Gabe and I recline against a log, our bodies leaning against one another. I lay my head on his shoulder. His head rests on mine. I inhale his musky scent and feel warm and safe. "I think this checks off more items on my list," I say.

It takes him a moment to respond. "Oh yeah," he drawls lazily.

"Nature-y hike, picnic, and vegging on a beach." I sigh and close my eyes, basking as golden, tree-filtered rays of sunlight warm my face.

He muses. "Yeah. We need that in our lives. Especially you."

I nudge his rib cage. "Says the boy trying to save his family's business, get into a competitive summer art program, and escort a pesky, high-maintenance First Daughter of the United States."

His eyes meet mine, a playful smile on his lips. "That last one is really tough," he teases.

"You should get hazard pay or something," I say, but the laughter on my lips freezes as I realize how close our faces are. How just an inch more and we'd be right back to where we were on that hilltop a week ago.

As his gaze searches mine, a surge of excitement tingles through my body. He leans close. "I thought maybe one of the bucket list items you were referring to was . . ." His voice trails off. His lips hover over mine.

I inhale his smoky, fresh-cut grass scent and sigh. "Yes, you can help me practice more."

His laugh is husky. "They say practice makes perf—" My lips press against his. His hands wrap around my waist and he pulls me close.

★ ★ ★

We spend the afternoon exploring the river, then coming back to the picnic blanket to snack, relax, and sneak in kisses whenever Elle isn't looking.

Elle must have caught on to her third-wheel vibes because her exploration trips get longer and longer. It's not until after we've polished off the last of the grapes that Gabriel and I are interrupted.

"Abby! Come here quick!" Elle's voice shouts from the trees across the river. I tilt my head. "How did my sister get to the other side of the river without us noticing?" I ask Gabe.

"We've been a bit distracted," he says. But I can tell he's also wondering the same.

Elle yells again. I feel bad having ignored her this entire afternoon. Gabe follows as I head toward a group of rocks that would lead us across the stream. I bite my lip. Old Abby would be nervous about falling. Operation Bucket List Abby says even if I fall, the water is low and I'll get a little wet. So what?

We find Elle in a clearing. I stop in my tracks, seeing she isn't alone. Billie, Kyle, and Jaisha wave hello. This explains why Elle's been gone in longer stretches. She found Kyle and crew.

My face warms and I wonder if they saw me and Gabe at our picnic.

"What are you doing here?" Gabe asks.

Kyle chuckles. "Bro, the Tinker trail." He points behind him and I'm relieved the Tinker trail is the opposite direction. They couldn't have seen Gabe and me on the banks together. I scan Kyle's and the twins' faces and they don't look like they suspect anything between me and Gabe. My stomach churns. Would it be bad if they saw us together? The only thing I know now is that I'm not ready to go into it's-complicated territory after such a blissful escape-into-alternate-reality kind of afternoon.

"See how much cooler the Tinker trail is," he says. I follow his gaze. Meanwhile, an excited Elle points at a depression in the ground that looks like a giant has stomped and left a footprint. The ground slopes downward, with loose stones and boulders along the way, and at the bottom there's a small hole that looks like a cave opening.

"Oh no. No. No. No," I say, immediately reading my sister's mind. "You are not going in a cave."

She points her phone, which is on flashlight mode, into the hole. Gabriel stands beside her and shakes his head with amazement. "It looks like a possible entrance into a cavern system," he says. "The closest cavern entrance is probably a couple miles away.

This may be the same system. How did you find this?" He looks at Kyle, who shrugs.

"I ran into everyone and we followed a weasel-looking thing," Elle explains.

Jaisha crouches like she is going down. "I'm gonna check it out."

Elle crouches beside her and inches closer to where the ground slopes down. "I'm going with."

"Oh no, you're not," I say in my best don't-argue-with-me mom voice. Elle looks like she is going to whine but I cut her off.

Gabe steps forward. "Elle, bad idea. Pretty sure avoiding dark empty caves is a First Daughter 101 thing. And I'd love to avoid jail time."

She rolls her eyes. "Fine. But can I at least take a couple photos in front of the entrance? This would be such a fun 'mysterious cave' post."

I study the entrance to the cavern. It's steep, but not as steep as the way we climbed to get to the river. "Well, if it's for your adoring fans," I tease.

No sooner do I finish my words than my sister jerks forward, arms flailing as she rolls down the incline toward the entrance of the cave. I don't know who's shrieking louder as she falls.

Gabriel slides down the incline to grab Elle, his bigger body in front of her and hands up, stopping her from tumbling farther.

Shaw is on the scene seconds later, pushing Kyle and the twins aside. Nessa pulls me back. It takes me a moment to register they've been nearby the entire time. Nessa's speaking rapidly into her walkie-talkie.

"Elle," I cry. "Are you okay?"

She whimpers and I see large bloody gashes on her elbows and knees as Shaw carries her out of the incline. He places her on the ground and examines her. My body shakes seeing all the blood. Shaw is checking her joints. "Doesn't appear to have broken anything," he says.

Nessa is already cleaning them with her field first aid kit. She sighs. "Nothing major but she should get medical attention."

Shaw picks her up again with ease. "Quite the tumble, but you're going to be fine, Elle. We're going to take you to the hospital to get you examined and patched up."

It's not until we're back at the parking lot that I realize I've been holding Gabe's hand the entire time. He squeezes my hand tight as Elle is loaded into Shaw's SUV. After he orders me to get in with her, I realize he wants me to leave Gabe behind.

"Come with us," I say. "You can get your truck later."

"Abby," Shaw warns.

Gabe shakes his head. "Go. Be with your sister. I'll meet you at the clinic."

I don't get to say goodbye as Nessa leads me firmly into the car.

"Rhapsody and Rapunzel are secure," Shaw says into his walkie-talkie.

As the truck speeds away, a garbled voice over the intercom informs my Secret Service agents that Rogers, as in Buck Rogers, is en route to the hospital. I trade glances with Elle as soon as we hear the code name.

Dad is on the way.

CHAPTER 22

"Daddy!" Elle exclaims as soon as he appears in the doorway, looking frazzled and wearing his Sunday golf attire. His security detail trails behind him.

My father is a national hero, but his watery eyes and the worry lines on his forehead make him look like any parent who finds their kid in the hospital. He strides into the room with the barest acknowledgment of the doctor or nurse, even me, as he rushes to Elle's bedside.

My kid sister breaks into tears and blubbers that she's fine.

I blink away my own tears. Elle is fine. Just a couple scrapes, and now we're awaiting some extra precautionary X-ray results, but the way Dad is hovering over her you'd think she broke both legs or something. He asks her several questions about her health until he's satisfied.

Then he asks the same questions of Dr. Sharma, whose voice is remarkably even, though her hands are clenched hard on her clipboard. Bet she wasn't expecting to attend to the president's family today.

When my dad is finally satisfied, he breaks into his First

Spouse smile and pumps Dr. Sharma's hand and then the nurse's with a hearty handshake. The faintest of blushes appear on their cheeks. It's hard to think of my dad as anything but a dork, but once upon a time he was kind of a heartthrob, so my mom claims.

He places both hands on his sandy-brown hair, a gesture I've seen millions of times as a way he calms himself down before his eyes land squarely on me.

"Hi, Dad," I say, my voice cracking. We've spoken almost daily, but finally seeing him in person reminds me how much I've missed him and Mom.

"Come here, pumpkin." He pulls me in for a hug. I melt into his bear hug and sniff peanut M&M's. Another one of his go-tos when he's anxious.

"You got here so quickly," I whisper.

"I was planning on surprising you girls with a visit soon," he says with a grin. "But when you hear your little girl took a spill and you're a licensed pilot and married to the commander in chief . . . there are certain things I can do quick." He taps his head. "Should've come today. I knew my Spidey sense was picking up something in the matrix." I narrow my eyes at him for mixing up his movies. He knows how annoying that is to me.

"It was hardly an accident," I protest. "Elle's clumsy butt tripped."

"I'm not the clumsy one," Elle says.

Dad sighs as he pulls back. His grip tightens around my arms. "Your mother wishes she was here."

"I know. We spoke to her before you came," I say. "She's tied up with some union negotiations."

I frown and follow my dad's gaze. My blood chills as I realize what's caught his attention. Gabe has been quietly sitting in the back of the room, unnoticed by Dad until now.

Dad releases me and turns his full scrutiny onto him. I feel bad for him as he stands taller and broader shouldered than usual. The only hint Gabriel's nervous is the red flush of his ears.

Meanwhile, I do my best to keep a neutral face, hoping Dad doesn't get any hey-we've-been-kissing vibes from us. Honestly, I haven't even worked out what's going on between Gabe and me, let alone what to tell my father. All I know is that it just happened, and it felt . . . oh, so right at the time.

I put myself in Dad's shoes as I examine Gabe's worn brown boots, rumpled cargo pants, dirty gray T-shirt, and his thick, longish dark hair matted with dirt and sweat. To me, sweaty and outdoorsy Gabriel is smoking hot, but to Dad? Judging by his pressed-together lips, I'm thinking he's not joining any fan clubs soon. In short, Gabe's outdoorsy-meets-edgy look is the polar opposite of, say, clean-cut Oliver Darby in a suit jacket and neatly cropped hair.

I wince as my father peers down his nose, a look I know means disapproval.

Elle steals a glance at me. She looks as nervous as I feel. I need to say something fast before we enter awkward silence territory, population everyone in this hospital room. "Dad, you remember Gabe Calabrese. He attended the state dinner with Tita Karra."

"I remember. The boy wearing Chuck Taylors with his tuxedo," Dad says, snapping his fingers.

"Yes, sir," Gabriel says. "It's nice to see you again."

My dad studies Gabe's outstretched hand a beat before

grasping it with a firm handshake. "You're the young man whose idea it was to take my girls on a hike?"

Elle and I protest at the same time. "Daddy, no," Elle says.

"Hiking was my idea," I add.

Dad guffaws. "Now I know I'm in an alternate universe. The two of you don't have an outdoorsy bone in your body."

I roll my eyes. "Not true. I wanted to try hiking for once. You always tell us to keep an open mind."

He side-eyes me. "I do, don't I?"

"Gabe was being a good host and guide," I say, my voice not as controlled as I'd like. My father studies me. My cheeks grow warm as I wonder if he suspects anything between me and Gabriel.

He turns his attention back to Gabriel, who stands his ground. "Yes, a good guide indeed. Our agents say if it weren't for you, my Elle could've had some serious injuries."

Gabriel blinks uncertainly. My father breaks into a smile and claps Gabriel heartily on the back. "Looks like you're a good guy to have around."

"Thank you, sir," Gabriel says.

My dad nods and turns back to Elle and me. "Let me catch up with your agents and then let's see if we can get out of here and find some dinner. I'm starving."

"We've got you covered," a familiar voice says as Tita Karra and Ruby rush in. Tita Karra wraps her arms around Elle. She whispers some words into her ear that make Elle cry happy tears.

Tita stands beside Ruby and addresses the room. "We're going to have barbecue and a bonfire at the inn. Gabe's mom has this hot sauce you'll adore," she adds.

My father's eyes have lit up. Dad loves his hot sauce. "How hot?"

"We've made many grown men cry." Ruby beams. She claps Gabe's back. "This one's our reigning hot-sauce champ." He rolls his eyes at his mom, but I can tell he's holding back his smile.

Dad guffaws. "Very well. We'll see how much heat Gabe can stand."

As my father leaves the room, I squeeze Gabe's shoulder. "I think he likes you," I say.

"What gave you that impression? The way he glares at me or his clenched fists?"

I chuckle. "For context, Oliver hates hot sauce. Maybe he wants to see if you can roll with him?"

He grimaces. "How hot can your dad roll?"

"He claims he lost his taste buds in space, so his tolerance for heat is really high." I grimace, feeling bad for Gabe.

"You mean I have to ingest nuclear-grade peppers to win his approval?" I hold back my smile as he grumbles about me sneaking in some milk to dinner.

★ ★ ★

Tita Karra and Ruby delivered on the BBQ. And the hot sauce. After four rounds of the sauce and Gabriel still standing, I could see the respect in Dad's eyes, which rose even further as Gabe discussed chicken wings. Another one of Dad's faves.

Fortunately, the rest of us get to enjoy Ruby's special honey BBQ sauce. I grin at Dad across the picnic table, polishing off his last rack. Elle sits next to him, doing the same—bib smeared with sauce and a few bandages dotting her arms from the gashes she got on the rocks. With her energy and appetite, you'd never guess she was at the hospital just this afternoon.

I spot Gabe a distance away, starting a fire at the inn's firepit. My breath catches as I watch him carrying a few logs. We left the hospital in separate vehicles, and I've hardly said a word to him since my father arrived. After all the excitement from Elle's fall, the kisses we shared by the river seem like a daydream, except it's not hard for me to recall the feel of Gabriel's lips pressed to mine.

"Penny for your thoughts," my dad says. He's watching me with interest. Does he suspect I was watching Gabe?

I force a smile. "I'm just excited for a bonfire. In fact, I'm going to head over now." I don't stay to hear Dad's response.

Gabriel is gone when I reach the firepit. I grab a seat on one of the logs facing the pit, forming a circle.

Ruby pokes at the small flames. I can feel the frustration roiling off her as the logs in the pit fail to catch fire. "Even starting and maintaining a fire takes patience," she says, mostly to herself.

"We need kindling," I say, rising from my chair to see if there are any sticks nearby, which is difficult given the only light is from the inn and the half-full moon above.

It wasn't until I moved to the White House that I learned starting a fire is not necessarily easy. I've watched our staff struggle at times to make sure the flames catch on and continue. That's where I learned about kindling. Sometimes creating a roaring fire needs help.

My search takes me around a large tree and out of sight of the firepit. I step on a branch that cracks under my shoes. There's a kindling candidate. I stoop to pick it up only to see another hand sweep it up first. I rise to my feet and find myself face to face with Gabe. "I got it," he says.

I'm tongue-tied. He's even more magnetic, if possible, thanks to the mix of moonlight and shadows on his face. I force my hands to my sides because all I really want to do is pull those cheekbones of his toward my face and continue what we started on the riverbank. His eyes are so soft and dreamy, it's probably a good thing his arms are full of wood to stop us from doing anything embarrassing.

A cloud must've moved because the moon's light grows brighter. I'm startled to see the inn's tree swing, empty and barely swaying on the other side of the tree. My chest tightens at seeing the place where Gabriel's grandparents swung together, so magically in love.

I sigh. "So romantic . . ."

Gabriel is silent and brooding as he studies the swing.

My nerves flare with anticipation. "Bet this would be a good place for more practice."

He avoids my gaze as he shakes his head. "This place deserves better than two people just . . . practicing."

I recoil, hearing anger and hurt in his voice. I must've offended him by suggesting we kiss here. "I'm sorry. I wasn't being serious, Gabriel."

"Nothing about our situation is serious, Abby," he says sharply.

A knot forms in my chest. "What do you mean?"

He lifts his face to the sky and takes a deep breath. "Nothing. Don't worry about it. I better get back, I think your dad is asking for some rocket fuel to start the fire."

As we round the tree, I realize it might've looked a little

suspicious for both of us to be walking in from the dark together. Fortunately, my father is nowhere in sight.

Ruby accepts Gabriel's kindling and gets to work. Moments later I'm clapping as the firepit roars to life. I grab a seat on the log nearest me and try to make eye contact with Gabriel to see if he'll join me, but his attention is elsewhere.

I feel a familiar hand on my shoulder as Dad takes a seat on the log next to me, his security detail behind him. Elle grabs a seat next to Tita Karra and Ruby. Gabe sits on the dirt, reclining on a log instead of sitting on the log with me and Dad. A few feet away, Shaw and Nessa are illuminated by the firepit's flames.

It's a pleasant summer night. The trees hum with the rhythmic chirps of the cicadas and the sky is an inky blue splattered with stars I could never see in the city.

My dad looks up, studying the night sky. He'd retired from the astronaut corps by the time I could read, but I still have vague dreamlike memories of him in a white suit, flying up to space. And of course, there's a ton of videos.

"Do you have a favorite star, Gabe?" he asks. "Abby said you're into astrophotography."

If only the darts in my eyes could prick Dad. Thanks for outing that I talk about Gabe with him. If he noticed anything awkward, Gabe doesn't look like it. He clears his throat. "The North Star seems to always be a good one," he says.

My father nods. "Yes. Polaris. It's gotten me out of a few jams."

"What about you, sir? What's your favorite?" Gabe asks.

Dad regards him. "I was actually thinking if I'd be able to see the space station passing by."

"Cool," Gabriel says, tilting his head to the sky.

Tita Karra snorts. "The world's tiniest bachelor pad is what my sister called it when they were dating."

Our group laughs as my father grins. "I was worried our relationship wouldn't take, but turns out absence does make the heart grow fonder."

"You mean Mom was always busy," Elle says.

"Yes, I suppose that counts," my dad muses. "Sometimes our duties take us away from the people we love. Like your mom."

"Do my friends count?" Elle whines. "It's like we're on different planets."

My dad rolls his eyes. "Yes, I guess so." He pauses. "And for Abby, Oliver counts too." I frown as Dad continues. "Sometimes you don't see your friends and loved ones, but you know they're there."

But I'm barely listening anymore as I go over my dad's words about people we love. Why did my father go out of his way to mention Oliver?

CHAPTER 23

The sun is barely risen when Dad leaves for the regional airport where his plane is parked. He's chipper and alert after a lifetime of having to be a morning person for his job. I'm sad to see him go, but he's meeting with a children's hospital and that's too important to skip. Ruby and I are the only ones downstairs to see him off after Dad insisted that Elle get her rest.

After Ruby hands him a bag of local breakfast items and gives a fond farewell, Dad wraps an arm around my shoulders and we walk down the porch steps. He hums, projecting he's in good spirits despite the both of us looking a little bleary-eyed. "This inn is fantastic," he muses as we stop at the foot of the stairs to say our goodbyes. "Your mom was not happy after the pizza delivery stunt, and adamant you all stay away from the press. I think you lucked out here at Mystic Hollow Inn." He hesitates.

I frown. "What?"

"You know your mom and I always do our due diligence."

I tilt my head. "Spill it, Dad."

He sighs. "About Gabe. Seems he was instrumental in some

huge news story here a couple years ago. He was the photographer."

I blink. "Yes, he said it was a story for his school paper."

Dad arches his brow. "It's not often a teenager scoops a major scandal that throws very powerful people into jail."

I frown, recalling the backstory he shared with me. "He said he worked on a story about a bully?" I'm at a loss for words because he didn't give me any details either.

My dad chuckles. "That's one word to call an ex-congressman."

I didn't realize his story was political. "Dad, is that what you meant about Gabriel taking photos of stars last night?" My head spins as I connect the dots. "Are you saying he's some lowlife tabloid photographer? I think Gabe helped put a real bad guy in jail."

"Yes, he did a good thing exposing corruption. But when journalists get big scoops, they tend to want more." He places his hands on my shoulders. His gaze holds mine. "Just be careful, honey, that's all I ask."

I struggle with what to say. Gabriel isn't working for his paper. He's applying to art school and needs to take photos of me for his portfolio. Yet only I'm in on his secret. Should that worry me? I take a deep breath.

"He's a good guy, Dad," I say, but I can still see the doubt in his eyes. "Is that why you mentioned Oliver last night?"

He frowns. "What?"

I cross my arms. "Last night at the firepit, you were talking about people we love. You mentioned Oliver."

My dad shakes his head. "Elle was talking about her friends.

Oliver is your friend, but . . ." He hesitates. "I have been suspecting maybe a bit more?"

My face reddens.

Dad closes his eyes like he's giving himself a pep talk. "Honey, I'm not here to interfere with your crushes, but you've been hanging out with Oliver a lot. And when Oliver tells me he may be coming to visit you . . ." His voice trails off.

My jaw drops. "Sorry? Did you say Oliver is coming to visit me? And why is he telling you and not me?"

He lifts his hands. "And that's where I officially step away from teenage drama. I talked with his dad about some new properties. Oliver was there. He mentioned he wanted to see you. Very casual. All chill. Not sus."

I groan. He kisses my cheek. "Take care of yourself and your sister, Abby." He pauses, head tilted in thought. "And even though you're technically grounded, allow yourself a little fun, okay? I'm glad that boy can stomach some serious firepower. Maybe he'll teach you to appreciate hot sauce."

I wave one last time as his car pulls away. And the feelings of uncertainty and doubt wash over me, like how I felt the first day I arrived at Mystic Hollow.

Dad was right.

Oliver's text arrives after lunch as Elle and I visit Mystic Hollow's florist shop to look for flowers for the jubilee. I'm instantly pulled away from my happy place among the fragrant blooms and potted plants in the shop's greenhouse seeing his text message.

You'll never guess where I am, he writes with a winky face emoji.

Instead of being excited, I'm full of nerves. *Pineapple farm eating pineapple ice cream?* I write.

Aloha, Hawai'i. I'm back in DC. He sends me a map with a pin in it. *ETA Mystic Hollow in three hours. Want to grab dinner?*

My hands shake as I type. The idea of my worlds colliding is more anxiety-inducing than relieving. *You don't have to come out here to visit me.*

I watch as gray dots dance on my screen as he types his response. *Sure I do. We're way overdue for a fancy dinner. Something you wanted to do this summer, right?*

I groan. I told him "foodie" dinner—of course Oliver would interpret that as "fancy" dinner. Though I was careful not to mention the bucket list to him. Knowing Oliver, he would've accidentally told others about my list. When I wrote the bullet I was thinking of a few "foodie" places in DC I read about on a food blog.

I tap my phone. *Fancy dinner? I'm in Mystic Hollow. They have a great burger joint.* The diner connected to Pat's ice cream parlor comes to mind.

I've got something better than burgers in mind . . . 😉. He leaves one more note about picking me up around five.

"Watch out," Elle says. I look up from my phone as I nearly collide into a rack of sunflowers. My sister is hunched over a bucket of tulips.

"Sorry. I was . . ." I lower my phone. "Oliver is going to take me to dinner tonight," I say.

Elle huffs as she gives me a look like she saw this coming. "Shocker. He's got a schedule to keep, after all."

I gasp. "What's that supposed to mean?"

She casually adds more flowers to her bucket. "It means he's like you, the human equivalent of Siri. Although you've been going off script this entire summer, which has been aaa-mazing."

I scoff. "Human equivalent of what?"

She looks me up and down. "You two always have an answer for everything. I'm pretty sure you were born with an itinerary embedded in those pretty heads of yours." My frown is Texas-sized. Is that really how she sees me, like a machine? Elle keeps going. "So, Oliver is probably freaking out that he's off schedule asking you to officially be his boo."

My jaw tightens. "Elle, that's so rude. Oliver is my friend, a real friend. Not some robot programmed to hang out with me. And as a 'real' friend he's keeping his promise to take me to a fancy parent-free dinner."

"Your list said 'foodie,' " she deadpans.

I groan. Even Elle knows there's a difference between fancy and foodie. "You know what I mean."

"But why?" she asks.

"He invited me. I agreed. Case closed. Stop making up problems."

"What do you girls think?" Mrs. Rey beams as she gestures at the large pot on her table. It's a display of golden flowers with the state flag of California displayed in the middle. "Each state flower will have its own pot. And we'll arrange all the pots, so they form a star," Mrs. Rey explains.

"Fifty states, fifty flowers," I muse, in keeping with our fifties theme. "It's going to be stunning."

"I agree," the florist responds eagerly. "You girls are so talented. All the great work you're doing for our town is so very much appreciated. I hope you make it back here next year, and the year after, and after."

My heart warms. "Definitely, Mrs. Rey, it feels so nice to be part of the community." And I mean it. I don't think I've ever spent so much time somewhere without my mom or her staff shadowing me. It feels—liberating.

Meanwhile, Mrs. Rey clasps her hands like her prayers have been answered. "Wonderful! And guess what? We're going to have some of your flower displays at the dance tonight to give people a little preview."

I open my mouth to respond, then shut it as I process her comment. "What dance, Mrs. Rey?"

She covers her mouth as she laughs. "I forget how isolated you girls are at that inn. Hasn't anyone told you about the Founder's Day Dance? It's tonight."

I flush. "Yes, I've been focused on the jubilee and lost track of time."

Mrs. Rey winks at me. "You should both be there. It'll be a lovely time, especially for kids your age."

Mrs. Rey lets us leave her shop only after we promise to attend tonight's dance. Elle is practically glowing. "How convenient

Oliver is taking you out to dinner tonight. Maybe you and your boyfriend can check off 'dance under the stars' too," she says. I elbow her. She scowls.

"Hey!" Gabriel waves at us two stores down. He's left Pat's ice cream parlor holding a stack of flyers. He approaches us, looking fit in a T-shirt and khaki shorts. We stop on the sidewalk to chat. "The pie contest is a hit," he says. "Bunch of folks have been asking for flyers." He holds up our latest advertisement about the jubilee.

"That's awesome," I say, but I don't feel it. I've felt a bit off since the tree swing last night and his "Abby isn't serious" comment. Something no one has ever accused me of. And then my dad's revelation about his journalism story didn't help.

He tilts his head, obviously detecting my hesitation, but fortunately he doesn't push. "Do you have anything else to take care of while we're in town?"

"Dress shopping," Elle says.

I give Elle a nudge as Gabriel shrugs. "Sure. Do you want me to wait for you?"

"For tonight's Founder's Day Dance," Elle continues. "I need a dress." Her tone is unusually harsh.

Gabriel hesitates. "I was going to mention the dance. Marge asked that I take photos tonight and—"

"Abby is going too," Elle interrupts. "She has a date."

Gabriel rocks back. "A date?"

"Tita Karra is going to meet us here to take us shopping," Elle says. "And then she'll take us home."

Gabriel nods, still refusing to make eye contact. "Sounds good.

I'm going to drop the rest of the flyers at Latte Love . . . See you later."

It isn't until Gabriel is out of earshot that I yell at Elle. "What was that? Why were you rubbing my dinner with Oliver in his face like that?"

She purses her lips. "Because it's not fair how you're treating Gabriel."

I gape at her. "Excuse me?"

"I saw you two at the river. He's totally into you and you were totally into him. And then you agree to go on a date with Oliver?"

I shake my head. "It's just dinner."

"Dinner. And then a dance. That's a date."

I sigh. "Gabriel and I . . . I mean, we're not exclusive. I don't know what we're doing. We called our kissing 'practice.' He doesn't want anything more with me."

"We called our kissing practice." Elle does a terrible impression of me as she glares my way. "You know, maybe you should hit the refresh button for your eyes because you clearly can't see."

My jaw drops as she saunters away. I should be used to her outbursts, but this one stings and I can't tell if it's because she's completely right about me and Gabriel, or completely wrong about me. I know there's something between me and Gabe, but I also know it can't go anywhere. How could it? I'm leaving at the end of the month and our paths will never cross again.

I stare at myself in my suite's mirror, wearing my new yellow dress and white strappy heels. Even an afternoon of shopping and pedicures has done little to lift my mood. Oliver will be arriving in twenty minutes to pick me up.

Tita Karra comes back to my room, holding her pearl necklace. I watch her reflection and frown as she approaches me. "Gabriel will understand, honey. We all knew you were a short-term guest." She clasps the necklace around my neck.

I flinch. So much to unpack in that statement. What does she know? I gulp. "Tita Karra, can I tell you something and you'll promise not to tell Mom?"

Her expression turns serious. "Of course, my dear. That's practically in the tita-niece handbook."

I take a deep breath. "I kissed Gabriel. And he kissed me back."

Tita's stone expression breaks into a soft smile. "I know, my dear. I think everyone knows, or at least suspected."

"Then how can you tell me Gabriel will understand?"

She wraps an arm around my shoulders. "Because you're young and you're allowed to have these fleeting moments. A summer romance? How very *young adult* of you. They can burn bright and hot like a firework, then extinguish just as quickly," she says gently.

I stare at her. "You think this is just a summer romance?"

Tita Karra looks me in the eye. "Only you can determine that." She hesitates. "But you and my godson are from two different worlds. And you will be returning to Washington soon and moving on with your life. Plus"—her hands fly to her hips—"I promised your mother I'd get you back in one piece. Believe me, I will."

I look at the mirror and force myself to smile at my reflection. There she is. Abigail Cary-Alzona. Prim. Proper. About to go on a date with Oliver Darby. The vice president's son and the boy who should be on the arm of the First Daughter. The one who makes perfect sense.

Tita Karra heads to my door. She tries to smile encouragingly. "You don't want a firework, sweetie. You want a star, a bright light that burns strong and steady."

I purse my lips. She must mean Gabriel is a temporary firework while Oliver is a constant glow. Her analogy makes sense, yet it doesn't make me feel better. I look out my window and appreciate the serenity of the inn's property bathed in sunlight. The constant, predictable sun. I flash a resigned smile. "I'm going to wait outside for Oliver."

She nods. "Of course. Elle and the rest of the family will see you at the dance. Enjoy your dinner date," she calls after me. I sigh. Even she acknowledges it's a date.

My chest tightens as I step outside. The driveway, fields, and trees glow with such warmth in the fading afternoon light. Gabriel called this time of day the golden hour. The perfect time to take photos. And he's right. It's like I'm in a dream.

I'm on autopilot as I walk down the porch and find myself by the large tree in front of the inn. The tree swing, with faded white wood, rocks gently. I smile and take a seat.

This is where Gabe's grandparents sat for their romantic photo. The chair is cool and creaks ever so slightly like a sigh. My legs dangle as I allow myself to sway in its inviting curves. I shut my eyes to feel the fading sunlight on my face and a gardenia-scented wind through my hair.

A loud click startles me. I turn to see a camera lens pointed my way. More clicks and I smile. Gabriel lowers his camera. "I think we have a winner," he says. My breath catches seeing how gorgeous he looks in the early evening sun. The way his dark hair glows with a fiery edge. The angles of his cheekbones. How his muscles are emphasized from the sunlight and shadows.

"Hold that," he says. He raises his camera again and steps closer. My smile disappears and instead I'm looking directly into the lens. He takes a few more shots and then lowers his camera. "Perfection," he says, voice low. "Most of the time when you look at a camera you're smiling."

"That's how I'm trained," I say. "To always smile when people are looking."

His eyes study mine. "Authenticity," he says. "That's when people are the most beautiful. When they're not forcing a smile." He takes another shot.

Our eyes meet and my mouth goes dry. Tita Karra said what we have is a summer romance. Something that burns hot, then will blow out and extinguish fast like a firework. But as we stare at one another it's like I'm gazing at the sun, a fire that has burned for billions of years.

And it's not fiery, passionate kisses I see. It's the tender image of Gabe's grandparents sitting side by side on this very swing I'm sitting on now. I stare at Gabriel, my chest tight, my heart full. I watch the Adam's apple in his throat bob as he struggles with his words too.

Gabriel is right. This swing isn't for practice kisses. The couples who sit here—are here for the real thing. My eyes shut as I lean toward him.

Maybe this will be a "for real" kiss? Maybe what we have is more than a summer romance. The swing shakes, startling me. I turn to find Oliver Darby wearing an expensive suit and his "vote for me" smile. I gasp as he slides next to me. "Awesome, you got us a photographer." He kisses my cheek. "You look gorgeous, Abby."

CHAPTER 24

I'm so startled by Oliver's presence I slide off the tree swing and not surprisingly fail to stick the landing. As I wobble, Gabriel rushes to my left arm, while Oliver grabs ahold of my right.

I look from boy to boy, unable to process my worlds colliding. Gabriel in worn dark jeans and a black T-shirt and Oliver in a perfectly tailored gray suit.

Gabe releases me first. He backs away, while Oliver steps close, chuckling. "That's my Abigail. I swear if it weren't for me, she'd have tripped at every one of her mom's campaign stops." Normally I'd correct Oliver about his exaggerations of my clumsiness, but I'm still at a loss for words.

Oliver practically snuck up on me and Gabe. Sure, nothing was happening between us, but we were having a moment. Weren't we?

Oliver clears his throat and offers Gabe a handshake. I see the defiance in Gabe's eyes, but he shakes his hand anyway in a quick, firm way like I've seen Mom do before a debate.

"Oliver," I say. "You remember Gabriel Calabrese. You met at the state dinner."

Oliver's forehead wrinkles a millisecond before a fake friendly smile crosses his face. "Yes! Of course. The boy in the sneakers, right?" He looks between us, laughing. "I thought you were doing some kind of portrait session." He looks Gabe up and down. "Though those angles looked more intimate than typical."

"Gabriel isn't taking official photos, these are . . . for private use," I say hurriedly. I don't want Oliver to think Gabriel is working for the media, but I also don't think I get to announce he's applying for an art program when Gabe hasn't even told his own mother.

Oliver frowns but says nothing more. "Abby, we'd better head out. We have reservations."

"Same," Gabriel says. "A bunch of us are hitting Mike's Biscuits before the dance."

Oliver chuckles. "I promised Abigail a fancy dinner and we're getting one at my family's resort. Chef LeMonde is preparing a special menu just for us."

My chest tightens. Of course we're going to the resort that is bankrupting Gabe's inn. I check on Gabriel, who refuses to meet my eyes. Oliver, who's never one for awkward silences, touches the small of my back. "We had better go."

Not knowing what to say to Gabe, I search for anything. "I'll see you at the dance."

Oliver perks up. "The Founder's Day thing?"

The storm in Gabriel's eyes makes me shiver. "Yes," he says, more like a challenge than a simple statement.

Oliver frowns as he looks at his watch. "Nice. We have dinner plans—"

"And so do I," Gabriel says. "Glad you can knock a few more items off your list, Abby." He mock bows before heading to his truck.

Oliver lifts his brows. "What list is this?"

I bite my lip. "Nothing. Don't worry about it." I'm relieved when he doesn't ask me anything further because honestly, I have no answers—only questions having to do with the boy who's left me, and not the one I'm walking away with.

I cast one last glance at Gabriel, then follow Oliver to his car.

Oliver's silver BMW convertible pulls into the circular driveway in front of a stately white marbled building. A water fountain lit by golden lights graces the resort's entrance along with exotic flowers and shrubs. The Commander Resort is all about high-end luxury, clean modern lines, and exclusivity. Unlike Mystic Hollow Inn, with its cozy elegance and historic charm, warm and inviting to all.

Valets in red uniforms hurry to open our doors as soon as Oliver parks. Soothing electronic music plays over speakers and the air smells like ginger and citrus—the signature Darby International Hotel scent. Of course, not part of the resort's staff are Shaw and Oliver's agent lurking nearby. It's a familiar sight given how much time me and Oliver have spent together, but I've come to like the Shaw and Nessa duo.

As I grip Oliver's arm and climb up the steps into the lobby, I imagine that this fulfills the expectations of what so many assumed—First Daughter Abigail Cary-Alzona on a date with her prince, Second Son Oliver Darby. Budding American power couple. A near-certain fate for anyone who's been watching these two teens grow up in each other's orbits.

Two attendants swing open the Commander's grand wood-and-glass doors, and we step into a modern rustic country-style lobby, complete with large wooden-beamed ceilings, ornate light fixtures, and massive oil paintings anchoring the space. A sharply dressed hotel manager greets us with a flourish, her heels clicking across the beautifully tiled floor.

I catch the knowing glances from staff and guests—subtle nods of approval, though no one makes a scene. The resort's manager appears and personally escorts us to the Commander's restaurant, aptly named Chief.

We enter a space that feels like a trendy urban restaurant: low ambient light, sleek modern furniture with dark accents, and upbeat dance music. It's exactly the kind of place I was thinking of going for my foodie, parent-free dinner. But having been enjoying the small-town charm of Mystic Hollow, this venue feels so out of place here. Or am I the one who's out of place?

We're seated at a table by a fancy fireplace. It's in a prime spot that seems like a see-and-be-seen kind of angle—not a private area like I expected. "Does this meet your expectations?" Oliver says with a knowing smile as we settle in. I nod. This certainly checks the box for a parent-free dinner, but I'm not 100 percent sure about my expectations. I had a very different vision for this evening.

My mind wanders to Mike's Biscuits, where Gabriel and his friends are probably enjoying hamburgers and the Pike Special from Pat's. "It's gorgeous," I mumble.

"Only the best for Abigail," he says. "You were missed in Hawai'i," he adds.

I stare at my golden plate settings. When I first arrived at Mystic Hollow, I would've said I missed being in Hawai'i, but now I realize I don't feel that way. Oliver continues, not at all waiting for my response. "But no worries. I've got plans for the rest of our summer once you're back in DC."

"I'll be traveling with my mom for most of July, remember? Italy and the Mediterranean region for a couple weeks and then a volunteer trip."

He grins. "I know. And wouldn't you know it? My family has over seven hundred hotels all over the world." I frown. Then why do they need to open one in Mystic Hollow and ruin Gabriel's inn? He just seems so oblivious to the situation.

I stammer, uncertain how to bring up the jubilee. "Oliver, I'm just—"

"Starving," Oliver finishes my sentence. "I know you and your hangry spells. Fortunately, Chef LeMonde has us covered."

Our dinner is exquisite in taste and in size. After seven courses, my taste buds have experienced a gastronomic tour de force, but because of the tiny portions, I can't say I'm exactly satisfied either. Quail legs and escargot can only go so far. The conversation's not much better. Oliver's talking about boats again, and law school.

I blink. *When did I start pretending that stuff was interesting?* It's like I dropped into his world and forgot there were other ones out there. Maybe Elle's right. Are we just like Siri in human form? Preprogrammed and predictable?

My stomach flutters and then growls. My face reddens. Oh no. I sincerely hope Oliver didn't hear that! A polite smile crosses Oliver's face. "Dessert," he says. He snaps his fingers at a server, who rushes forward like he was summoned by a king. The entitlement—was that always there? "Would you ask LeMonde for a tray of his desserts?"

"Actually—" I interrupt. Oliver blinks. I know he's not used to being interrupted, but now and then I pull rank. Which I decide to do now. "I have an idea."

Mike's Biscuits n' Burgers is busy. The restaurant glows with warm, inviting lights, old-school music, and laughter as Oliver pulls into a parking spot. My shoulders start to relax as I hop out of the car. This is where I wanted to be tonight. As I tug Oliver toward the diner, he glances at Pat's ice cream parlor next door and frowns. "Are you going to the right place?"

I smile. "Absolutely. They have the best fries."

Oliver frowns. "You said we're getting dessert."

I remember I thought the same thing when Gabriel introduced

me to dipping my French fries in ice cream. "The ice cream parlor and diner are owned by the same family—the two businesses are connected inside like a food hall," I explain, waving him to follow me. "Dessert is called the Pike Special. You'll see!"

As we step inside, it's an inviting scene, even with our security detail lurking in the back. People in red booths enjoying hearty burgers and even heartier laughs. Families. Couples. And toward the back, I see a tall booth and recognize Kyle and the twins, but not the people sitting across from them. I don't see Gabe, and I don't want to look obvious searching for him.

Kyle sees me and hollers my name. Billie does the same, and her twin, Jaisha, sticks her head out and gestures for me to join them. I turn to Oliver, who looks uneasy until he meets my eyes and grins reassuringly. "This reminds me of that diner we visited in Buffalo," he says.

I nudge him forward. "But no parents or press watching us," I say. No one to perform for. No one to have to impress. Although that diner had the best chicken wings.

"Abby," a voice calls from near the counter. Pat in his white cap waves hello. "Good to see you, kid. You look like you could use a Pike."

"Yes!" I glance at Oliver. "Make that two."

I turn my attention toward Kyle's table and notice everyone getting up to leave. Including Gabriel. Apparently, he was in Kyle's booth, and I couldn't see him from the entrance. Of course, he looks hot in his fitted black button-up and sneakers. Suddenly, I'm very self-conscious of how close I am to Oliver. We're practically arm in arm. Gabe offers the briefest of smiles as he walks past us. "I'm late." He taps his camera. I recall he's taking photos of the dance tonight as he rushes out of Mike's door.

Kyle offers me a fist bump. "You missed our high school paper reunion. We were brainstorming some breaking news–worthy headlines." His grin is all teeth. I notice the twins brimming with excitement. Billie rubs her hands together nervously, while Jaisha's stare is laser-focused on Oliver. I sigh. People often get that way when the dashing Oliver Darby is around.

"Sorry to miss the fun," I say, meaning it. "I was with—"

"Oliver Darby." The twins finish my sentence for me. Of course they're eager to meet Oliver. As I look around the diner, I'm greeted with more smiles and waves, except for our agents now posted at the two exits. The twins gush over Oliver—he's taller in person. He's nicer in person. Etc. Etc. We've both heard it all before.

Oliver grins. "Thanks very much, you're too kind. You girls are taller and nicer in person too," he teases. The girls sigh at the good old Oliver Darby charm. My bestie knows how to please.

Meanwhile, an apologetic look crosses Kyle's face. "We have to take off. Our friend's band is about to perform."

"Oh, no worries. We're just getting dessert to go," I say. "See you at the dance."

Kyle nods. "Sweet. And maybe do us a favor and save a dance for our boy Gabe. He's been grumpy all night."

"And save me a dance too." Jaisha winks at Oliver. I watch as the group heads out. I'm grateful Oliver doesn't say anything about Kyle's comment, but I feel his eyes on me.

"Abby Special," Pat hollers. I'm grateful for the distraction. I head to the counter, where Pat has two large drinks in a takeaway tray and a white bag waiting for me.

I arch a brow. "An Abby Special?"

He laughs. "Yeah, it's a Pike Special, but 'to-go,' just like you."

I feign shock. "If this is your way of telling me to slow down, I get the picture."

"Not at all, my dear," says a man in a restaurant uniform. The name "Mike" is embroidered on his shirt. This must be the Mike from Mike's Biscuits. He grins as he joins Pat. "We see you and know you're going places. Just don't forget about us in Mystic Hollow."

My chest tightens with joy. "I'll never forget you." After Oliver insists on a huge tip, I wave the bag in his face as we exit.

His nose wrinkles. "Grease."

I scoff. "You mean heaven."

The town square looks like a postcard. Strings of white lights twinkle from the lampposts and the trees. Vendors sell fresh buttery popcorn from bright red carts, next to colorful stands with sugary clouds of cotton candy, boba tea, and other mouthwatering treats. A band performs on the gazebo's stage, facing the bubbling fountain and dance floor where a vibrant crowd sways to the beats.

I spot the flower displays I helped design with Mrs. Rey around the gazebo, and they look spectacular. We decided to display just a few examples at tonight's dance to promote the jubilee. The florist is nearby, and I give her a thumbs-up. It's just flowers, but it feels amazing contributing to tonight's dance. Like a little piece of me belongs here.

My heart warms at the scene before me. The dance floor has been laid on the ground, where a bunch of folks watch the performance. Several dance. "Isn't this adorable," I gush.

Oliver nods in approval. "Perfect. I'm glad we're here. I was going to tell you—"

"Abby! Oliver!" a familiar voice shouts, interrupting Oliver. Elle beckons us onto the dance floor with Tita Karra and Ruby. I can't help my large grin. I was so worried I ruined Elle's summer, but from the looks of it she's having the time of her life. "Come join us," she shrieks. Oliver waves back, pleased to see them.

Meanwhile, I hold up our dessert bag, letting her know we're going to eat first.

Oliver and I sit down on a bench. "Elle looks well," he says, and genuinely means it.

"She's having the best of times." I show him how to dip the fries in his chocolate shake. He wrinkles his nose.

"You look like you've adapted to this place too." He holds up his fry. "Not sure this is my thing, to be honest."

"What? It's sweet and savory," I say. He dips his fry and studies the drip of ice cream like it's a chemistry experiment. I demonstrate again and close my eyes to savor the magic: salty crisp fry meets rich, sweet chocolate.

A loud click and flash of light startles me.

"Didn't think you all would make it," a voice nearby says. I sigh. I don't need to look to know it's Gabriel with his camera. I swallow my fry, feeling sheepish being caught acting so silly. "I wanted to show Oliver the 'Abby Special' and the town," I say.

"Nice." Gabriel arches a thick brow as he looks at Oliver.

"Maybe it would be good for you to get to know the local businesses since you're part of the community now." But the tone in Gabriel's voice suggests Oliver isn't part of the community at all.

And Oliver knows it. His jaw hardens as he assesses Gabriel. "Actually, my uncle's resort is making progress getting to know the community." He stands up so he's eye to eye with him. "A number of businesses have decided to help him with his Fourth of July festival. In fact, we just heard from the mayor that the Commander is going to be hosting the Fourth of July fireworks display this year."

I practically jump to my feet. "What?"

Oliver doesn't look at me as he stares at Gabriel. "The Commander is going to host the Fourth of July fireworks. Mayor Lee and the management at Grand Meadows all agreed we'd be the better location."

My insides are roiling. The inn was banking on hosting the fireworks. Ruby had a meeting with the mayor this afternoon, but we never did hear how it went. And from the look on Gabriel's face, it appears he didn't hear the news either. Our silence is interrupted as a waltz begins to play. My chest tightens thinking about the last time Gabriel and I danced together. His hands intertwined with mine, heat radiating from his body and gaze. But now, there's only cold when I look at him. "I'm sorry, Gabriel—"

"It's the waltz," Gabriel says, interrupting me. "Here's your chance to finally dance under the stars."

"Gabriel, please—" I stop mid-sentence. Our eyes meet and the betrayal in Gabriel's gaze is palpable—that expression the one he wore when we first met. Two people from completely different worlds. And now my date, Oliver Darby, just announced his family has practically ruined the inn by taking the fireworks show from them.

"Practice time is over," Gabriel says, his tone final.

Oliver frowns but offers me his hand. "For once, an excellent idea." I ignore Oliver and shiver despite the summer heat. Gabe and I have been referring to our time together and our kisses as "practice" for my real boyfriend. He's always believed I would end up with Oliver.

I look at my old friend, grinning down at me. Have I believed that too?

Gabriel steps aside, sweeping an arm toward the dance floor. "After you, Pineapple Princess," he murmurs, low enough that only I can hear as Oliver leads me to the dance floor. The crowd parts like we're royalty as murmurs and cheers from partygoers fill the night air. This is it. Our entrance. Our moment. My and Oliver's adoring public, but all I can think about is a certain photographer hanging in the background and the betrayal in his eyes.

The music stops and there's a commotion on the stage. Mayor Lee has the microphone. A bright smile on his face. "Sorry to interrupt, everyone, but I want to formally acknowledge our very special guests this evening."

If everyone wasn't already paying attention to us, they are now. "We're honored to have the First Daughters with us. There's Eleanor." My sister waves with both hands, a huge grin plastered on her face, as the crowd claps. Mayor Lee chuckles and then points toward me. "And of course, Abigail Cary-Alzona with Vice

President Darby's son, Oliver. Let's welcome our guests to Mystic Hollow!"

Oliver dips his head in acknowledgment at the round of applause. I force a grin and do the same. Abigail Cary-Alzona First Daughter mode. Smile on the outside, cringe on the inside.

Mayor Lee continues, "And speaking of the Darby family, I'm pleased to share they will be hosting this year's regional fireworks show." My chest tightens as the mayor confirms what Oliver had shared moments ago. It's real. The inn lost the fireworks show.

The crowd erupts into cheers, except for a few people: Marge, who stands near the gazebo looking decidedly displeased, my family, and Gabriel and his mom.

The mayor looks up at the sky with a very pleased smile. "As a token of their new role, the Darby family has arranged for a surprise demonstration. Everyone, can you help me count down from ten?"

Oliver squeezes my hand. "Check this out, Abby. We arranged a nice touch for tonight's activities."

As the crowd reaches "one," a huge glare shoots up into the sky, followed by two others. Loud pops followed by bursts of light. My jaw drops. Oliver's family has arranged fireworks for tonight's dance. Leave it to the Darbys to make an impression with a bang. Oliver grins. "This is just a small taste of what the Fourth fireworks show will look like."

Music begins to play, and the mayor invites everyone to the dance floor as the fireworks burst above. Oliver spins me around.

Among the crowd of happy onlookers, I catch my sister looking very disappointed. And Gabriel is nowhere to be seen.

It's a struggle to dance with Oliver. Not only because I'm sick to my stomach about the devastating news he delivered to Gabriel in the most ostentatious way possible, but because I can't focus on the dance moves like I usually do. Oliver counts the steps aloud so I can hear, trying to get me to focus. He's not Gabriel. Dancing with Oliver doesn't feel natural. And the fireworks above are not helping with my footwork.

This is the scene I had envisioned in my head for years, isn't it? Fireworks and dancing. A warm summer evening, laughter, and the smell of jasmine and citronella candles. This should be the most romantic moment of my life, but by the time the song is over I find myself rushing off the dance floor.

Oliver is close behind. "Abby, are you okay?" I look over his shoulder to confirm no one is nearby, then as an extra precaution pull him behind a tree out of view. Excitement and confusion cross his face. "What are you—"

"Why did you gloat to Gabriel about the fireworks?" I interrupt him, practically stabbing a finger into his chest.

"Abby, you'll wrinkle my shirt." He laughs nervously.

His shirt? Is that what he's worried about? I throw up my arms. "You knew Gabe's family was trying to host the fireworks display. His inn needed that boost to help keep their family business afloat."

Oliver arches a brow before speaking. "I didn't know anything about his family business. Honest. Our only intention is to help the community by sponsoring the fireworks." As he talks about the facilities at the Commander, I'm reminded how skilled Oliver is at talking with people. Charming, strategic—the kind of boy who was born to shake hands and win votes. The kind of boy I'm supposed to end up with.

"Abby, if Gabriel's family hosted, they'd have to pour in huge amounts of resources. Fireworks are expensive. This is a win-win for everyone," he says, ending his speech.

"This is a win-win for everyone?" I mimic Oliver's clipped voice.

He makes a face. "Seriously, Abby? Did you just try to impersonate me?"

I groan, doing my best to compose myself. "I just wanted you to hear how ridiculous this situation is. The owners of Grand Meadows were going to foot the bill," I say through gritted teeth. "Gabe's family wasn't going to pay for the show. This is a win for you and a loss for Gabriel."

"You mean a loss for his business. Besides, do you really blame Grand Meadows for going with us? They're a small business too."

My silence is my answer. Of course Grand Meadows would prefer to not foot the bill. Going with Oliver's family means they don't have to spend another dime. That's why Grand Meadows chose his family's resort.

But the anger in me is still bubbling. I ask Shaw to get the car. My agent, who's been a respectful distance away from me the entire night, suddenly becomes visible.

"Abby," Oliver calls after me. "Let's talk."

But I'm done talking. I need to find Gabriel and we need to figure out a plan. Now.

I am not giving up on the jubilee.

CHAPTER 25

My hands fly across my phone, texting Erin, my mom's old campaign staffer, for any assistance or ideas they might have for the jubilee. It's early evening on the West Coast. I know they're definitely still answering work calls, even on a Saturday.

Shaw drives the SUV in silence, but I catch the worry in his eyes each time he glances at me in the rearview mirror. When we arrive at the Mystic Hollow Inn, I walk inside to find Ruby and Tita Karra sitting together on the couch, cups of tea in hand. I'm embarrassed to interrupt them, as the two look like they're having some quiet time together. Ruby manages a smile. "Abby, dear. I thought you were still at the dance."

"I came back early," I say, wanting to avoid her sad eyes. "Is Gabriel around?"

Ruby clears her throat. "He went outside. Not sure if he's here still."

I hesitate. "I'm sorry about the fireworks show. I know you really worked hard to be the host."

"It's a real blow, but we're going to be fine. Don't you worry." Her tone doesn't convince me. Ruby nods at the door. "I think Gabe mentioned doing some evening shots of the inn."

I apologize one more time and head out. The night air is thick with humidity and loud with the trill of cicadas chirping from the groves of trees in the distance. The moonlight casts a brilliant white glow on the grassy fields surrounding the house. I check the back of the inn and see Gabe's green truck empty and dark. Meaning he's outside on the property somewhere.

There's only so many places he could be. I check the picnic area to the side of the house. Then the Honeymoon Cottage, where my phone pings. It's the one place on the property where we have the barest of phone reception.

Erin has responded to me, hopefully with good news about possible jubilee participation, but I'll open their message later. Gabe is my priority now.

I glance at the garden, but I know he isn't there. I walk toward the giant oak tree with the inn's well-worn tree swing. As I approach the large, sturdy tree and the firepit and logs surrounding it, my chest tightens as the happier memories of this place come to mind. It's only been a few weeks, yet the inn already feels like home.

The creak of metal confirms my hunch as I see the white swing swaying back and forth. Gabriel lies sprawled across it, eyes fixed on the stars, his body bathed in silver moonlight. My pulse quickens at the sight of him, here alone. Just the two of us, in this place that means more than words.

"Abby, what are you doing here?" Gabe says. His voice has a slight tremor. We stare sadly at one another until I'm finally able to respond.

"I didn't know Oliver's family had booked the fireworks display," I tell him. "I'm so sorry."

With a loud sigh, he returns his gaze to the sky. "It's not your fault, Abby."

My stomach knots up. "Still, I feel awful. There has to be something we can do."

He shakes his head, resigned. "I spoke to Mom when I got back. Mayor Lee broke the news to her this afternoon. All day she's been getting messages from vendors that they're leaving our event and going to participate in the Commander Resort's festival."

"But we have the pie competition and the flowers," I say, my voice cracking.

Gabriel's shoulders slump. "They're leaving. They know people will spend their time and money at the Commander's bigger event. The business council is considering leaving too."

My jaw drops. "We can't give up. We'll figure something out. We'll have more attractions at our event."

The swing creaks loudly as Gabriel sits up. "Abby, I think you and your network have done enough. We already knew the inn was in trouble. Nothing has changed our situation."

I frown. "So, what? You're going to just give up?"

He runs a hand through his hair. "I don't know, Abby. My mom and I will work something out." But from his tone, I can tell he doesn't even believe himself.

I remember the text from Erin that I received by the honeymoon suite. I check the message, hoping there's some good news.

My jaw drops at the image on my phone. It's me holding a red Solo cup, with the most unflattering face, and dancing at Kyle's lake house. And there are more photos. I swipe and see me making kissy faces at the camera with Gabriel in several selfies. And our nighttime astrophotography photo shoot. Me posing in Gabe's hoodie atop the honeymoon suite. It's so oversized it looks like I'm wearing only the hoodie. Gabe and me picnicking on the river, looking very cozy.

I swipe and swipe. Finally, there's photos of me arguing with Oliver just earlier at the Founder's Day Dance.

These images just dropped, Erin wrote with several brain-exploding emojis. It feels like time stands still as I study each photo like a nightmare unfolding before my eyes. Of course, I have no reception so I can't call them to ask where they saw these photos, but I'm sure by now they're everywhere.

My hands shake. That photo. Gabriel took it. He must've taken the other images too. I look up and meet his gaze, a fiery fury coursing through my veins. He's far enough that he can't see the contents of my phone, but he must know something's off because he's completely still, with a confused look on his face. "Abby, what is it?"

I hold up my phone and show him the images. "These photos just showed up online," I say. He squints as I scroll through. His eyes flick across the images—pausing on the photos taken at our private picnic.

"Where did those come from? How—"

I jerk my phone away from him. "You were that upset with me you had to post these photos?"

Gabe's eyes widen as he shakes his head. "No, Abby. This is some kind of mistake."

I show him the selfie of us making kissy faces. "Who else had this photo?"

He stares, like a campaign worker caught without a statement. "I don't know—"

I scroll through the photos again. The screenshot of one post shows five hundred comments, but I know better than to read them.

Loud footsteps approach and I turn to see Shaw. "Excuse me, Abby. You have a call from the White House."

My blood chills. How do I explain this to my mother? She trusted me to behave out here. Those photos are completely taken out of context, but even if I explain I know the damage is done.

"We didn't do anything wrong," Gabe says.

I give him the most withering look. "Gabe, I'm sorry about your family's business, but how could you do this? I trusted you."

"Abby, wait—" Gabe calls after me. But I don't stop walking. I need to talk to my mom. I need to get away. I follow Shaw into his SUV, where my mom is on the line on a satellite phone. I settle into the leather seat, wiping the hot tears on my face. Shaw hands me the phone.

"Abby, what on earth is going on out there?" my mother exclaims.

"Mom," I sniffle, unable to collect my thoughts. I gaze at the inn with its white-wood siding, softly weathered after decades of sun and love. The wide wraparound porch that always feels like an open-armed welcome. I've grown so much these past few weeks at Mystic Hollow. I've done amazing things that I'll never forget. But this isn't where I belong. This isn't my world. Gabe is right. Practice is over.

"Mom, I want to come home."

CHAPTER 26

I run up the inn's stairs one last time to grab the essentials from my room. I take a photograph with my mind to remember our Blue Ridge Suite. The elegant yet cozy room was my home for these past few weeks. I remember how isolated I felt when I first arrived, and now just how much I've grown to appreciate the simple space, the slow stretches of time.

Down the hallway and the staircase, my chest tightens as I pass the photo of Gabriel's grandparents. I don't stop to study it like I usually do. Besides, it's not like the image of the happy couple swinging isn't burned into my mind.

At the foyer, Ruby, Tita Karra, and Elle are assembled. Elle and I give a quick but gracious goodbye to Ruby. My eyes water. Her hug is strong and comforting. She's too polite to pry further when we say our parents need us home. "We enjoyed hosting you. Come back anytime," Ruby says.

Tita Karra whispers in my ear as she hugs me. "We'll talk to him and get to the bottom of the situation." My throat tightens, wondering what kind of trouble Gabe will face with his photos. "I'll come to visit you as soon as I can."

I bury my head under her chin. "You'll be fine," she says, lifting my chin. "You'll both be fine." I nod, knowing she isn't talking about me and Elle; she's talking about me and Gabriel.

As I head to our SUV, I spot Gabriel. He's started a fire at the firepit. He's too far away for me to see the details of his face, but his shoulders are slumped as he stands up. My feet stop and we stare at each other from a distance. The fire casts him in a red-and-orange glow like the sunlight when we kissed on the hilltop. I blink angry tears away, hating how I looked forward to his company, how I kissed those lips, how I trusted him.

Gabe raises his hand to say goodbye, but I look away. There's nothing further to say. I hop into the car next to Elle, slamming the door with a satisfying thud.

Shaw peers at me from the rearview mirror. "I can call in some favors? Get his truck towed, or at least a few parking tickets," he offers.

"What? No." My laugh is rueful. "He's not worth it. Besides, it was always going to end between me and him." My voice cracks. It's a true statement. We were never going to be in each other's lives after this summer. I just didn't think it would end this way.

This time I see Nessa looking at me in the mirror. Eyebrows pinched and lips pursed like she's holding back her thoughts. Finally, she taps Shaw to start the car.

I sigh, relieved to go home. Elle leans her head on my shoulder as we speed away. At least I'll always have my sister.

It's after midnight when Elle and I get back to the White House. Our parents are still up, waiting in the Residence's living room on the sofa. They clearly had a late night too, still in their formal wear, though Mom's heels are kicked off and Dad's dress shirt is rolled up at the sleeves. If we hadn't come home, I bet they'd be upstairs by now.

Dad envelops us in a big hug. Mom joins in and I'm feeling ten again, when we used to have these big group hugs. I'm sad when Dad lets go and Mom pulls me and Elle to sit between them. We're silent a moment, not sure where to start. Finally, I go, because the tension is real.

"Mom, before you say anything, you have to know those photos are completely out of context. I was not drinking at that party. Just because a cup is red doesn't mean it's got alcohol. And those pictures with Oliver were from a totally private moment and we had an argument. It happens with you and Dad; it happens with friends. We're allowed to disagree just like everyone else."

"And the photos with Gabe?" Dad asks.

"I know how it looks—but it's not like that. We were just being goofy. I had like three iced coffees and multiple brain freezes and we were just being silly."

"Seriously, Dad. If you had the double mocha caramel coffees, you'd be a little bonkers too," Elle chimes in.

My father shakes his head. "Elle, why don't you go to bed, honey. Your mom and I need to speak with your sister."

Elle pouts. "Dad, Gabe's a good guy."

"Eleanor," my mother warns, voice sharp and cold. She doesn't need to be the most powerful person in the world to make her point. Her disappointed-mom tone is good enough. Elle rises grumpily and stomps out. I watch her go with some regret. It would've been nice having some backup.

My mom leans back. Her hand goes to her forehead, and I feel instantly guilty. I've broken rule number one. Mom has so much on her plate and for me to give her another headache makes me feel terrible. "Mom, I'm so sorry. I didn't think Gabe would ever dream of releasing those images. He was upset because Oliver's family stole the fireworks show from his inn."

"I spoke to Ben," my mom says, referring to Oliver's dad. "He explained to me the situation with the Calabreses and their jubilee."

I sigh. "That's the same event I was volunteering to help."

Her laugh is empty. "I'm sorry, Abby, I had no idea there was such a conflict of interest with the inn and resort hosting dueling festivals. Otherwise, I wouldn't have agreed to let you volunteer."

"Conflict of interest?"

She rubs her temples. "I don't want to go into politics, dear. These photos complicate matters for me and the vice president.

"Tomorrow my staff is going on the Sunday morning news shows. They were supposed to talk about my WAKE-UP Bill, but now they're prepping for questions about my daughter's relationship with the vice president's son and her wild party antics."

"Mom, none of this is real news," I complain.

"No, it's not, Abby," my dad says. "But you know people will do anything to paint your mother in a bad light." He waves a hand in the air like he's reading a headline. "FDOTUS Protesting Mother's Economic Policies. FDOTUS Doesn't Agree with

Mom's Economic Adviser." He sounds defeated. "Or just good old-fashioned FDOTUS Caught Cheating on the Vice President's Son."

I look at my mother, who shakes her head in dismay. I know she hates the false coverage too. "Why? What business do they have asking about your teenage daughter's friends?" I whimper.

"None," my parents say at the same time.

My dad leans forward. "But it's salacious clickbait. And these kinds of things were another reason we insisted you're not allowed to have a boyfriend until you're at least a senior in high school."

"Mom, is it possible people are blowing this up bigger than it really is?" I ask. "I was just helping a small-town festival."

"I know, sweetie," Mom says, tone sharp. "But you competing against the Darbys is news to some people."

"It wasn't anything like that. It's completely blown out of proportion."

She nods emphatically. "And that's what we're going to say. We're going to remind everyone you're a seventeen-year-old teenage girl and your life is totally off-limits."

My dad cuts in. "But as we do damage control, this puts your mother's own agenda at risk, and we lose precious time—"

"When we're on defense," I say, finishing his sentence. "I know." I cross my arms and look away. "When I'm the president's daughter I don't get to make mistakes."

My mother sighs. "I'm sorry, Abby."

My eyes blur. "I just wanted a normal summer." My mother pulls me in, and I can't help myself as I nestle my head on her shoulder, dripping tears on her gown.

"I never thought Gabriel would share those photos. I trusted him."

She rubs my back. "Honey, honey. It's okay. You can't read minds."

"And to be fair, we don't know if Gabe was behind the photos," my dad says.

"They're selfies taken on his phone," I say sadly. "No one else would have them."

Mom nods. "I agree with your father. We don't know for sure it was Gabe, but whoever turned in those photos probably made a lot of money."

She doesn't need to say anything further. I've connected the dots. Gabriel's family business is struggling. The jubilee is practically tanked, and they needed the money.

"Gabe has a history of breaking news stories. Like the time he busted the congressman," I say. I place my head in my hands. This whole time he was pretending to want to go to art school, but maybe he was really biding his time, and his plan was always to expose me.

"Listen to me, Abby," my mom says, voice firm but loving. "You never asked for this life. Your father and I know you will make mistakes. We all do. It's human. It's natural. We want you to have as normal a life as possible."

"She's right," my dad adds, his tone gentler. "Our communications team is the best in the world. They'll handle the press—just like they did with the pineapple story. But sweetheart, for the next couple of days you'll need to follow our lead."

I sniffle. "How is that different from every other day, Dad?"

My parents exchange looks, but there's nothing they can say. A bitter taste fills my mouth. Rapunzel has returned to the White House. And she's going to keep boys like Gabe out of her tower.

★ ★ ★

I spend the next day wallowing in my room, wearing my fluffy tie-dyed robe and watching old episodes of *The Great British Baking Show*. Oliver finally stops texting me after his twentieth try. His texts alternate between "are you okay" and "these images were photoshopped, right?" But I don't have the mental space to talk to him or anyone now.

Dad has been checking on me periodically. Even the promise of ice cream doesn't move me. The only thing that gets my attention is Elle, and that's because her bedroom is right across from mine and she's quite loud. I let her slink into my room, and we sit on the bed together silently. "It wasn't him," she finally says.

"Elle," I warn.

"I don't believe it." She's insistent. "Why would he do that?"

I sigh. "His family needed the money."

"But he was really into you. It was so obvious."

"Elle, I told you we were just practicing." My face reddens I'm so embarrassed.

She blinks. "You still believe that?"

"My unofficial bucket list," I sputter. "He saw it and knew all the things there, first kiss, dance under the stars. Except we mutually agreed that I was supposed to do those items with my boyfriend." I shudder. "And since he wasn't technically my boyfriend, we called those kisses practice . . . y'know. For the real thing."

Elle's eyes are wide. "Is this an upperclassman thing? Why do you all have to make things so confusing?"

"They were his words," I say, frowning. Or were they mine?

"Whatever you two had, it was real. I felt it. Didn't you?" I stare at my hands, my throat welling up. I did feel it. It did feel real. More real than anything I've felt with Oliver. With anyone. I bury my head in my pillow and let Elle turn up the music.

★ ★ ★

On Monday morning, a firm knock on my door startles me out of bed at seven a.m. I recognize the voice of Tom, one of Mom's social secretaries, at the door. I groan. Now I know I'm back at the White House.

I pull on my robe and open my door, where he's standing in a tailored suit.

"Good morning, Abby. I'm so glad you're back with us," he says with a toothy smile.

"What do you want?"

He chuckles. "I'll cut to the chase. Your mother thought it would be a good idea for you to keep busy today." He hands me a sheet of paper with a list. He knows me and my preference for lists quite well.

He goes over the day's agenda—an eat-healthy initiative, tea with a foreign dignitary. The last item makes him grin.

"As you know, your mother's initiative in the arts has created a presidential young scholars' program. A group of those young scholars will be visiting the White House in a couple of hours, and we'd love to have you meet this distinguished group."

I cross my arms. "Basically, she wants a bunch of photo ops showing I'm 'back to normal.'"

He blinks. "It's a very strategic schedule, Abby."

"Sure," I mutter, taking the list. I shut the door. Back to First Daughter mode.

CHAPTER 27

The morning goes by in a blur. Not five minutes after Tom leaves, I hear another knock. It's one of Mom's staff with a dress for me to wear. I don't recognize it, so it must mean our comms people are being extra attentive to my presentation today.

It's a classic Ralph Lauren green-and-navy-blue dress. It's stylish and cute, but after wearing tank tops and shorts for the past month, I'm feeling some whiplash. Another staff member stops by to help with my hair. I sigh. Time to switch to "autopilot" as I get told what to wear, where to go, and what to say.

Shortly after I'm dressed, I'm led to the Treaty Room to discuss Dad's eating-healthy initiative. I admire the delicious breakfast food displayed, but it's a stark contrast to the stacks of pancakes and ham biscuits I've been noshing on the past few weeks. I smile and say the minimum as my dad leads the discussion. One reporter dares to ask me a question, and it's simply, "How are you feeling today, Abby?"

"I'm well, thank you for asking." Smile, nod. Done.

"How's your summer going?" another asks.

I pause. Not great, to be honest. A boy who I trusted betrayed me and yet somehow, I can't stop thinking of him. "Also well," I say.

"Any comment about your relationship with Oliver Darby?" the reporter follows up.

My body tenses as all the cameras in the room focus on me. I guess I'll be making the five o'clock news again. I force another smile. "Oliver and I are doing well."

"How about we focus on an issue important to families and children?" my father interrupts. Dad meets my gaze and I flash him an appreciative smile. I do my best to fade into the background.

★ ★ ★

The tea with visiting dignitaries in the White House Treaty Room is a prim and proper affair, which I pass with flying colors because it requires me to sit pretty, nod, smile, and offer gracious thanks while my mother leads the discussion. And all the reporters here have the sense to focus on Mom and her guests.

I sit and hold my teacup as I've been taught. Only once does my hand feel shaky. Fortunately, one of the staff is nearby and offers me a refill so I can lower my cup. The tea runs five minutes behind schedule.

"Thank you, Abby, for doing this. We won't be in DC much longer," my mom says in my ear before leaving for her next appointment.

She's referring to our trip to Italy right after the White House Independence Day Gala, but it's not hard for my mind to think more dramatically. We only have three more years before her second term is done. And for two of those years, I'll be away at college. And then in a high-powered career. And then the other half of a power couple. My life is already planned. It's practically written in the stars.

A firm hand taps my shoulder. "Hey, do you want me to find that journalist who asked about your summer and throw him out?" I laugh and gaze at Shaw, whose arched brow looks like a weapon.

"No, let's just force him to eat pineapple pizza," I joke before sighing. "I'm pretty sure my next appointment is starting soon. Better go before Mom's team has a heart attack."

It's not until we enter the White House Blue Room that I remember the group we're meeting next. It's the US Presidential Art Scholars.

I'm happy to see they're closer to my age. College students from across the country who've won scholarships for different forms of arts. I'm thankful none of them give any I-saw-you-in-the-news vibes as we shake hands.

I meet painters, sculptors, poets, and photography scholars, which of course makes me think of Gabriel. As my father speaks, I smile as I listen in the background.

I try not to be awkward as they talk about their work, but all I can think about is Gabriel. How much he would enjoy being here with his people. And how I wish I could call him up and FaceTime him. But you're not supposed to want to talk with the guy who betrayed you. You shouldn't care about his future. He's not supposed to be running through your mind like this.

"For what it's worth, the artistry of the photographs is first class," one of the group's chaperones says to me.

The voice is familiar. My father continues to address the students, so a quick side conversation is fine. "I'm sorry, Professor . . ." My eyes widen with recognition. It's the art philanthropist from Italy who Gabe and I met at the state dinner.

"Luca Ferro," he says with a grin.

"Of course, so good to see you again," I say.

He laughs. "I just snuck in now. The Presidential Scholars will be doing an international exchange with the Firenze Accademia."

I recognize that name immediately. The Firenze Accademia is the art school Gabe wants to go to. I compose myself. "Which photographs do you mean?" I ask.

He looks apologetic. "The ones about your summer." His smile is soft. "I think you're entitled to be a kid just like any other. And I'm sorry those photos are not ones you wanted shared, but I thought you'd like to know that a few of them are very, very good." He grins. "I remember meeting this young man at dinner with you. From the way he spoke, I could tell he knew a great deal about photography. Now I see the evidence."

My ears perk up. "Please tell me more, Signor Ferro."

"The night sky, astrophotography in particular, it takes a lot of skill. And to also have you appear in the photograph as well." He shakes his head with a respectful gaze. "He's quite talented. I'd love to see more of his work."

I blush. I recall that evening so vividly, but I had no idea how much effort Gabe was putting into those shots to capture them—it's flattering to think about it. And for Signor Ferro to commend him and wish to see more of his work? It would be great to pass this news to Gabe, wouldn't it? Ferro is exactly the kind of person who could help Gabe get into the Accademia. My belly flutters with anxiety. What if I contact Gabe, but he ignores me? And why would I talk to him after he sold me out?

"Thank you, Signor Ferro. It's so kind of you to say, but Gabe and me . . . Well, you saw those photos. We're not exactly talking . . ." My voice trails off.

He grins. "Of course. But I also saw the two of you at dinner. You two are beautiful dance partners." He produces a card from his blazer pocket. "Just in case." I smile politely as I accept the card. I imagine it burning a hole in my pocket.

I'm mindlessly staring at the cake showcase on TV when I see the reflection of someone gliding into my room. "Ano 'yan? Is that supposed to be a troll?" Tita Karra asks, pointing at the lumpy green cake figure on the screen.

"It's an alien," I tell her. "The theme for this round is Out of This World."

"If this was a Filipino contestant, they would've made a kapre. They're green and lumpy." She plops on my bed. Seeing Tita Karra makes my stomach lurch. She's transformed from her Mystic Hollow look, jeans and plaid, to a chic and polished pantsuit. She grabs my hand and squeezes it. "Come out to the living room. We're setting up for Monopoly."

Monopoly? Does she want to rub Gabe's favorite board game in my face? "I'm not in the mood," I say.

She pulls me up. "You will be when I share some news." I

follow her to the living room. It's an inviting scene. Mom, Dad, and Elle in pajamas, sitting around a coffee table. It's so rare we spend time like this together I feel guilty for wanting to sit this out.

Mom smiles at me and Tita Karra. "Oh good. I was in the mood to embarrass my sister this evening."

Tita Karra rolls her eyes but sits on a cushion eagerly. "Speaking of embarrassing," she says. "I have some information you'll want to hear about the photographs of Abby."

The room goes pin-drop silent. My mom squints. "Do I need to get our lawyers on the phone?"

"No." Tita Karra waves her hand dismissively. "It wasn't Gabe who sold the photos."

Elle screeches. "I knew it!"

My mouth goes dry. "But those were his photos. I was in them. I know he took them."

Tita Karra nods. "Gabriel took the photos, but he didn't sell them. It was Kyle."

I rock back. "Kyle? How did he—"

"Kyle worked with Gabriel on a few news stories. He still had access to Gabriel's cloud storage. He downloaded those photos without Gabriel's knowledge."

I cover my face. "Why would Kyle do this?" But the answer comes to me immediately. Kyle wanted another big story like the one he and Gabriel broke about the congressman.

I look at Tita Karra for confirmation. "So it wasn't Gabriel."

She nods and rummages through her purse and puts a manila folder on the table, and then gestures for me to open it. I swallow as I empty the contents onto the Monopoly board. Photos spill onto the coffee table. They're photos of me. My mother holds them up and murmurs with appreciation. Even Dad comments that the kid has an eye.

I stare at the photos, me awash in sunlight, eating ice cream. Quiet, private, happy moments and pure elation. All the things I felt when I was with him.

The last photo in the stack nearly slips from my hands. It's me, sitting at the edge of a hill, eyes on the horizon. My profile, my pose . . . it's identical to the one of my great-grandmother Liwayway when she was my age. Tears sting my eyes. Gabe remembered that photo from the night we first met. And somehow, he re-created it—a quiet tribute to her, and to my family's history.

My mom's eyes water as I show her the image. I gasp finding writing on the back: *Abby, I promised I wouldn't share any of these without your approval, but I thought you'd like copies to add to your family collection. —G*

P.S. I think you have a lot in common with your brave lola.

I smile through my tears as I stare at the stacks and stacks of images in shock. It must've taken him days to pull this together. Some of the photos were on his digital camera, but for others he used his dad's analog camera and would've had to develop them in a darkroom.

My mother squeezes my shoulder. "He's very talented," she offers with a look of appreciation and apology.

"He is." I hold up an image of me smiling in front of the inn's pineapple sign. "These photos, the Mystic Hollow Inn, and the jubilee. They all represent the things you and I love about this country: remembering our history, building community, and serving our neighbors whether they're in a city or a small town," I say. "Gabe was able to capture that spirit—along with some carefree summer days. What's more American than teenagers enjoying some independence?" I pause and am thrilled as my family's slow clap turns into a thunderous applause straight from a teen flick. I smile, glad to see Gabriel's photos don't inspire just me.

My chest tightens as I think of him and Mystic Hollow. I fix my attention on Tita. "How's the jubilee coming along?"

She bites her lip. "After the fireworks show going to the Darbys and the controversy of the photos, Ruby decided to cancel the jubilee. The guests who did book with them are canceling their rooms."

I cover my face. "I ruined their business."

"Honey, no, you did not," Mom responds gently. "It sounds like they've been in trouble for a while."

"I just wish there was something I could—" I stop mid-sentence as I remember my own advice: It's not what you got, it's who you know.

I turn to my mother. "Mom, I have a proposal for you."

CHAPTER 28

It takes less than twenty-four hours for my mom and her staff to approve my plan, which included receiving an apology letter from Kyle five hours ago that was shared with the press.

Dad and I are currently in the White House kitchen, pulling out cookie dough. Mom smells like coffee and doughnuts when I hug her, a sign that she's been extra nice to her staff when she's had last-minute requests. Giving people sweets as an incentive is still something she does even as president. "Mom, thank you, thank you, salamat po." I happy dance in my slippers.

"Mahal kita, anak," Mom says as she pulls me close. I sigh, feeling her love oozing from every pore.

"Let's give the Calabreses a call?" she says, motioning me to follow her. It's a little after five p.m. The plan is a no-go if Ruby doesn't agree. The sooner they agree the better, but my chest tightens, and I know what I must do. "Actually, Mom and Dad, there's something I want to do in person."

I give my father a pleading look. "Daddy, remember when you missed my fifth birthday? I never called in a favor after that."

“Sweetie, you know I was in space.” But he looks pained, and I know he still feels guilty.

I got him.

★ ★ ★

Dad lands his personal aircraft in the Mystic Hollow regional airport one and a half hours later. The agents on our plane disembark, including Shaw and Nessa, who meet with a local team that has our cars ready.

If he weren’t so harried looking, I’d think Shaw was happy to be back. I breathe in the fresh air and admire the summer sky—still streaked with orange fading to purple.

My father disembarks from his plane, stretching and looking happy that he was able to flex his pilot muscles tonight. I wrap him in a big hug. “Daddy, do you mind if I . . .”

He smiles. “Go on, honey. Finish your mission.” I peck him on the cheek and I’m off. Nessa has the SUV door open. My stomach fills with anxiety and excitement as we pull in front of the inn. I’m happy to see the windows, framed by their now-familiar shutters, lit with a warm and inviting glow.

Ruby flies out the front door. “Abby,” she gushes. “You all didn’t have to do this.” Then, lowering her voice, she adds, “Your mother called us.” And I know what a big deal it is when the president—my mom—makes that call.

“We wanted to,” I insist, squeezing her hand.

“I’m so sorry for everything. The photos. The invasion of your privacy.”

"You have nothing to apologize for. The past few weeks have been the best in my life. It wasn't your fault," I say, glancing around. "And it wasn't Gabriel's."

Ruby steps back with a knowing smile. "Gabe's not here. He said something about *cosmic photographs* before he left. If you know where to find him, then I think you should be the one to break the news," she says with a wink.

I'm glad it's evening, hoping it covers my flushed face. If Gabe is photographing the cosmos, then I know exactly where he is.

★ ★ ★

The Milky Way must be visible tonight. The memory rushes back to me of Gabriel describing the astronomical event he wanted to capture on film—he called it a portrait framed by the cosmos. The business card for Signor Ferro burns in my pocket. I can't wait to give it to him.

Shaw and Nessa don't look thrilled when I tell them where we're going. "It's an open field in the middle of nowhere," I say.

"Exactly," Shaw grumbles. "My allergies are already protesting."

Nessa grins. "Stop it," she chides. "We wish you and Gabe good luck."

"We may even reconsider his code name," Shaw adds.

I laugh. "Actually, I think Rascal is growing on him."

The drive up the hill is dark, windy, and a bit nerve-racking, not just because of the treetops blocking the night sky but also because of the anticipation of apologizing to Gabe. What if he doesn't accept my apology? What if he's realized being friends with me is too hard? I've spoken in front of national TV cameras, stood on debate stages, yet somehow telling Gabe how I feel is the scariest thing I've ever done.

Finally, we reach the gravelly parking lot where—just as I pictured it—Gabe's green truck is parked. The field nearby is away from as much light pollution and people as possible. A place he'd never taken anyone before—until meeting me. Gabe made changes I never appreciated. How could I have not noticed this before?

I have the wrong kind of shoes on as I jog through the trees. My wedge sandals wobble with every step, but even Clumsyrella Abby isn't stopping now. I push through the branches and suddenly there it is: the meadow. I stop in my tracks. Soft, tall grass and a gentle, warm breeze brush against my bare legs. If the meadow was a golden haven at sunset, at night it's a starlit dreamscape. The sky is so bright and alive, I feel like I could reach up and touch the brilliant, milky-white band stretching across it and walk its trails of stars like a path into the universe. I'm so distracted it takes me a minute to realize Gabe is nowhere in sight.

But this is where he said he'd take his astrophotography photos, isn't it? My chest feels hollow as doubt creeps in. We were taking practice photos at the honeymoon suite, but I could've sworn he said he would come here for the shower. Did I get the wrong location?

I scan the meadow and see some rocks I hadn't noticed before sticking up where the hill begins to slope down. I squint and my heart races. A camera bag is sitting atop the rock. My legs are moving before my mind even registers. A camera bag. He's here. He's here! I'm racing toward the rock.

"Gabriel, where are—" I screech as I trip over a rock. My arms fly wildly, trying to regain balance.

One moment I'm flying—then I'm not. I gasp, realizing I've landed somewhere warm, solid, and familiar. His comforting scent of mint gum and smoky wood wraps around me.

I lift my head from Gabriel's chest and peer up at his amused eyes. "Hi," I whisper.

"Hi back." His brows furrow. "Are you okay?"

"I am, but my shoe isn't." I lift my foot where the strap on my sandal has broken.

He chuckles. "So, we broke in those hiking boots because . . . ?"

I wiggle in his arms. "True, but where's the fun in that? Besides, I already checked 'nature-y' off my list." I take a deep breath. "But I'm not here to talk about my to-do list or my shoes."

He helps me to my feet. The amusement in his eyes quickly melts into confusion.

"Why are you here?"

My body trembles, feeling more nervous now than when I give a nationally televised interview. "I wanted to apologize for assuming you were the one to post the photos."

His gaze sharpens. "It was Kyle. He wanted to relive his big journalism scoop."

My head bows. "I know. He sent my mother an apology letter. But I shouldn't have . . . I jumped to conclusions without even talking with you."

He sighs. "Abby, I've known you for only a few weeks and I've seen the pressure you live under. I understand why you thought the way you did. You didn't have to come here to tell me this. A text or DM would've been fine."

I scoff. "You want me to just slide into your DMs to apologize?"

He shoves his hands into his pockets. "We both knew this was temporary. Your future is mapped out. Your summer is all set. You're making progress on that list of yours . . . you don't need me for Operation Bucket List." He falters. "Not that you need me."

My eyes narrow. "Of course I don't need you to rescue my list, but I really, really wanted your help." I put a hand on his arm. "We made a deal. I gave you permission to use those photos for your portfolio. You promised to help me finish what I started."

He arches a brow. "We've completed almost everything on your list. I thought we did pretty good."

I place a hand on his cheek. "There's one more we can add now." Before he can say anything, I tiptoe up to kiss him and melt into that magical, safe, and fiery place.

Finally, he pulls away. "Are you saying this kiss isn't practice?" he asks.

I stare deeply into his eyes. "This is definitely not practice . . . if that's okay with you?"

Gabriel's hands circle around my waist and he pulls me close.

When we finally come up for air, his hands reach mine. He guides my left hand to his shoulder, then gently takes my right hand, extending our arms into a dance position. "How about we complete another bucket list item?" he asks.

And we dance under the stars.

CHAPTER 29

My eyes flutter open as sunlight creeps through red curtains. I blink, trying to remember where I am, and my gaze finally lands on a heart-shaped pillow on a nearby couch, which is the perfect reminder.

I chuckle. With the inn's manor house fully booked with my mother's advance team and press pool, I've been assigned to stay the night in Mystic Hollow's Honeymoon Cottage, which is isolated and away from the frenzy. And a location that Shaw and Nessa prefer.

Sneaking out of a tiny cabin—with a team of agents monitoring every inch—is not an easy feat. Not that I was planning on going anywhere after my dance under the stars with Gabe.

I smile, recalling how we spun and swayed beneath the night sky, then collapsed on his blanket to gaze at the stars.

My bed jiggles as my sister hops on. Elle is wearing the sneakers I should've been wearing last night. "If you're going to do a grand gesture, at least wear the proper foot attire."

I give her the stink eye. "I couldn't focus on anything other than getting to Gabe."

This earns me a croon, plus a "that is sooo romantic" from her. I give my sister a glance and realize she's already dressed for the day. "Why didn't you wake me up?"

She twirls a strand of her hair. "You looked like you needed your beauty sleep after a late night." I throw a pillow at her. "Elle! We have a lot to do."

A knock on the cabin door interrupts us. "Don't open the door," I tell Elle. "I'm not ready for visitors." She rolls her eyes and does the exact opposite of what I've asked.

Tita Karra smiles in the doorway. "Goodness, I miss you two. The manor house is so loud."

"How is Ruby doing?" I ask as she walks in. "I hope it's not too much for them?"

"Are you kidding? The two of them are happier than I've seen them in a while. It's been a long time since their hotel has been fully booked."

Her hands land on her hips. "Abby, how come you're not dressed?"

"Tita, she had a late night," Elle teases.

Someone clears their throat. My heart leaps seeing who it is. "Hope I'm not interrupting?" Gabe asks in the doorway. He's carrying a tray of coffee and a box of doughnuts. Elle's eyes light up.

"Mayor Lee is here and brought some treats," he says as Elle takes the food off his hands. Behind him are Jaisha and Billie, holding more goodies.

The twins look supremely apologetic as they duck their heads inside. I gesture for them to join us inside the cabin. Billie enters first. "We're so sorry about Kyle and the photos."

"It wasn't your fault," I say.

Jaisha shakes her head. "We're sort of responsible. I mean, I am. I'd been egging Kyle on about being a one-hit wonder and I probably reminded him about having access to Gabe's cloud during a nasty staff meeting."

Billie arches a brow. "Probably? You said Gabe's newspaper folder had more talent after one semester than Kyle did his entire life."

Jaisha shrugged. "Well, it's true."

I chuckle. "It's all good. I think things ended better than could be expected." I glance at Gabe, whose dazzling smile melts me.

Jaisha makes an *ooh la la* sound. "Does that mean things with you and Oliver are over?"

"There never was a me and Oliver," I tell them.

Billie hides a grin behind her hand while Jaisha leans in. "Really. How would you like to clear the record with me—with an exclusive interview?"

"Jaisha," Gabe warns.

She shrugs. "Thought I'd try." She nods at her twin, and the two of them leave to join the other volunteers. I peek out the door and feel my chest tighten with happiness. Marge is already at work, guiding volunteers as they set up tables, and even her partner, Mayor Lee, chips in. Mrs. Rey arranges her flower display with Pat's help. Mike is assembling the ice cream and biscuits food booth. My heart swells at the sight—so many familiar faces from Mystic Hollow, people I've worked alongside, now woven into the fabric of this town I've come to love.

Tita Karra taps my arm. "You've made your mark on this town, anak," she says. "And you've made some good friends." She leans close so only I can hear. "Maybe he's more like a star than a firework," she says.

My cheeks flush, recalling Tita's analogy—a romance that burns steady like a star or explodes and disappears like a firework. "He's my North Star," I reply.

Elle runs out the door as she shouts, "They're here."

Tita winks at me, then pats Gabe on the shoulder as she follows my sister. "Looks like the Darbys made it," she says. I glance at Gabriel—he nods, even looks happy to see Oliver's family helping with the jubilee.

After a tense call from my mother, Oliver's family—eager for any sign of peace after what looked like a falling-out between me and Oliver—jumped at the chance to help.

My mother agreed to focus her economic priority speech specifically on her rural and small towns initiatives in Mystic Hollow, where she would highlight her plans for small business owners, like the Calabreses, and one idea inspired by me.

As part of her visit, she would stay at the Darby family's Commander Resort on July third for photo ops and meetings, then deliver a speech at Gabriel's inn the morning of July fourth to kick off the jubilee festival.

In return, Oliver's family agreed to let the Calabreses host the daytime Fourth of July festivities, while their resort would host the evening fireworks celebration. It's a win-win for both businesses and the entire community. But right now, there's only one community member on my mind.

I wrap my arms around Gabe's waist. "This is amazing, but there's still a lot of work to do."

Gabriel's eyes are half-hooded as his leans forward, angling for a kiss. "I'm sorry? What work?"

I giggle and push him away. "Gabriel, focus." I pull out my phone to show him my list. But instead of looking at my list, he swipes a finger across my screen to lock it. Then he pulls me close. "I have a suggestion. Maybe you don't use a checklist for this event?" He grins.

I feign anger. "Gabriel, one of my mother's talking points—inspired by me, by the way—is an initiative to get more young people to volunteer in local communities. I can't blow off my duties if she's making me an example."

He chuckles. "Fine, how about a compromise?"

I tilt my head. "Okay, I'm listening."

"We complete another item off your list." He steps close. The heat from his body and glow in his eyes are an unfair negotiating tactic as I match his step forward.

"Two items," I counter.

He throws his hands up. "Okay, two items. But I get one more photo shoot for my portfolio," he says, his eyes twinkling.

"Another photo shoot? Gabe, we only have twenty-four hours before the jubilee."

He intertwines our fingers. "It won't be until late tonight."

He pulls me close. “You’ll need to meet me at the tree swing.” I shiver with delight. Posing in the same place as his grandparents’ famous photograph would be an honor.

“You have a deal,” I say as I sigh into our kiss.

Like our photo shoot that night on the tree swing, the jubilee the next day is a sweet success. My mother’s visit to Mystic Hollow attracted people from all over the state and even across the borders, with some very loyal pie eaters for our Fifty States Pie-Eating Contest.

Though our celebrity chef fell through for the contest, everyone seemed to enjoy his replacement, my father, who had no problem describing himself as an amateur baker, in addition to being a First Gentleman and a former astronaut. #Lifegoals.

The small businesses and every member of the Main Street Makers Business Council were thrilled to meet my mother, especially Marge, who promptly declared herself president of her fan club.

And for Elle, the crowning achievement was beating me and Oliver at a game of Frog Launch on the midway, but not before shamelessly flirting with the boy running the game.

I purse my lips as Elle waves away the stuffed bear in the boy’s hand and points at the prizes behind him.

Oliver chuckles. “Apparently, her large panda stuffy needs a large frog friend.”

I smile at my bestie, who’s wearing his familiar country fair outfit—khakis and a fitted cornflower-blue polo that doesn't hide his athletic build. He looks every bit the part of the dashing vice president's son. I decided to go a little off script today with my white cutoff shorts and sneakers. I toss my rubber frog in the air. "One more game? I see a large dolphin stuffy on the prize board calling our name."

He laughs and puts his hands in his pockets. "Nah, I'm good, Abby. I mean, I did get to swim with real ones while you were shoveling a ton of horse sh—" I elbow him in the ribs and he joins my giggles until he abruptly stops.

I follow his gaze and see Gabriel in full photographer mode, grinning as he takes photos of a mom and her baby wearing the cutest red-white-and-blue dress and headband. Oliver tilts his head. "Not a bad way to meet constituents," he says thoughtfully. His face melts into a full-on smirk as he teases me.

"Or just be an active and caring member of the community," I retort.

He sits on the game counter, so we're eye level. "Have you seen the latest headlines about you?" he asks.

I cover my face. "No. I'm making more news? Are they angry we're not together?" I remove my hands slowly and gaze at him. "Are you angry?"

His body stiffens, but I know that twitch he does with his mouth when he's holding back a smile. He holds up his phone so I can read the headline: "First Daughter Puts Community First." My eyes tear up as I read on about being a "vital voice for young people."

Oliver chuckles. "Seems you've changed the narrative with

your volunteer work here. I'm glad they're talking positively about you and not focusing on us as a couple. Takes some pressure off, doesn't it?"

I nod. "I have to show Gabe this. He'll be proud to see our work being praised." I pause to give my friend a hug before running off. We don't need to say anything further, thanks to our best-friends mind-melding abilities—we both want the other to be happy.

"I'm good, Abby," Oliver says, pulling away. "And I'm starting to see the appeal of Mystic Hollow." He nods behind me. I twist to see Kyle and the twins enthusiastically waving at him to come join them, water balloons gleaming in their hands. I arch a brow at him. "You sure you're going to stay here and not come to my mom's party?"

He stands up like he's about to make a declaration. "Absolutely. It's the Commander's inaugural fireworks show. I'm happy to represent my family. And besides"—he nods in Gabriel's direction—"better him than me dealing with your two left feet on the dance floor."

He walks away and grabs a couple water balloons from Kyle's bucket. I debate whether to tell them that Oliver is a star quarterback, but I'm sure Kyle will learn the hard way.

"You guys going to be okay?" I find Gabriel standing not far away. A look of hesitation in his eyes. I don't hesitate as I wrap my arms around his neck.

"Totally. Besides, Oliver's never had a hard time making friends." I nod behind me, where he's clowning around with Kyle and the twins.

I grab my phone and find the article Oliver showed me. Gabe skims it, and I watch a smile spread across his gorgeous face. "You did it, Abby. And I agree, you are an inspiration, and not just for young people." I shriek as he lifts me in the air and spins. I stretch out my arms, close my eyes, empty my mind of any worries or cares. And enjoy a perfect summer day.

Later that afternoon, an ecstatic Ruby closes out the carnival with a heartfelt thanks and the exciting announcement that the jubilee has had its largest attendance ever—and the inn is officially booked for the rest of the summer. I laugh as I experience the largest group hug ever as Elle, Tita, Marge, and several others cheer.

Ruby also graciously invites all the guests to watch the fireworks show at the Commander later this evening, and I know that's the cue for me and my family to head back to DC for the party back at the White House.

As we head to Mystic Hollow's regional airport, we find Marge, Mayor Lee, Pat, and Mike waiting for us on the tarmac. Each one of them gets the biggest bear hug from me, followed by Gabriel, Elle, Tita Karra, and Ruby like a conga line of well-wishes before our group boards the plane. As I embrace each of my new friends, I promise a special tour of the White House and my return to Mystic Hollow for their pumpkin festival.

Pat hands me a bag. I giggle seeing the *Abby Special* printed on the to-go container. "It's official. You're part of Mystic Hollow," he says.

Smiling, I glance at Gabriel. "I already feel that way for more reasons than one." I hold up my ice cream container and our group says "brain freeze" as we pose for Gabe's camera.

As we settle on the plane, I smile to myself as Elle acts as tour guide and flight attendant for Ruby and Tita Karra.

I cozy up beside Gabriel and he whispers in my ear, "I was wrong."

I smirk. "Let me count the ways," I tease.

But he ignores me as his copper eyes hold mine. "You do belong in Mystic Hollow." I lean my head on his shoulder and we watch the world grow smaller outside our window.

It's a short flight from Mystic Hollow to DC, so I plan to savor every minute with Gabe before my mom's big Fourth of July party.

My dad's voice pipes over the plane's speaker. "Folks, looks like we've got a special treat. We're going to fly through some early fireworks shows."

Our group gasps as we look outside the plane's windows. Bursts of light brighten the ground below as our plane flies through orange-and-pink sunset-kissed skies.

Gabriel's hand wraps around mine and he doesn't let go. Not on the plane, not on the dance floor at the White House's gala, and not when we sneak upstairs to the Residence.

Alone at last, we dance on the Truman Balcony of the White House to the sound of firecrackers and the brilliant bursts of light stretching high into the sky.

I stare at the strong planes of Gabe's face as the glare of fireworks casts delicious shadows over his cheeks. To think, we only met just a few weeks ago and now here we are, twisting and turning in matching Chuck Taylors. He laughs and asks me what I'm thinking.

"I'm just mentally checking off my bucket list," I reply.

He laughs. “You know, I might be developing a list of my own you can help me with.”

“Does it involve ordering a pizza?” I tease.

“Oh, that’s definitely on the list, but it’s not the first item.” His voice trails off as he dips his head for a firework-packed, toe-curling kiss.

Abby's Unofficial Summer Bucket List

⬇(Pg. 2 For My Eyes Only)

Progress Report

- ☒ 1. Enjoy a laid-back picnic
- ☒ 2. Veg out at the beach
- ☒ 3. Get brain-freeze induced by fancy whipped-cream-smothered coffee latte (the perfect summer drink)
- ☐ 4. Chill and savor ice cream in a huge waffle cone (the perfect summer indulgence) **(incomplete: technically not in a cone!)**
- ☒ 5. Dine at top foodie restaurant (no parents)
- ☒ 6. Stay up all night (not studying)
- ☒ 7. Watch the sun set (not rushed)
- ☒ 8. Go stargazing (no agenda)
- ☒ 9. Dance under the stars (alone or with someone special . . .) **(With Gabe)** ♥
- ☐ 10. First date? **(Incomplete: will make an official date soon)** ♥
- ☒ 11. First kiss??? **(lots of practice with Gabe)**
- ☒ 12. Be spontaneous. For once. **(Try multiple times. Thanks to my summer in Mystic Hollow.)**

EPILOGUE

"Actually, my mom helped me check off this bucket list item," I say, licking my cold, creamy ice cream as it melts down my large waffle cone and drips onto my hand.

"No way! Does Pat's Famous Ice Cream mean nothing to you?" Gabriel teases.

"But we didn't *have* ice cream in a cone," I point out. "The bucket list item was specifically ice cream *in a cone.*"

"Ice cream, you say?" Gabriel scoots his metal café chair closer and kisses the side of my mouth, where some chocolate remains. "Hate to break it to you, but if we're getting all technical, that's gelato, not ice cream."

I pretend to pout. "Ice cream isn't ice cream. Pizza isn't pizza."

"We fail Operation Bucket List again," Gabe adds.

"Then we'll have to conduct more ice cream recon missions," I exclaim. "You did help with one more item on my list this evening, though. This is our official first date."

He counts on his fingers. "So, the picnic, our multiple photo shoots, the gala dance—"

"Didn't count. Because we never said those were dates."

"Wow, guess you've been keeping score." His eyes lock on mine. "And your first kiss? Did we technically check that box off?"

I waggle my brows. "If I don't check that box off, does that mean we get to keep practicing until it's real?"

"I do like the sound of that," he says, leaning forward for more "practice."

The locals sipping their Aperol spritzes beneath striped umbrellas nearby seem like they couldn't care less about our sickly sweet PDA. Nessa, in a breezy sundress, and Shaw, rocking shorts and a polo, are here, of course—perfectly incognito. And with glasses of lemonade and panini with prosciutto and mozzarella, they actually look like they're enjoying themselves. They didn't get Hawai'i, but no one's complaining now.

I lean my head on Gabe's shoulder, blissed out in the Italian coastal town we're vacationing in, the buildings cascading down the hillside like a painting. Narrow cobblestone streets wind around houses, occasionally revealing a sudden, breathtaking glimpse of the moonlight-drenched sea.

Couples stroll hand in hand and someone nearby strums a guitar. The breeze is a comforting blend of salt, citrus, and espresso. Everything moves a little slower, as if the whole town is in no hurry to leave summer behind. Sitting next to Gabe, I feel the same.

Gabe takes several photos of the town and then one of me, switching between his father's analog camera and his digital one.

I squint. "I thought you were done with your application."

He grins. "Those were for my mom." I grin too, glad Ruby is now fully in the know about supporting Gabe's art school plans.

After the runaway success of the jubilee, Tita Karra's investors came through, giving Ruby enough breathing room to hire more staff and freeing Gabe from his duties. And after she saw her son's phenomenal photos, including shots captured with his father's old camera, it came as no surprise he was interested in applying to a prestigious art academy. What *was* a surprise was Gabe's invitation to interview for one of their coveted fellowships. It could've been done virtually, but since I happened to be headed this way, still chasing the final items on my bucket list, I convinced Gabe to turn it into an in-person visit.

He doesn't say it, but I know the occasional twitching of his hands is him nervously waiting to hear back from the school. Something tells me Professor Ferro is going to come through for him. I just know it. Meanwhile, I do everything I can to distract him.

"And what about that last photo of me? Still trying to make some easy money with the tabloids?" I tease.

Now I've got his attention. "Please, I'd make more in an interview on CNN," he jokes. "A tell-all exclusive about my time with the Pineapple Princess."

"You're really the worst," I say. "Plus, pineapples are starting to grow on me. After all, that prickly, cheery fruit brought me to you." My back sinks into his body. I turn so I can see his face. His smile makes my blood hum.

I sigh with contentment. "Thank you," I say, looking him deep in his copper eyes.

"Of course. I'll never kiss and tell, Abby. Just kiss," he teases.

"No, not about that." I squeeze his hands, matching the

intense happiness tightening in my chest. "Until I met you, my life had been one big checklist with a schedule that was perfectly planned, but also mind-numbing." I gaze out at the sea, where two boats bob in the waves. "I wanted to impress my parents, but you taught me to also live for myself."

He pulls me close. "If it weren't for you, I wouldn't be here, let alone have pressed send on my application. You're my muse, Abby. You inspired me to follow my dreams and"—he waggles his brows—"I've got a portfolio full of photos of you." I laugh as he shows me my "brain freeze" scrunched-up face on his phone.

A swift movement catches my eye as Nessa touches her ear with a look of concern. She flashes Shaw a pained look as she climbs onto her Vespa. Seconds later I know the source of her chagrin.

A delighted Elle shrieks as she zooms by aboard a red Vespa, holding on to the back of a boy I've never seen.

I trade glances with Gabriel. "Sit this one out?"

He shrugs. "I seem to recall 'be spontaneous' on your bucket list?"

"I think we've checked that one off multiple times," I deadpan.

"Except you're never one to turn down extra credit," he teases. He's not wrong.

Gearing up for another exciting summer night underneath the stars with my very own certified smokeshow photographer, I grab my helmet and head for our Vespa nearby.

Besides, there's no reason Operation Bucket List can't last longer than one summer. Or that we can't keep adding new goals.

As Gabe climbs on behind me, I give him a sly grin. "One more pose?" I lean in, and he's already guessed what I had in mind as our lips press together and his camera clicks.

In fact, I think we've just snapped the first photo of what comes next.

ACKNOWLEDGMENTS

Clearly, publishing a book is not a one-person job. I had a whole committee, multiple subcommittees, and the occasional emergency session (complete with late-night snacks) to help me craft this debut novel of my heart. There are so many people to thank, and I'll try to name as many as possible before the orchestra rises, the lights dim, and I'm ushered offstage.

To my brilliant and storied editor, Wendy Loggia: Thank you for believing in me and spotting the spark in this DC love story. Your keen eye and editorial superpowers helped bring Abby and Gabe to life with more heart, charm, and star-spangled flair than I ever imagined. From first draft chaos to launch day jitters, I love working and creating with you.

Thank you to my phenomenal agent, Ann Rose, for holding my hand through every twist and turn of this journey. Your wisdom, tenacity, and unwavering belief in me have been nothing short of magical—and I'm so grateful to have you in my corner.

I'm deeply grateful to my publishing team at Delacorte Romance who championed this book like it was running for office. Thank you, Makena Cioni (go, Team Jess), Rebecca Gudelis,

Casey Moses, Cathy Bobak, Tamar Schwartz, Liz Sutton, and Jamie Johnson, for expertly guiding this wide-eyed debut author through the complex corridors of the book world—no security clearance required.

To my exceptional cover artist, Chloe Quinn: Thank you for turning emotional fireworks into visual magic—Abby and Gabe have never looked more explosive.

Thank you to my "Research Committee" of DC insiders Stephanie Vance, Jessica D., Shannon, and those-who-shall-remain-nameless who've worked at 1700 Pennsylvania Avenue (the People's House: A White House Experience) and 1600 Pennsylvania Avenue (the White House) for answering my strange and random questions about life in the Residence.

This book was fueled by the brilliance, banter, and borderline-unhinged group chats shared with me by my writer friends: C. H. Barron, Nicole Green, Jen Steiner, Joyana Peters, Katie Sivinski, and Wendra Chambers—thanks for being key critique partners on my "Debut Committee."

Endless thanks to the brilliant authors and industry pros who helped me get here, including my SCBWI Mid-Atlantic crew—especially Erin Teagan, Val Patterson, and Julie Scheina. Thanks to the WriteMentor community; and to my outstanding mentor, Marisa Noelle, thanks for being the first author to validate my writing aspirations. Shout-outs to Stuart White, George Jreije, and my "COVID class." Thanks to the Author Mentor Match community, who lifted my writing to the next level, and the one-and-only Tracy Badua for being a mentor and a friend. Jenna Lee-Yun, Tiara Blue, Jenny Mattern, Stephanie Sosa, Ryan Black, Nedda

Lewers—thank you for talking me off countless ledges and distracting me with memes.

Thank you to all the Rosebuds authors, including my DMV crew Charlene Thomas, Erin Becker, Sky Sprayberry. Stefany Valentine, you have a special place in my heart. To my friends in the Filipino community, including authors Tif Marcelo, Kess Costales, Maan Gabriel, Maida Malby, Taj McCoy, Anna Lapera, Isabelle Wong, and Reinalyn and Adrianna. And to Team Sloth, Y. M. Resnik, Linh Pham, Cecile Ferro, and Julie Tieu—thanks for the cookies, holiday cards, and support over the years.

I can hear the music swelling, but I cannot leave the stage without thanking my most important group of supporters: my family. To Mom, who always found the time to take me to the library. Your example taught me to be strong. You gave me the confidence to find my voice and pursue my dreams. To my big brothers, Ron and Ken, for letting me beat them up when we were kids and for always being in my corner. To my kid brother, Rex—thanks for styling me (and my characters) so well!

To my brilliant, talented partner and smokeshow, Brian—your unwavering love and support has been nothing short of heroic. From holding down the fort every weekend to taking on the full weight of parenting while I locked myself away to write, you made space for this dream to grow. (Plus inspired a lot of the banter in these pages!) I couldn't have done this without you—and I wouldn't have wanted to. You are my wonderwall.

When I first visited Washington, DC, as a wide-eyed middle schooler, it was love at first sight. Like many, I was awed by the grandeur of the monuments—but what truly captivated me was the deeper story: the nation's history, the promise of the American dream, and the enduring ideals behind our democratic institutions. This novel is first and foremost meant to be a fun love story, but it's also inspired by loving this country—a hard thing to do sometimes, especially when it doesn't feel like your country is loving you back.

To the readers and dreamers, who read to find brighter places—you are not alone. To all those still showing up, still believing, still working to make this country better—thank you from the bottom of my heart.